TALES OF
OLD SARAJEVO

ISAK SAMOKOVLIJA

TALES OF
OLD SARAJEVO

with an Introduction by
Ivo Andrić

edited by
Zdenko Lešić

translated by
Celia Hawkesworth and
Christina Pribićević-Zorić

VALLENTINE MITCHELL
LONDON • PORTLAND, OR

First published in 1997 in Great Britain by
VALLENTINE MITCHELL & CO. LTD
900 Eastern Avenue
London IG2 7HH

and in the United States of America by
VALLENTINE MITCHELL
c/o ISBS
5804 N.E. Hassalo Street
Portland, Oregon 97213-3644

British Library Cataloguing in Publication Data

Samokovlija, Isak
  Tales of old Sarajevo
  1. Samokovlija, Isak – Translations into English 2. Sephardim
  – Bosnia and Hercegovina – Sarajevo – Fiction 3. Holocaust,
  Jewish (1939–1945) – Bosnia and Hercegovina – Sarajevo –
  Fiction
  I. Title II. Lesic, Zdenko
  891.8'2'3'52 [F]

  ISBN 0853033323 (cloth)
  ISBN 0853033315 (paper)

Library of Congress Cataloging-in-Publication Data

Samokovlija, Isak.
  [Short stories. English. Selections]
  Tales of old Sarajevo / Isak Samokovlija ; with an introduction by
  Ivo Andrić ; edited by Zdenko Lešić ; translated by Celia
  Hawkesworth and Christina Pribićević-Zorić.
      p.   cm.
  ISBN 0-85303-332-3. — ISBN 0-85303-331-5 (pbk.)
      1. Sarajevo (Bosnia and Hercegovina)—Fiction. 2. Samokovlija,
  Isak—Translations into English. I. Lešić, Zdenko.
  II. Hawkesworth, Celia, 1942–   . III. Pribićević-Zorić, Christina.
  IV. Title.
  PG1418.S3A25   1997
  891.8'2354—dc21   97-17737
                                                                    CIP

Typeset by Vitaset, Paddock Wood, Kent
Printed in Great Britain by
Bookcraft (Bath) Ltd, Midsomer Norton, Avon

For the community of Sephardic Jews of Bosnia
who disappeared in the Holocaust
and now live only in Samokovlija's stories

Contents

List of Illustrations

Photographs provided by the Jewish Museum, Belgrade,
and La Benevolencija, London

Acknowledgements

The editor wishes to thank Branko Danon and Daria Stojnic, president of the Jewish society 'Friends of La Benevolencija', in London, for their generous assistance in the preparation and production of this book. He also thanks Professor Dr Rikica Samokovlija-Najdanovic for the kind authorisation of this edition of her father's short stories. The editor's special thanks are due to Cheryl R. Mariner of World Jewish Relief, and Jeff Shear, of Jewish Care, for their encouragement and support. Further acknowledgements are due to Milica Kraus, curator of the Jewish Museum in Belgrade for providing photographs for this book, and to the Andrić Foundation in Belgrade for permission to translate and print Ivo Andrić's short article on Isak Samokovlija and the Sarajevo Sephardim.

Translators' Note

The stories in this collection presented the translators with certain
technical questions. They contain many words and phrases in
foreign languages: Arabic, Hebrew, Spanish (the Sephardic Jewish
Ladino). These reflect the variety of cultures concentrated in
Sarajevo. In some instances we decided to translate them, but for
the most part we have left them (marked in italics) and provided a
short glossary at the end of the book. Some Ladino sentences have
been left without a gloss in the hope that they will be understood.
The remaining dilemmas concern the names of people and places:
the original Serbo-Croatian uses diacritic marks to differentiate
certain letters. Since the names of many characters are not themselves Slav, we decided to transliterate them in a way that would
ease their pronunciation for English-language readers (e.g.
Hanucha) and to use established English versions of Jewish names
as appropriate (e.g. Samuel, Miriam). Place names were another
matter, however: it seemed to make little sense to transliterate
Sarajevo as Sarayevo, for instance. Despite the ensuing inconsis-
tence, we have settled for the original spelling of place names, so
that they may be identified on a map, but we have omitted dia-
critics as unnecessarily confusing. Readers will therefore find the
main Sarajevo market written Bascarsija in preference to either
Baščaršija or Bashcharshiya. We hope that such a solution will make
for smooth reading of the stories, which is of course our main
concern.

CHRISTINA PRIBIĆEVIĆ-ZORIĆ
CELIA HAWKESWORTH

IVO ANDRIĆ (1892–1975) is a major twentieth-century European writer, winner of the Nobel Prize for Literature in 1961. Born in Bosnia of Roman Catholic parents, he grew up alongside Orthodox Christians, Muslims and Jews in Visegrad and Sarajevo. His first work appeared in 1914 and he published six volumes of short stories and five novels, as well as verse, essays and reflective prose.

CELIA HAWKESWORTH is Senior Lecturer in Serbo-Croat, School of Slavonic and East European Studies, University of London. Among her recent translations are *The Damned Yard* (Forest Books), *Conversation with Goya* (Menard), and *Bosnian Chronicle* (Harvill), all by Ivo Andrić, and *In the Jaws of Life* by Dubravka Ugresić (Virago).

ZDENKO LEŠIĆ was Professor of the Theory of Literature at the University of Sarajevo before being forced to leave in 1993. He also co-edited the most prominent Bosnian literary journal, *Izraz*. Recently he edited *Children of Atlantis, Voices from the Former Yugoslavia* (Central European University Press, Budapest, London, New York, 1995).

CHRISTINA PRIBIĆEVIĆ-ZORIĆ is a broadcaster based in London. Her translations include the award-winning *Dictionary of the Khazars* (Hamish Hamilton) by Milorad Pavic, and *The Taste of a Man* (Little, Brown) by Slavenka Drakulić.

IVO ANDRIĆ

Isak Samokovlija and
The Bosnian Sephardim

There is no need here to say much about the short stories of
Isak Samokovlija. So vibrant and exquisite in their simplicity, they
speak clearly and simply for and of themselves. I shall confine
myself merely to saying a few words about the environment which
spawned this Bosnian writer of Jewish origin, who depicted the life
and mentality of Bosnian Sephardic Jews.

When the Jews were expelled from Spain at the end of the
fifteenth century, they sought refuge in countries which had not
established the persecution of Jews as a principle, and which at
least tolerated them. One such country was what was then Turkey.
By the first half of the sixteenth century, banished Spanish Jews
started appearing in major Balkan cities, including Sarajevo,
whence they later moved to smaller Bosnian towns. Their position
in Bosnia was not very different from that of other non-Muslims;
what made it more difficult was that these Spanish Jews were small
in number, isolated in a foreign land, with no blood, religious or
language ties with other non-Muslims. In order to survive under
such conditions, these Jewish refugees had to cope and bend with
the wind even more than the Christians. Crowded into a kind of
ghetto, into the Great Courtyard as it was known, surrounded by
the prejudices and superstitions of their fellow citizens of other
religions, oppressed and exploited by the ruling Ottoman caste,
necessity and the instinct for self-defence made them retreat
behind the rampart-like wall of their own Jewish and Spanish
traditions, beliefs and prejudices.

With time, the cultural reserves they had brought with them from

1

the old country, from Spain, began to dim and fade but, cultivating them with unusual love under what were adverse conditions, by and large they managed to preserve these traditions until not long ago. In Turkish times, their spiritual life, like that of our other peoples, was largely confined to a relative knowledge of religious texts (in this case Hebraic) and to the rote performance of ritual.

Like a thin curtain that was more solid than any wall, the incomprehensible Hebrew letters concealed the religious part of their life which they preserved through the centuries. Their other such curtain was the Spanish language. For more than four centuries they protected and preserved their mother–stepmother tongue, even though they could neither develop it nor prevent its ossification and corruption. This was the language in which they sang wedding and love songs, romance songs from their native Andalusia; it was the language they used in their private lives and business dealings.

These two distant, foreign scripts and languages were, like everything else for them, a means for self-preservation and self-identity, like two codes in the long, difficult war of their life.

Of course, this community could not escape the influence of the people with whom it had lived for centuries. The exigencies of common life and daily communication inevitably led to the infiltration of Slav and Turkish language elements and customs into their lives. For, although they used Hebrew in the synagogue, and Spanish at home, they still had to speak 'Bosnian' with the people, and Turkish with officials. Such were the demands life placed upon them. Newcomers, different from the rest of us, they became one of us.

And yet, they lived without real schools or any real possibilities for a cultural life of their own. Under Ottoman rule, and later under Austro-Hungarian occupation, the law virtually denied them access to higher public or state office, steering them instead towards manual labour, a limited number of crafts and, in particular, retail and wholesale trade.

By force of circumstance, necessity and custom, theirs was a small, closed community of hard-earned, painstakingly guarded and always endangered wealth and, even more, of dire poverty. All this was bound to affect their development. And yet it failed to corrupt them as a whole, to corrode their community either spiritually or physically. And when, with the advent of the nineteenth

2

century and modernisation, their living conditions slightly improved, but only slightly, they demonstrated, despite the backwardness imposed on them and our other peoples, sure signs of their energy and talent, their feeling for the new and their innate desire for progress.

In more recent times, Serbo-Croat literacy developed among the Sephardim as it did among the rest of Bosnia-Herzegovina's people. In the past fifty years, they have produced any number of intellectual, cultural, even scientific figures and artists. Foremost among them, without any doubt, is the harmonious, profoundly humane Isak Samokovlija, one of the best writers Bosnia-Herzegovina has given our literature.

During the Second World War, however, the dark, murderous onslaught of racism managed to disperse and destroy the Bosnian Sephardim, unprepared and unaccustomed as they were to this sort of fight. They had always wanted simply to live their lives, yet throughout their tortuous history they had always been deprived of a part of life. This time they were deprived of life itself.

Today, the only remaining trace of Bosnia's Sephardic Jews is their big old cemetery that stands on the steep slope rising above Sarajevo's Miljacka River, where for over a hundred years generations of Sephardim were buried. But the heavy tombstones and their inscriptions, which say little as it is, are fading and disappearing with each passing day. Those lying in these graves are doubly dead and alone, because among the living they have no one to come and visit them. At the top of the cemetery now stands a white marble pyramid, the last monument to the destroyed Bosnian Sephardic community. Its inscription explains their fate: 'To Jewish fallen soldiers and victims of fascism – Jasenovac – Stara Gradiska – Djakovo – Jadovno – Loborgrad – Auschwitz – Bergen-Belsen.' That is the tragic death camp geography of the Bosnian Sephardim whose community was so brutally wiped out.

It is our good fortune (and this shows the importance and nature of art, and in this case of literature), that Bosnia-Herzegovina's Sephardic community gave literature a writer of such worth, thereby preserving its distinctive identity in his work. In terms of both its artistic power and importance as a human record, this work deserves to be received, read and learned in all cultural environments.

Translated by Christina Pribićević-Zorić

3

The Kaddish

I

They buried her into the darkness itself. As Miko was leaving the cemetery an old Jew took him by the hand. The man called out to his wife from the door: 'I've brought him home ... I couldn't leave him out there in the road ... an orphan ...'

It took the woman a moment to absorb his words and then a glow appeared in her eyes!

'Good, Señor Judah!'

She made the boy a bed next to the children and gave him dinner. Miko fell fast asleep as though nothing had changed in his life. He simply fell silent, his head bowed.

Later they discovered that he had epilepsy and, not wishing him to frighten the children, they removed Miko. And so he was passed on from house to house. Children ran away from him, and he would hide in the flower and vegetable gardens, and behind the tombstones in the cemetery.

When even Biño the tinsmith would not take him in, not even for money, they sent him away from their little town. Thus it was that he found himself here in the city, and got to know its streets. He passed from hand to hand like a tarnished coin, turning as dark as a gypsy. He would go out early, be it winter or summer, to make the rounds of the *mahalas* and city centre, stocky in his blue chintz outfit which buttoned up at the back, prompting the children to pluck at the patterned shirt underneath. He peered out of his small eyes like a blind man groping his way through a sunny day. He went

4

barefoot and always carried pieces of coloured glass and scraps of cloth in his hand, crying out in a drawl (when the children teased him): 'Nooo, I don't waaant to … I don't waaant to!' His voice was like a screeching bird's. He would hold up his hands, fingers splayed, as if defending himself against attack from the air.

That is how he was when Sarucha found him.

'So you are Tia Bea's grandchild, are you? May God be good to her in that other world! And he's got epilepsy, you say. Well, what can one do? The trials sent by God … blessed be His name! … just have to be borne. I will take him in for the sake of my own soul, and for the sake of his grandmother – may God be good to her in that other world!'

Sarucha took him home with her. They entered the courtyard and sat down at the bottom of the wooden stairs.

'Sit down, Miko mine, sit down. I am old and asthmatic, I have to rest … these wretched stairs will be the end of me … and I will die before my time … Sit down, my child, sit down … I knew your grandma … I knew her well … she was a midwife, a good woman, may they be good to her in that other world! She was my midwife, for my one child, I never had any more … yes, son, it was God's will … His will … And she nursed me back to health. I came down with a fever after the baby was born. I was bed-ridden from the third day after *Sukkoth* till just before *Purim* … Had it not been for her, for your grandma, I don't think I would have lived to praise the Lord. With God's help she put me back on my feet again. She gave me herbal brandy to drink and I recovered, my boy, I recovered … Later both the child and Señor Liacho died …'

Sarucha burst into tears, and Miko drew his legs together, pulled up his knees, crossed his arms on top of them and rested his head. When they reached the top of the stairs, Sarucha took him into the kitchen. There she cut his hair with scissors, bathed him with hot water over the copper basin and took him, swathed in a sheet, to a little room where she lay him down on the mattress. She brought him bread and cheese to eat.

When Miko had fallen asleep, Sarucha kneeled down beside him and gazed at his face.

'He has sent you to me … He, Lord of the Universe … for you to say the *kaddish* when my time comes. He who rules the world, our Lord, has sent you, for there to be someone to say the *kaddish* for me and for Señor Liacho, and in return I will take care of you and save you from poverty.'

Sarucha burst into tears right there next to the child, who was sleeping so sweetly and peacefully, perhaps for the first time since his mother died. The blank face and thick lips were brushed by the shadow of a smile.

'Smile, my child, smile, God gave everyone a Sabbath – His day of joy, which He created and graced with the holy *Torah*'. Again Sarucha sobbed, like all old women who thus express the sorrow and the warmth which sometimes touch their hearts.

After a while she rose to her feet, lifted the arched lid of her treasure chest and took out a small bundle. The soft jingling of the Turkish gold coins echoed in the silence.

'Sarucha will use one of these to buy you clothes, my child', she said solemnly and, chanting, placed a gold *rushpa* on Miko's brow, sliding it down over his cheek.

She remembered that Miko had not kissed the *mezuzah* upon entering the house. She went to the door, placed two fingers on the small rectangular glass, then raised them to her lips and kissed them. She stared at the letters inside, but as the *mezuzah* hung in the shadow she went back to fetch a candle. She stood there gazing at it for a long time, with candle in hand, and then again she placed two fingers on the *mezuzah*, carried the fingers across the room and, kneeling down next to the child, pressed them against his lips. Startled, Miko cried out in that drawling way of his: 'I don't waaant to ...' and began to pull his hands out from under the covers.

'*Los malachim que lo guarden*', whispered Sarucha as if in prayer, and prepared for bed.

Sarucha had suffered great hardship. When she was widowed she had had to accept charity. Later some good people had helped her and she eventually became known as 'la tradeswoman'. She went from house to house selling chintz, fine silk, kerchiefs and shawls, earning enough to eat, and even to put aside a little something for her old age. She had not abandoned her occupation even now. Having devoted herself to trade, it was as if she had committed herself to a life of passing from one courtyard to another, one street to another, squeezing her heavy, lumbering frame through the side gates, offering her wares to Muslim and Spanish homes at a cheap price, but only for ready cash. Death was always on her mind and whenever she felt her chest tighten and started to wheeze, she would be scared. That was why Miko had so gladdened her heart. Now she would have someone to be by her side, she would not be alone at night, she would have someone to read the *kaddish* ... the *kaddish* ... to read the prayer.

When Liacho died, her greatest sorrow had been that there was no one to read the *kaddish* for him: 'I did everything I could for him, but God did not let me do the most important thing', she would say. Her first child had died, and she never bore either male or female again. She went to the *khoja* and to the rabbi, she jotted down everything they said, she drank all the herbs they recommended, she even went to the spa in Priboj, but all to no avail. She remained barren. And as she did not conceal her defect, no one wanted her after Señor Liacho died, although she was not yet forty.

In the morning she got up and, not wanting to disturb Miko, tiptoed into the kitchen where she opened the window and looked down into the gardens below. She wanted to see a face, to say hello, to say a word, to anybody, to the first person who appeared at a window or on one of the rickety wooden verandas. It was still early. The arrogant, defiant crow of the roosters had only just pierced the air, and a white thin mist was threading its way through the plums and quinces, their leaves still wet with dew. The blush of morning rose above the Yellow Fortress. Sarucha inhaled the fresh air. It smelled of something, a herb, a flower, wallflowers, pumpkins ... she tried to remember what it was. She thought of a time which had long since passed. She sighed deeply. Suddenly something soft and warm brushed her bare leg. She bent down, her face red, and the purring olive cat leaped into her arms.

Sarucha held it and pressed it against her cheek.

II

Miko grew into a quiet, doleful boy.

At first everything in Sarucha's house came to life. The cobwebs disappeared from the corners. Two pots of redolent young rue stood on the window sill. The little meat-pie pans came back from the tinsmith looking like new, and on Fridays Sarucha rose early and spent all day preparing for the holy Sabbath. She only just managed to finish everything by nightfall. She washed Miko with a cheap bar of scented soap, dressed him in his clean underwear, Saturday suit and smartly blocked fez, and then changed her own clothes, wrapped a silk scarf around her cap, lit the lamp and descended with Miko to wait at the bottom of the stairs for Rebbe Yako.

Old Yako came every Friday evening straight from temple to recite the *kiddush* in the widow's house. In his faded green cloth *jubbah*, he looked taller and thinner than he was. He climbed the steps slowly, humming a Sabbath hymn. When Sarucha kissed his hand he blessed her in the manner of the great rabbis and famous *shaliahs*. He placed his hand slowly on her cap, closed his blue eyes, furrowed his brow, tossed back his head and recited the Hebrew blessing in a ringing voice.

After completing the *kiddush* he would leave, solemn and mysterious, and for Sarucha it was as if a saint or the legendary Elijah the Prophet himself had visited her house. She would watch his departing figure disappear, but those blue eyes with their white lashes, that wrinkled face framed by the white beard and side curls under the fez would float before her eyes long after he had gone.

'Miko mine, Rebbe Yako will easily teach you how to read, easily, my boy', she would say and then add: 'Shabbat Shalom, Miko!'

Miko would walk over, kiss her hand, sit down next to her on the wooden bench, and eat his dinner in silence, while Sarucha talked about how wonderful it would be once Miko learned how to read the prayers, recite the *kiddush* and sing the songs of David.

'Will you work hard, Miko?'

'Yes', Miko replied, shyly dipping crusts of bread into his fish chowder.

After dinner Sarucha would spread out the mattresses and Miko would take the pieces of glass from his pockets and hold them up to the light of the lamp:

'Oh, oh, Tia, red, red! Look! Look! Oh, oh, green, green ... yellow, yellow ... oh, oh ...'

And Rebbe Yako started coming every day. He brought with him a thin little book and Miko started learning the alphabet. They would sit at the bottom of the stairs – Sarucha returned early from her rounds – the rebbe would rock back and forth and repeat with

8

Miko: 'A*leph* – wing, *beth* – mouth, *gimel* – tooth, *daleth* – hammer', and so on down to the last letter, to *tav* – crippled leg, and then go back and do it all over again, and again, until they heard Sarucha rattling the cups and coffee-pot upstairs, preparing to come down.

Rebbe Yako would take out his handkerchief, wipe his mouth, moustache and beard, and say:

'That's enough for today, my child. Kiss the book and say amen!'

Miko would close the book, put it aside and lift the olive cat onto his lap. His head was spinning. All the bold angular Hebrew letters and their symbols seemed to fly out at him from the darkness, and he lost consciousness in a bedlam of wings, mouths, hammers, thick lines and thin, points and corners. His head jogged rhythmically up and down, his ears ringing with: 'A*leph, beth, gimel, daleth* ...' And so he would doze off.

'What do I think? Well, good woman, first of all ours is a difficult law. It is not easy to learn to read our sacred letters. And Miko? God is great. God has given an abundance of brains to some and He has given at least some to everyone, including Miko. Today, tomorrow, Miko too will learn something. Something; we don't really know very much ourselves. What do the rest of us know, good woman? Barely enough to fathom the depth and greatness of our holy *Torah*', Rebbe Yako would say.

But Miko made poor progress and was wasting away.

He lost weight and looked wan. All day long he would amble around the courtyard, climb the fence and look into the next-door gardens, and when he heard Sarucha's footsteps around the hour of *ikindia*, the Muslim afternoon prayer, he would run sluggishly to the closed courtyard gate and start hopping from one foot to the other: 'The street, I want to go out, Tia, dear Tia, out into the street ...'

Sarucha would take him by the hand and lead him to the bottom of the stairs.

'Wait a minute, boy, wait Miko mine, I've brought you something ...'

And she would take out a cube of Turkish delight or a lollipop or some fruit, and Miko would stop to eat it, to lick it, his tongue darting out at the candied stick, now and then repeating wildly, as if in a dream:

'Into the street ... the street ...'

Then one day he disappeared. The olive cat searched the house for him, and when it noticed the broken window, it jumped onto the sill, miaowed several times and then returned downstairs to lie in the sun and wait for Sarucha. When she did not find Miko at home Sarucha went out of her mind. She flailed her arms, checked with the neighbours and finally, exhausted and gasping, sat down and wept.

Just before nightfall Miko entered the courtyard as incorporeal as a shadow. The cat leaped down from Sarucha's lap. Startled, she said:

'Miko ... oh ... my poor Miko ... Sinner that I am ... where have you been? ...'

Miko quietly and very slowly crossed the courtyard, carrying a fez full of glass fragments as if it were a cup full of water, saying:

'Red, red ... oh, oh ... yellow, yellow ... oh, oh ... Tia ... Tia ... red ...'

That winter Sarucha fell ill. There was a wheezing in her chest. She wailed: 'I'm going to die and you're not paying attention, you're not studying, you don't even know the *kaddish* yet ... oh, sinner that I am ... And you're back to your old ways, you're big. All summer I paid Rebbe Yako ... and all you do is loll around ... God Almighty, I'm going to die, die ...'

Sarucha was convulsed with coughing. Miko sat contritely by her side, resting his head on his knees, slowly drawing out the words and saying softly to himself: '*Aaaleph ... beeeth ... giiimel ... daaaleth* ...', thinking that he was saying the greatest of prayers for Tia Sarucha's recovery. All through her illness, he would go down to the bottom of the stairs, take the little book from inside his shirt, sit down and recite the Hebrew letters. Every so often he would look up at the sky and heave a great sigh. In the evening, when Sarucha started to moan and groan again, and to cough, he would snuggle up to her and, after long hesitation, say: 'Tia, don't be afraid ... Don't be afraid, Tia ... you won't die ...', and then he would resume his prayer: '*Aleph, beth, gimel, daleth* ...'

Sarucha recovered time and again.

And so their life continued until the second summer, when Miko took to traipsing around town. He stayed out all day; Sarucha combed the area, asking around for him, and only just managed to find him. And where was he? He was sitting by the road, watching

10

the children swim in the Miljacka River. Coated in dust and sweat, he was tapping a stone on the ground, gazing at the water. The other children squealed, screamed, splashed in the water, jumped off the rocks, swam, went diving, and those who did not know how to keep afloat puffed up their wet trunks and then carefully lowered themselves into the water, floating like big colourful bubbles.

'My, oh my, sinner that I am, what on earth will become of you?! Why did I ever take you in? Good God! Why, you're no longer a child … no you're not …' Sarucha scolded him, gasping, wet under her shawl.

She took him home; on the way she got him some Turkish hazelnuts and when they reached the stairs she sat him down on the bottom step, stroking his face, and said to him fondly:

'Well, Miko, it's time for you to mend your ways, make a poor sad woman happy and open your eyes; I'll adopt you as my very own, so that you are not orphaned a second time, without knowing your mother … Miko, open your eyes and look into mine. All this will be yours; God gave it, all I ask of Him is an easy death … Do you hear me, Miko? All of it, everything will be yours, the house, the courtyard, the chest and everything inside it, and there is a lot inside it, Miko, yes there is; you'll be able to open a shop of your own … Do you hear me, Miko?'

Miko was sitting beside her, stroking the cat with one hand, and turning over a piece of glass with the other.

'It's me who will die first, me!'

'God forbid', cried Sarucha getting up. 'God forbid! Look, Miko, you are getting your life back, you are!' She took his hand in hers and stroked it: 'You won't die, no you won't, God willing you will recover completely, yes you will, you'll grow up to be a man … and Zimbula has a girl in Sterluca, Miko mine; never mind that she is cross-eyed, she will be a girl like her mother and you can get married and have children, born right here; may the first one be a boy, and when you promise him to our Lord may this house and this courtyard burst into song and the sound of music and may you live long, Miko, and be here to say the *kaddish* for me … the *kaddish*…for me and for Señor Liacho…'

Sarucha clasped his head in her hands to kiss him on the brow, and choked with elation, he laughed, opened his mouth, drew two

11

or three breaths, then twitched, turned his foot, clenched his fists, rolled back his eyes until only the whites showed and toppled over in a faint, jerking and twitching in pain. He had an epileptic fit whenever he felt joy.

For a while Miko was better. He did not leave the house, until one morning he disappeared again. He went into the city's back streets, and even down to the Turkish cemetery. At nightfall he crept back into the house and slept under the stairs, only to disappear again at daybreak. Sometimes the Muslim children would chase him away with stones and he would come home all bloody and go to Tia Sarucha with head bowed, repentant. Sarucha lost hope, she saw that nothing would come of him and she scolded and berated him, and when he had had enough he would leave the house again.

III

They were picking plums and making jam when word spread among the Jews that Miko the epileptic was in the new hospital, the one built by the Austrians behind Mustai-Bey's plum orchard. They immediately ran to tell Sarucha, but she was in bed herself. Her legs were as swollen as pillars.

'Oh my', she wailed, 'oh my, sinner that I am, for this to happen to me just now!'

She offered the woman taking care of her a whole *sechser* to go and see how he was, but the young woman refused, frightened and offended that Sarucha could even think of such a thing.

'You surprise me, Tia Sarucha, you of all people! How can you even think of a woman going there, for God's sake, to a hospital on the outskirts of town? ... God forbid!'

For the first time the town started taking an interest in what would happen to Miko. He was the first Spanish Jew to be in hospital. The eldest member of the *hevra kaddisha* decided that the sexton should go there daily and inquire whether the Spaniard, Miko Pardo – the epileptic – had died. He needed to be buried according to Jewish law and what did those Krauts up there know about that? According to Jewish law he had to be buried immediately, as soon as the soul departed from the body. But those people up there might leave him for two or three days. God forbid such a thing should happen to a Jew, even if it was just Miko the epileptic! And so the decision was taken and every morning the sexton walked around the iron railings of the hospital gate. People walked in and out, but he just bided his time until the gate-keeper asked him what he wanted.

'Has that fellow … Pardo … Miko … the Spaniard … the epileptic…died?'

And every time the sexton came back with fresh news. They had shut Miko up in that building where they amputate legs, cut open stomachs and take out eyes. The guess was that they must have sliced off a piece of his intestine, or opened up his head to see where the epilepsy came from. Some said he had been bitten by an adder in the Turkish cemetery at the foot of Sedrenik and that they had amputated his leg just below the knee.

Months went by.

Summer drew to a close and Sarucha's olive cat amused itself alone at the bottom of the stairs. Upstairs Sarucha was moaning, but down below the sun was still warm and the cat could stretch out contentedly in the noon-day heat. Reclining on its side, stretching out its paws, it squinted with golden-green eyes, the black pupils barely visible thin lines. Its sprawling stomach rose and fell, its little nipples pink among the fine grey fur. The courtyard gate squeaked, the cat lazily turned its head and suddenly it leaped to its feet btistling, as if a dog was coming its way. It was Miko. Tall, his eyes bright, a strange smile on his face. When he knocked at the door and stepped into the room, Sarucha almost fainted. He walked over to her bed, all tall and thin now, and kissed her hand. Sarucha looked at him. He had changed so much. His skin had become white, there was an openness about him, his lips had thinned out. He was wearing a thin yellow suit and red-laced canvas shoes.

When she got over the shock she burst into tears. Stroking his face and head she said:

'Miko mine, dear … Miko … See what you've reduced me to? … See? …' Sarucha uncovered her legs.

There lay two strangely deformed legs, swollen, chalk-white, bloated with water, cold, with a cadaverous sheen.

'Everything will be all right, Tia Sarucha, everything, don't you worry! Look, feel here … that's where they hit me with the rock …

the Turks ... up by the wooden mosque .... Whack, the rock hit me and ... when I woke up I was lying in bed. My head was wrapped in cotton ... I'm fine now, I feel lighter, as if something fell out of my head ... yes, Tia Sarucha, everything will be all right now ... everything ...'

Miko lay his head on her breast and burst into tears. Sarucha stroked his hair and when he stopped sobbing, she asked him:

'Miko, will you recite the *kaddish* for me when I die, will you know how now ... will you?'

'Yes, I will', said Miko, his tears muffling the words.

Sarucha pulled herself up.

'Come now, son, get up, open the old chest; here are the keys. There is a book at the bottom ... take it out, son ...'

Miko held the book out to her and she took it with both hands, lifted it to her lips and kissed it. For a long while she stroked the silver-studded crimson velvet binding, and then she held it out to him.

'Here, Miko, take it, it's from Señor Liacho ... for you to be a good Jew and to pray to our Lord, to live in His glory ...'

Miko kissed her hand and Sarucha started to cry.

From that day on Miko never strayed far from the house again. He nursed the patient, roasted coffee for her, made her swollen legs comfortable, changed the compresses on her head, fed her soup made by the neighbours, brewed herbs for her, sat by her side all night reading from the prayer book, speaking the Hebrew words, singing to himself, drawing out the word endings and rolling his eyes.

When old Tia Sarucha began to turn blue, the women had to practically drag him out of the room so that he would not see her dead. Sad, pale, sleepless and hungry, he stood hunched by the door, the book under his arm. From inside came the choking, strangling sound of her death rattle. Miko began to shake and, pulling himself away, he staggered down the stairs. At the bottom of the steps he stopped. The evening sun bathed him in its warm red glow. Miko shivered as if he had a fever. He listened for any sound from the room upstairs, then he turned around and gazed at the sky. Its beautiful russet redness filled his eyes, pouring into him as if he were a bottomless pit, and within two or three seconds, as if saturated, big red stains appeared on his cheeks. Miko then opened the velvet prayer book, found his place, and began to read the *kaddish*, the prayer for the dead.

He read it aloud, word by drawn-out word, in a strange kind of chant, entranced. He opened and closed his eyes, swaying back and forth on his toes. His cheeks went red, and a white foam gathered in the corners of his mouth. His entire body shook.

Entering the courtyard gate, passers-by, Jews and Muslims, looked at Miko in wonder. His sad, solemn voice rose and fell into the silence of the flushed evening.

'... Amen ... ye. .. e. .. sheme ... rabba...'

Thus he sang until he had completed the prayer. Then silence descended. A furry butterfly flapped its orange wings against the white wall. Miko closed the book, kissed it, stood on his toes, lifted his arms up in the air and stood there like that for a minute; then, as if broken into four, his body collapsed at the bottom of the stairs. People ran over to him. Some offered their keys. Avdaga the baker, who made soft white bread rolls at the corner in Pehlivanusha St., crouched down beside Miko, picked up his wrist and felt it.

'No, *djanum*, it's not epilepsy. There's no need for the key! It's over, he's burst an artery. It's *damla*, a stroke, a bad stroke', he said lowering the arm. '*Allah rahmetile*! May God rest his soul.'

They covered him with a white sheet; upstairs a door opened and in a subdued voice a woman told the people in the courtyard:

'Tell them to pour out the water. Sarucha has left the living. May God have mercy on her soul!'

In the spring they dragged everything away from Sarucha's house. They put a new lock on the courtyard gate and peace descended. Rays of sunshine broke through the cracks in the roof and little rings of light glittered like gold coins on the rafters in the dark attic. The door stood wide open. Every so often one of the old oak columns would groan. At the bottom of the stairs the olive cat was basking in the sun. It had carried its litter down from the attic, one by one. Lying on its side, it squinted, a fluffy little kitten hanging from each of its nipples.

It was noon.

To the sound of an accordion being played in one of the white blossom gardens, the new cathedral in town down below struck the hour:

Dong ... dong ... dong ...

Ong ... ong ... ong ... came the mysterious echo from Sarucha's house.

Gently sprouting from the dried-up stalk of rue in the cracked flowerpot on the window sill was a new serrated leaf. Passing by Sarucha's big house, people with a discerning sense of smell knew from its scent that spring had arrived.

Translated by Christina Pribićević-Zorić

From Spring to Spring

One could imagine his life from the manner of his death, and people simply shrugged their shoulders in that manly way that was their wont when dealing with someone else's pain, but the children were stunned by the unexpected news that his corpse had been winched up from the depths of a well.

It was spring, the one before had run rampant, and in between the two everything possible had come crashing down on his head. Crashing down until it subsided. It had all been spun and woven long ago and when the threads were stretched tight, suddenly and malevolently, fate like a spider drank its fill of blood and claimed its due for having had to wait from one century to the next. There is no point in asking why. Thousands of reasons will swarm like ants, white and black, winged and wingless, to dissuade you from your freedom.

He had lived for two or three very ordinary, small pleasures. They had come his way just a few times in all those long years. Everything else had come at will.

* * *

Spring that year – which is when this story about him and his wife Luna begins – was hot, with big drops of bountiful rain, plenty of sun and joy. Both day and night. Life was bursting forth everywhere and everywhere one could feel a rush in the air. That spring even the yellow kernels in his pocket sprouted. Amazed, he took them out, held them in the palm of his hand and looked at them. They had sprouted tiny, shiny little tails.

'They're shoots ... shoots ...', the thought quietly burgeoned in his mind, growing happily as if in a hothouse. He was glad that something was germinating and growing from being in contact with him and his warmth. He crouched right there in the street, in the glow of the sun, and looked at them.

'They're growing, they're growing', the cry of joy fluttered inside him without fuss or words, when suddenly he felt something block out the sun. Lifting his head he saw Rabbi Perera leaning over his hand. The rabbi was putting on his glasses to see better.

'Those kernels are alive, alive my Haimacho!', the rabbi said solemnly. 'Plant them in the earth, plant them. If you toss them into the dust you will kill as many lives as there are kernels. You must plant them and say the prayer prescribed for leaving seeds. May they bear fruit and grow, because our Lord loves the creation and reproduction of life.'

Haimacho's joy vanished instantaneously. Like the goldbug run over by clattering wheels as it spreads open its metallic wings, stretching out the underlying thin little interlacing veins just when it is about to fly off into the shimmering air and buzz around in the rampage of spring, so it vanished.

He rose lazily to his feet, leaving the rabbi to return his glasses piously to their worn case, and was followed by thundering voices saying: 'seeds ... leaving seeds, creation ... reproduction ...'

For the first time since his marriage, it was as if something had unwittingly mocked his sterility.

He let his arms hang limply by his side and, still frowning, walked on in fear of committing some wrong, when who should appear at the very first corner but Long Luna, his wife's namesake, who sold rue. This woman, with her broad hips, waddled up to him and offered him rue from her basket.

'Smell it, Haimacho, smell it! This year God blessed every living thing, everything that moves and grows. Smell it, rue has never smelled like this before! Take a sprig home to your Luna! The smell will drive her crazy and you'll know you've got a woman ...'

The smell of the rue filled his nostrils, but when he saw the mocking glint in her eyes he jumped aside as if to leap clear of a madwoman. He took the shortest route home and as soon as he reached the courtyard he threw the kernels onto the cobblestones. They spilled everywhere and a white hen came scampering out of the garden to collect them. When she had finished pecking the last kernel, she raised her head, twisted her neck and cocked an eye at him. Horrified and unsettled, he gazed wide-eyed into the terrible eye of the hen.

I

The *Talmud* is full of wondrous stories about fish, and Jewish women know how to cook them in a great variety of ways. Some are famous in town for their skill, and on Sabbath evenings few homes are without this well-made dish.

The mop-headed Jew delivered fish all over the *mahala*. He slipped past houses, fences and people like a secret. He trudged quietly down streets, through town and across courtyards. Always the same, always in the same suit, with his long side curls and wispy beard, he performed the job importantly, as importantly as his fellow Jews ate that same fish in their homes at night after prayer in temple, sitting silently and listening to the soft crackle of the flames rising up in the large lamp above the table.

Except for Fridays he had no real occupation the rest of the week. He would just roam around to see what odd jobs or news he could pick up and was always one of the first in temple, morning and night. There he felt worthy and in his rightful place. Were it not for these constant prayers, his sure and saintly deportment would (in his opinion) have no basis. Hence, he would always enter the temple bowing deeply to the holy chest where they kept the *Torah* and then, with the greatest reverence, lift a corner of the embroidered, gold-threaded cloth and press his lips to it.

He also liked the memorial services held in private houses. He would rock back and forth along with everyone else, read for the salvation of the souls of all the dead, drink Turkish coffee and *rakija*, and wrap up the yellow cakes and odd coin they handed out at the end of the prayer.

On Fridays he would pull tight the belt on his trousers, check his shoes and walk in the street with a bounce to his step.

Everyone knew his spot in the square next to the fishmonger.

He used to potter around there as a child, and later he would crouch there placidly, push the basket in front of him and wait. The customers would come of themselves: 'Haimacho, please take this fish to my house for me! With measured movements, he would take the fish, examine the gills to see whether they were pink and fresh, then slowly and carefully lay them out in the basket so that he always knew which fish belonged to whom. He liked this work and when he got a *huchen* or speckled trout to carry, both his hands and his eyes would leap with joy.

He enjoyed the fish and the fact that housewives would look forward to the sound of his knock. He would knock on the courtyard door according to the value and kind of fish he was carrying, and from his knock housewives could guess what he had on offer. He would meet them half-way by trying to match their appetites.

'Come in, Haimacho, come in. The *pastel* is just out of the oven, have some, here's a fork ...' That was how he was welcomed by Floreta, whose favourite fish was pike. 'Pike is a fatty fish, the best fish!'

Haimacho would laugh good-naturedly at the old woman; he knew that other housewives had their soft spots. Each liked a different size and variety of fish. He also knew that all these good, mild-mannered, quiet women could be terrible and even turn purple with anger if he showed up with minnows or chubs. And that happened sometimes. Such Fridays always made him unhappy. Opening the courtyard door as if it was his fault that there was not a better choice of fish, he would creep across the washed cobblestones and quake in front of the housewives.

'Oh dear ... (he would close his eyes), oh ... of all days, that it should be this Friday ... and we have a guest coming tonight, the *shaliah* from Jerusalem ... Even carp, even carp would be out of place for such an occasion, let alone these miserable minnows ... take them away ... and take yourself away with them ...'

That is how the women would greet him on such Fridays and silently he would leave the fish and depart. As he went from door to door he kept thinking that Rabbi Perera should look in the *Torah* or *Talmud* to see whether they said something about it being forbidden to eat minnows, the way it is forbidden to eat crabs and eels.

'Maybe it's written somewhere ... maybe ...' He would talk to himself like that, contending that the rabbis in the *halakha* should discuss the matter and remove this calamity from Jewish homes.

He was always a-tingle when he carried *huchen*. There was a spring to his step and he showed them to each house where, after accepting a glass of *rakija* from the happy housewife, he would turn around in the kitchen, look at everything that was being prepared for the big dinner and fill his nostrils with the hot smells of roast meat, thin layers of pastry and rare dishes usually prepared to celebrate happy betrothals and major holidays.

Grinning to himself he would then go down into town and say: 'The *huchen* are a joy, a pleasure. Their scales are small and silvery, their stomachs milky white, and their eyes are alive. Alive. Even when the *huchen* are dead, their eyes are still alive, staring out freely, without fear...whereas trout have sad eyes ...'

That is how such Fridays would end, wrapping in his handkerchief the white *zwanzigs* he would get as his earnings from the richer tradesmen.

At home he would wash (at the well in summertime), change into his Sabbath suit (which had belonged to his late father), go to temple and then to dinner at Señor Kucha's, who on the Sabbath shared his table with the poor.

II

Having seen him frequently at memorial services, Yahiel Ganhiz judged him to be ready for marriage and one day took him by the hand like a child and led him straight from temple to his house. Haimacho, who looked minute next to the huge Yahiel, simply gazed up at him and said not a word.

'I have some good brandy left over from *Pesach* and it's cold this morning ...'

They entered the house in silence. Pushing aside a stack of unbound books, Haimacho sat down on the bench and Yahiel, with his big head, huge torso and heavy hand, grabbed the wooden hammer and banged on the ceiling. A little later he said in his thick voice:

'Haimacho, son of the cobbler Eliazar Papo, I invited you for breakfast. Please pay me that honour. Sit down, sit down!'

21

Haimacho had just risen to his feet; his little donkey was moaning outside like an empty barrel. From the sound of the glass bowl rattling on the shelf, it was clearly cracked. Then Yahiel's wife came in.

'Good day, Haimacho!', she said, carrying in the salt, bread and a plate of hard-boiled eggs.

'Good day, Haimacho, you have come at a good time!'

'Good day, Haimacho!', she said bringing a napkin for him to wipe his mouth.

'And bring in the *rakija*, woman, the one left over from Pesach! Haimacho is a rare guest, it is not every day that he comes.'

The woman brought in the bottle and two glasses and then departed.

Yahiel filled the glasses and then raised his in a toast:

'*Lehaim!*'

'*Lehaim!*'

They drank down the first glass. Each peeled an egg.

'Haimacho, your father was a widower for many years and never remarried. He left behind one child ...'

Haimacho listened and ate his egg.

'You, Haimacho, are that child! But you stopped being a child long ago ... you're not even a boy any more!'

Yahiel poured out two more glasses, put a piece of bread and a bit of egg in his mouth, and when he finished chewing, swallowed it down and continued speaking.

'You are getting on, Haimacho, you are not young any more and it is almost too late for you to marry a young girl.'

'Too late! Too late!', Haimacho repeated, rising to his feet.

'And a man needs a woman in the house! Yes, he does. A man falls apart without a woman, like a book without a binding. Here, look! The first to go are the front pages, the book gets dog-eared, the threads break and it all falls apart. Yes, yes ... that's how it is, my Haimacho, and then one doesn't know where the *Haggadah* begins and the *Shefoch* ends. And the song of the goat? No trace of it, no trace at all ... Look!' Yahiel pointed to some old tattered books.

Haimacho nodded his head!

'On *Shevuoth* the Israelites received the Law, and for a Jew a wife is the law. Are you a good Jew? Yes, you are. And Luna? Luna,

22

Machebohor's daughter, is a good girl, a hard-working girl. Pock-marked women bring luck, they bring peace to the house. They do not talk much, and they ask for nothing. It suffices to buy them a ring, the most ordinary ring ...'

When they finished breakfast Yahiel took Haimacho's hand and raised him to his feet from the bench.

'Go now, Haimacho, and think about it!' At the door he added: 'The girl is as firm and round as an apple'. He patted him on the shoulder: 'Round ... firm ...', he said once more, smiling, and then quickly shut the door on him.

After that day, Haimacho would often close the curtain on the window, lock the door and secretly open the chest. Every time he counted the *zwanzigs* and copper coins he would be pleased that there was so much, enough even to feed a wife. Really, he should stop going to Señor Kucha's on the Sabbath. He could take Liacho there and tell Señor Kucha: 'I will eat at home from now on, but you be good to this man'. That is what he could do and that is what he would do. The wife, his wife, could cook, light the lamp, and he would recite the *kiddush* in his own home ...

Such were the thoughts in his mind, but when he stepped out of the house his decisions would evaporate, and the sight of Yahiel Ganhiz, that giant of a man, would frighten him even from a distance. He would steer clear of him whenever he could, and when Yahiel's voice boomed anywhere near him, he would duck down and slowly slip away, regardless of whether it was a café or a memorial service.

It was around this time that, walking down Buka Street at the foot of Mejtas cemetery, he remembered a conversation he had had as a child. He had been sitting there with the other children, and Chucho, the fez-maker's son, was saying he had noticed that Rosika had started to grow breasts ...'like two little buns ... and I pinched her, yes I did, I swear ... I swear on my mother's life!' That is what Chucho said, then he stood up, pounded his chest and said with a swagger: 'When I grow up I'll take her for my wife. I will, I tell you, I'll take her for my wife. You'll see! I'm going to pinch her again, I am!' Chucho's eyes burned with fire, and little Haimacho went home, cuddled up miserably to his grandmother, who had raised him since he was an orphan, buried his head in her lap and burst into tears.

23

And so Haimacho became more and more afraid of Yahiel, who now kept a close watch on him even in temple, and if he caught Haimacho's eye he would raise his hoarse voice in prayer like a warning and everyone would turn around to see what was the matter, and Haimacho would cover himself with his *tallit* and hide behind his book.

But this torture did not last long, because the enormous book-binder would suddenly move to another seat and even when leaving the temple would ignore Haimacho. In vain did Haimacho now try to approach him. Yahiel did not want to see him. And then one day, not knowing why himself, Haimacho made straight for the man's house. On his way he kept thinking about the stack of green paper on top of which lay an old, thick, leather-bound book.

Yahiel was pressing newly-bound prayer books between two boards of wood and as soon he saw Haimacho he straightened his back and held up his hand.

'Wait a minute, my good Jew, let me tell you right away that there is no money in it. Luna can sew, and let her work if you need her to! You understand? She's got no money. None.'

This time Haimacho was not deafened by the thundering voice so much as startled that Yahiel had broached the subject immediately. Opening the door he had decided at the last minute to ask for a book, but now he was flustered and said nothing.

Sizing him up with a stern eye, Yahiel said scornfully:

'So? You're after money, like everyone else! Your Friday earnings aren't enough for you … that's it, isn't it!?'

Haimacho thought that Yahiel must know about the *zwanzigs* he had saved, and, staring at the ground, he mumbled:

'I don't need any money …'

Yahiel laughed with loud satisfaction.

'I knew you were an honest man … I knew it …' He patted him on the back and wished him the best of luck. Haimacho stood there as if rooted to the spot and the faintest smile crossed his face.

III

Nothing in Haimacho's little house changed, even when they brought Luna there one night after the wedding dinner which had been held at the home of the bookbinder, Yahiel Ganhiz. For the first

24

time in his life, Haimacho, the groom, was inebriated, not because someone had deliberately tried to get him drunk but because he himself was feeling heavy-hearted and wanted to drink, and because it did not take much to make him drunk. That evening both Sara, with her tambourine, and the old Spanish dance for two, looked sad to him. Yet the whole house was in high spirits, echoed by the loud chatter, shrieking children, women singing, clinking glasses and rattling dishes, because Yahiel had laid out a very good dinner. There were dishes of fish, so that Haimacho's and Luna's offspring might multiply, and salted roast almonds, so that everyone would keep drinking.

With their stomachs full and thirst quenched, the naturally boisterous guests had let themselves go completely, as if this was their last party and they intended to take full advantage of it. Haimacho was upset by it all and, sitting beside Luna, he merely smiled at these people who were filling their mouths, wiping their greasy chins and lifting their glasses to toast him and Luna. Sara, who provided the entertainment at such celebrations in the homes of the poor, banged away tirelessly at her tambourine and after every song wiped her sweaty, greasy face with a crumpled handkerchief, and straightened her cap with its long wide tassel trailing down her back. For the tenth time now she sang the wedding song: 'O *que relumbror de novia hermosa* ...' Straining her voice as she sang, she turned each time to Haimacho and Luna, rolling her eyes meaningfully. The whole room would again go crazy, some tapping the rhythm with forks against their glasses, others clapping their hands, while the children, sprawled out on the floor, banged their plates on the planks until Yahiel Ganhiz's entire house was rocking as if afloat.

Haimacho gripped the bench, his eyes glued to Sara's big throat which was straining like a pair of bellows; he was afraid it might burst and a black clot of blood would come spurting out. But every time Yahiel called out: *Novio!*, he would pick up a glass in a fluster, clink it with him and drain the small tapered brandy glass down to the last drop. In the end Luna removed the glass from his hand, but by then Haimacho had already had enough. Everything in the room was moving and seemed to be spinning, rising, falling, tilting, tumbling, it was as if even Luna was falling into his lap and he was catching her in his arms, feeling how big, full and fleshy her breasts

25

were. The thought of them sobered him up, and he huddled on the bench, scared that he would have to pinch those breasts like Chucho, the fez-maker's son.

So it was that on his wedding night Haimacho was half-sober, tired and bloated when he locked the door. After the wedding party left the courtyard, his whole room began to sway to the beat of the evening's songs and he sat down half-dead on the divan, while Luna stood shyly by the stove ...

Only a few days later, Luna ventured to tell him that the two of them would have no children. She said it quite suddenly somehow, after dinner when they were sitting silently, each in their own corner of the room. He looked Luna straight in the eye and asked her warily why not?

'God did not make you that way, Haimacho', replied Luna coldly. Dropping her voice, she added: 'You are a *monjo!*', and turned red with embarrassment.

Thereafter, Luna slept alone on blankets in the corner, but Haimacho lived in the hope that God would give him children. He spent his *zwanzigs*, earned others, squatted near the fishmonger, checked the gills of the fish and, hauling his little basket onto his back, made the rounds of the *mahala*. This calmed him and he reconciled himself to not having children, because even before the end of nine months, slowly, bit by bit, he had discovered his secret, without getting too upset about it. Unperturbed, he continued to look forward to the Sabbath and holidays, smiling contentedly whenever he bought fruit for dinner and wine for *kiddush*, and when he washed and dressed for the Sabbath he was happiest, and would look like a new man when he returned from temple in the evening and, like the real man of the house, would happily call out to Luna from the veranda, with the Sabbath greeting: '*Shabbat Shalom!*'

While delivering his fish, he had even composed an entire litany of prayers and when his basket was nice and full, he would walk down the street whispering to himself, as if mumbling one of the psalms of David: 'May they multiply like the sand and the fish in the sea, may everyone multiply to whom the Lord has given the gift of birth, as He has given them eyes to see with, ears to hear with, a soul to breathe with! May they multiply and may they give birth, and we shall rejoice with them and not envy them, because

it is the will of the Lord, *Adonai Sabaoth*, for us to be without offspring
and to glorify His name in our own way. Amen!'

He would walk around like some kind of secret, all withdrawing
into himself, while Luna stayed at home, sad and lonely, singing
her song '*Anderlet*', sewing colourful, billowy pantaloons and silk
tops for the women and girls of the Muslim *mahala*.

And then came that frenzied spring.

IV

It came rolling in. Almost overnight it spilled over the *mahala*, the
courtyards, the gardens and the rooftops. Fruit trees suddenly
blossomed, the grass turned green. Girls opened their windows,
song filled the air, the squeals of children were everywhere.

And with the blossom could be noticed these two things: it was
as if it had blushed from the torrid songs of the young girls, and it
was as if, now ripe, its petals began to fall from the loud squeals
and shrieks of the children.

The children went wild. Spring had them in a spin and they chased
each other down the streets, jumped over fences and hedges,
scrambled onto rooftops and simply would not talk in any calm,
intelligent way, but rather kept squealing and tearing around. They
would go down the street and begin to whinny, like colts which
had broken out of the courtyard and gone racing around the
corner.

At the top of the street, Muslim children blew on the whistles
they had made out of willow, while down by Sada's well a horde of
Jewish children disentangled themselves, running around, squealing in a hundred voices. These children, who were barefoot and
lived in dank little houses, were feeling the warm cobblestones
under their feet for the very first time and it brought a glow to their
eyes. And the whole *mahala* came to life with them. Like one and
the same cry passing from mouth to mouth, spring flooded into
the *mahala*, sweeping everything in its path.

The crests of the roosters that jumped into the street from the
courtyards were as red as the brightest blood. They crowed, they
ran around furiously in circles, flapped their wings, dropping first
the right one and then the left, their strong feathers scraping the

27

cobblestones, while the hens congregated, nodding their heads approvingly, some of them clucking, roosting, looking as if their crops were full of seeds. Yellow and white butterflies appeared in the street, fluttering in front of the windows, flitting down into the gardens where they were chased by sparrows which they deliberately grazed with just the tips of their wings.

Old people, asthmatic and racked by coughing, breathed more easily. The flow of blood in their hard arteries was warmer, smoother.

'Ah … aah … aaah …', they rejoiced, as they lifted their heads and straightened their stooped backs.

Sara, the poorest and noisest woman in the *mahala*, having shooed her five hungry children into the street before *aksham*, picked up her tambourine, hid it under her long shawl and left the house. She turned into the first courtyard and immediately burst into song, banging away at her tambourine: '*Asuerico de quince anos*' … she sang, swayed, lifted her voice and body, and beat on her tambourine. In an instant the fragrant air quivered, housewives appeared at their windows, the strains of the *sevdalinka* soared, the pulse quickened and the young girls clasped hands.

The children came running in, the courtyard filled up, Sara sat herself down on a bright cushion in front of the door, the girls all around her, and the courtyard went mad.

In all this spring madness, Haimacho felt somewhat uneasy. Ever since the day he had tossed down the grains of corn, he had been roaming around the *mahala* like a beaten dog. Down at the foot of the *mahala*, where small houses were wedged in among the buildings, his Luna was sitting by the open window, gazing at a patch of sky and the wisp of green that spilled down from Brijeg.

As she sat by the window the breeze tickled her neck, the breeze that blew up there like a memory. Up there was where she had been raised, and spring was running so rampant up there this year that it seemed to reach her even down here. She could hear the leaves rustling in the mulberry tree, smell the lilacs which were already in bloom, smell the soap the girls washed their breasts with in spring time, smell the rue they used as adornment, and there would be the smell of the wallflowers now too. A sniff of the air told her that the wallflowers were as red as a girl's cheek, that their blossoms were full, not four-leaved and small. She had loved the smell of wallflowers ever since she had been a young girl, when her thighs had begun to sway and her step had become small and shy. She knew that the wallflowers were now being taken out into the sun in flower boxes: you crumbled the surrounding soil with your fingers and sprinkled it with water, and then they would blossom at the same time as the lilacs. She loved wallflowers, both red and white. She liked the red better. She would gaze at their colour and feel as if her own blood had that same redness and that same fragrance. Her blood had a fragrance, it was the fragrance of youth, but she had never wanted anyone to detect it. She was a shy girl. All budding girls are shy, but she had another reason as well. She was pockmarked, ugly. However, that was no reason for her not to smell the wallflowers and listen to the blood rush to her cheeks and caress the tips of her ripe breasts.

Her face had pockmarks and God knows what it would have looked like without them. It was something she thought about a great deal. She would lock herself into her room, face the mirror, unbutton her vest and shirt, and look to see whether there were any such marks on her breasts or her shoulders, and what unpocked skin was like. And she would see that the skin on her chest was white, that her breasts were round and firm, and her nipples small and pink. That is what she would see. She also had a black mole near her underarm, and peering out from her armpit were curly little hairs which were always damp. She would examine all this shyly in the mirror, bit by bit, baring first one side of her breast and then the other, and when the whole breast would spill out of her shirt she would tremble with fear, cover it quickly with her hand and pull her shirt back over it.

Still, she knew she was ugly, not so much because of the pockmarks as because of her half-white eye. Her right eye was normal, pretty, large and dark, but her left eye was disfigured by a scar. And so, being pockmarked and disfigured, she was the quietest and most timid of all the girls. She would hide in one of the rooms and seldom venture out to mingle with the other girls who were healthy, pretty and alluring. It was then that she fell in love with her sad song about Anderlet! She had fallen in love with the song because it was plaintive and doleful, because the very melody made her feel as if something was crying out inside her, grieving, hurting. Sitting at home alone with her needlework, she would close her eyes happily and begin: 'Anderle-e-e-t, my Anderl-e-e-e-t.'

29

She was not sad, even though one spring after another went by, even though one girl after another got married and her youth went the way of the shrivelling wallflowers, red and white. She waited, quiet and patient. And when they married her off to Haimacho she did not particularly rejoice. It was as if she expected her life to be what it had become after her wedding night. She was not disillusioned and she lived side by side with Haimacho, turning into the embodiment of peace, into a phenomenon.

And now, for the first time in four long years, this spring when the grains of corn in Haimacho's pocket sprouted, something stirred inside her, it was growing here at the window, in the sun, in the air flowing down from Banjski Brijeg, from Bjelave all the way down to these small, tiny houses hidden behind the three-storey buildings. Returning from the *mahala*, she would open wide the window in the little room and sit alone on the bench cushion, her legs folded beneath her, gazing with her right eye at the greenery and blossoming fruit trees.

She would slap some redness into her sallow cheeks.

And the bright little chintz curtain, pulled to one side, would flutter like a little flag behind her back, occasionally tickling her cheek. She would never even notice when Haimacho entered the room.

V

Spring burst forth and swelled. It penetrated even the most hidden corners, it came in through the doors and the windows, it crept into the soul and the eyes, and even into certain invisible extremities of the body which spread out like roots into the fresh, fragrant air of morning and night. One such evening, Haimacho found Luna in the courtyard replanting a young shoot into a red clay flowerpot.

'It's a carnation, a carnation!', said Luna, rising to her feet with a sigh, as if crouching had tired her. The way she looked at him with her black right eye and white left one unnerved Haimacho.

'So?', he asked surprised, and had the feeling that this was not his Luna standing there but somebody else.

'Nothing …', said Luna, picking up the flowerpot and running quickly up the stairs and into the kitchen.

Luna had been to the *mahala* that day: 'It's a carnation, a carnation, its flower is as red as if you had dripped blood onto it', the Dervish-effendi's wife had said, handing Luna the cutting. 'Here, wrap it up in this wet cloth, it will flower within a month. My *haji* likes to smell it even now, and the children like it too. Ask my daughters-in-law ...', the Hadji-Dervish-effendi's wife chuckled, with a meaningful look. Luna laughed. She sensed it was a joke, blushed and when she was alone with Hashia for a fitting for silk pantaloons and a velvet vest, she asked her timidly, blushing but still curious, what the *haji's* wife had meant about the carnation. Shaking with laughter, Hashia collapsed on the divan. Luna dropped down next to her, her heart heavy somehow, and on the verge of tears. 'Oh, nothing, Lunia', (that was how her name was spoken in Muslim homes). 'Nothing! We're supposed to wear carnations when we get ready for bed at night in our chambers. The *haji's* sons like the smell of carnations and won't kiss us unless they hear the flower brush their ear. That's all it is, dear!'

Luna pondered this at the window, in the kitchen, in the courtyard and all spring long she smelled the wallflowers and the carnations, remembered her youth and thought of the chambers of the *haji's* daughters-in-law. She felt the stirrings of passion, it flowed through her body, burning inside her like a fire.

At dusk, the *mahalas* began to sob with song, with the sounds of the *zurle* and the accordion. And with the approach of summer, hot and humid, a glow came to Luna's right eye, she started to stand tall and look younger. At *ikindia* she would go to Muslim houses, deliver her sewing, sip coffee and sweet sherbet in the gardens, sit on the *kilims* sweating under her arms and her breasts and, to the sound of clattering glasses, cups and coffee-pots, secretly unbutton her robes to breathe more easily. The girls and young women, all decked out in their colourful airy pantaloons and thin white blouses, excitable, their cheeks flushed, their eyes sparkling under thinly drawn black eyebrows, sang one song after another in their soaring voices, pinched each other, giggled, ran up to the wooden screens to peak through the holes out into the street. And standing in the streets were the young men, decked out in their new *bairam* vests and trousers, with silk sashes around their waists and a flower in the hand, and speaking caressingly to the girls through the crack in the door. The children were shouting.

31

VI

Haimacho was becoming increasingly uneasy. It was as if he had a bad premonition. That spring he walked around as if he was not of this world, as if he was in someone else's skin, as if now for the first time something had hurled him into this wonderful place full of vivacious people and red with the first cherries.

'*Ashlamas! Ashlamas!*' His ears rang with the cry that echoed all over town. The fruit-sellers had filled their woven baskets with the first cherries of spring, red and big, sprinkling them with water so that the droplets would cling to them like red pearls. '*Ashlamas! Ashlamas!*', they cried. People passed by, children and adults, their hearts fluttering, their eyes aglow. Everyone remembered last year's *ashlamas*, those sweet harbingers of early summer.

Haimacho too walked by the overflowing baskets and was tempted to stop and take a cherry, bite into it, suck its sweet juice and then say to the fruit-seller: 'Well, give me a pound, a pound of those with the little stalks, those in that basket, a pound, and pour them into my kerchief ...' He did this every year. He would hold the kerchief by the corners, get a loaf of bread, squat in the burning sun next to the bakery and chew with his mouth full, while the pigeons swooped down in front of him, cooing and waiting for him to toss them a crumb of bread or a handful of corn.

His heart ached for the same thing this year, but he had a feeling that he would not find the *ashlamas* sweet, that the sun would not warm him like last year and that the pigeons would be too afraid to come and eat out of his hand.

Walking through town, he caught himself thinking about the *mahalas* above, eavesdropping on conversations behind their tall wooden fences, standing on his toes to catch a glimpse of what he was determined to see. When he snapped out of this mood he had the feeling he had lost consciousness and was unable to remember the streets he had taken. And often, when he suddenly came to like this, he would notice a Muslim in a red fez nearby, with sleeves rolled up and looped onto his vest, chest bare, bronzed by the wind and the sun, but the skin was white under his shirt.

On such days he would ask Luna when night fell whether she had gone to the *mahala*.

'Yes, I was there!', Luna would answer freely and loudly, and his head would begin to throb.

Summer became increasingly electric.

The days blazed with sun and dazzling light, the nights were hot, only occasionally ruffled by a cool breeze. Down in Cemalusa the hubbub would diminish in the evening, conversations would lose their stridency, and the strains of passionate song, accompanied by the wailing of violin and a tambourine, would waft sporadically through the open doors of the tavern. One could hear a woman's voice and from its sound tell how the dancer was turning her painted face aside, while her eyes, glassy and ringed with blue, would flash, beckoning one minute, looking away the next, her thighs wiggling as she lifted her whole body, standing on her toes and bending backwards. A cry from the drunken crowd would occasionally pierce the darkness of the streets like a bolt of lightning, hitting the window glass.

When the evening sky turned red up in the *mahala*, the voice of the *muezzin* would spill out from the minaret as softly and quietly as a whisper, the fragrance of the roses would fill the courtyards, a child's thin, wavering voice would ring out, a demure female tune would be answered by a powerful male song, interlaced with the sound of the *zurle*; the dogs would be barking, with fires crackling in the gardens, calls echoing in the air, the tambourine beating out its rhythm, the accordion stretched to its limits, while people would stroll down the streets, as if reborn, vibrant and young, swinging long white lanterns in their hands.

Haimacho went to bed right after *aksham*, but he could not fall asleep. What was Luna doing, he wondered, tossing and turning on his mattress.

One Friday he too suddenly felt a tingle of delight and joy. He forgot everything that had been eating away at his heart and soul like a worm, and the blood in his veins turned warm. His hands began to tremble, his eyes opened wide, shining with a red and green light, and wherever he looked he found a sense of kinship with everything, with people and objects, corners and cobblestones.

He had left the house that day with his usual heavy heart, and even in the temple his troubling thoughts had interfered with his prayers. Hoisting his empty basket on his back, he went to

33

Salihbey square where the fishmongers were. Suddenly, his heart almost stopped! A crowd had gathered around Sason's stall and was peering at something. At first Haimacho thought it must be a big *huchen* that had been brought for sale, and a frown darkened his brow, because he did not like seeing fish cut up and sold in pieces (which often was the only way big fish could be sold). He had composed himself, heard Sason's intermittent cry: 'Live fish! Live fish! Live trout! ... C-o-m-e and get it ... C-o-m-e and get it ...', rushed over, pushed his way through the crowd and peered into the trough which was almost brimful with water. The trough was teeming with live fish. Their dark grey backs, smooth and slimy, half-protruded from the water. Swirling around with their pink fins, opening wide their mouths, lifting their armour to reveal the red, finely serrated gills under-neath, the golden rings in their eyes shining, their bellies flashing white, their tails swishing, the live fish swimming in the trough were terrified, banging their heads against the wood, grazing past each other, leaping out of the water. His eyes almost popping out of his head, Haimacho put his hands on his hips, gaped and watched, his legs shaking. He was seeing live fish for the first time in his life. The very first time!

'Live fish! Live fish!', Sason cried, then picked up a small net and scooped out some fish. The trout flapped around in the net, their heads and tails sticking out of the holes, gasping for air, their silvery, nacre bellies flashing white.

'Haimacho, please ... Haimacho ...', cried old Kucho, the money-changer, a string with two pike hanging from one finger. But Haimacho did not hear him. He was agog; the blood throbbed in his veins. He barely managed to take the fish in his hands. Dazed, he turned it over, looked at it and put it into his basket. He did not sit down; with basket in hand, he went back to the trough and peered into it again.

When the fish had been sold, when his customers had had their fill of the smell, Haimacho stood up with a cheerful smile (he had about twenty fine trout), scooped up some water in his hand from the trough, splashed it on the fish which were still alive in his basket, hoisted the basket onto his back and left.

The half-live fish flapped around in the basket, which leaked water down Haimacho's back. Haimacho stopped at each well he came to, lowered his basket, removed the wet cloth from it, scooped water into both hands and poured it on the trout. He opened his hands so that the water would stream straight into their mouths. The fish opened their clean pink mouths, fixing him with their stare. Haimacho called over the children and they gathered around, leaned over to look, pushed and shoved, almost knocking over both the basket and Haimacho himself.

And so he went his way, joyful, happy as never before; he took off his tunic, covered his head with a handkerchief, and tucked his fez under his belt. He was soaking with sweat, especially his face. It trickled down his side curls and onto the wisps of his russet beard, but his eyes shone bright and twinkled. His shirt stuck to his torso, sweat trickled down his back, but he just kept listening for the sound of the live trout flapping around in the basket, and he felt good somehow, he did not find the climb up the steep streets difficult today, he was not scorched by the sun and he knocked at every door gingerly, cheerfully, as if he was bringing everyone the joy that had so profusely filled his soul.

But the poor housewives, unaccustomed to seeing him like this, took fright. They thought: 'There's Haimacho carrying *huchen* or carp, not chub; Señor Dudo must be having guests for dinner!'

'Oh, I'm ruined! My spinach pie has burned and the lamb could be a cat it's so scrawny!', wailed Dudo's Renucha, opening the kitchen door. 'What is it, what are you carrying Haimacho? Something good, God willing! Come in, come in ...'

'Nothing, nothing, Tia Renucha. Here, I've got live fish, live trout ... live ones ... I'm taking them to the Macedonian ... Look ... Give me some water to splash over them ...', Haimacho said, all out of breath.

And so Haimacho went from yard to yard, red in the face, dripping with sweat and water, whispering his litany, to which now for the first time he added the words 'live fish'. 'May you multiply like the sand and the live fish in the sea, all of you to whom God has given the gift of birth, as He has given you eyes to see with, ears to listen with, a soul to breathe with. May you multiply like the sand and the live fish in the sea and may we rejoice with you and not envy you, for it is the Lord's will that we who have no offspring shall not have any and that we shall glorify His name in our own way. Amen!'

VII

That same Friday the following occurred as well.

Luna's cheeks were already flushed. As she moved from yard to yard and garden to garden, Luna began to sigh for love. She opened her arms, not yet knowing to whom. At dusk, when she would leave her companions for home, she would turn around to watch the women enter their chambers and she would sigh. Blossoming timidly and secretly inside her was the desire to be in one of those chambers herself, where the wide open windows let in the cool evening air with its fragrance of flowers and of pears arranged on shelves. If only she could be in such a room, waiting, reclining on a mattress ...

She would bypass the Jewish *mahala* on her way back, and when she got home, she would toss and turn on her blankets, yearning for a hand to caress her, burning with almost wanton passion for anyone to hold her in his arms and make her weak at the knees. The nights were humid and sometimes she would sleep on the veranda, her breathing laboured as if she had a fever, and she would uncover her thighs to cool down.

She knew that Haimacho saw something was happening to her. At first she was careful not to let him know what was troubling her but later she stopped caring. Still, ever since the day that she had met Alia, when she had found him crouching in a corner of the Dervish-effendi's courtyard, happily munching a crust of bread made with fresh wheat, she had become apprehensive again and very withdrawn at home because she did not want Haimacho to know her thoughts or her dreams. But inside they were tearing her apart.

That particular Friday when Haimacho had seen live fish for the first time and in his delight had forgotten all his brooding mis- givings, Luna returned home from the *mahala* beside herself. She felt as if her clothes were torn, hanging and falling off her. Her arms, breasts, thighs and joints hurt, and when she thought of what had happened to her she felt faint. Her legs would barely hold her.

Nightfall was still far off, but in view of preparations for the Sabbath, Luna was afraid she would find Haimacho by the well where he washed. She pulled her shawl over her head and walked in terror of collapsing right in the middle of the courtyard as soon as she saw him. She fanned herself with the ends of her shawl to cool down, because she was on fire and wet with sweat. Luna could smell the soap she had washed with in his bathroom and also his sweat (because he had thrown her head back on his shoulder), and she wanted to get his smell out of her clothes.

She opened the yard door, and as she walked in and down the steps the courtyard began to spin before her eyes. Luna managed to collect herself enough to see that no one was there. She threw off her shawl, shoved the basin and soap in front of the door, grabbed a ready change of clothes from the next room and shut herself up in the kitchen. There she collapsed on the chest in the corner and began to shake from head to foot. She shook so hard that the kitchen dishes began to clatter. Luna felt a wave of relief, thought fleetingly of everything she had experienced only shortly before, then abruptly rose to her feet and began to undress. She stripped down to her waist, wrapped a scarf around her head, poured water from the bucket into the basin and, examining her forearms for any visible bruises, began to splash water on herself and soap her breasts, shoulders and neck. Next she slipped off her skirt and stockings, washed herself all over and quickly put on her Sabbath clothes. She again checked the blouse she had been wearing, rolled it up carefully and put it away in the chest. She wrapped a silk scarf over the cap on her head and, smelling strongly of almond soap, walked out of the kitchen, her step lighter and surer as she crossed the doorstep. Just then, Haimacho, gasping from the heat, was coming up the steps. He was carrying his basket. Flustered, Luna went into the other room. She started tidying up and appeared not to hear him call.

'Luna', Haimacho called out again, opening the door. 'Here, put this water-melon in some water!'

Haimacho gave her the water-melon with both hands; taking it Luna wanted to say something, but her voice failed her. She pressed the water-melon against her cheek and just managed to say:

'It's so cold!'

'It's still not cold enough, no, it's not. Put it in some water and let it stand for two hours until dinner. And change the water regularly so that it stays cold! A water-melon is nothing if it isn't cold!'

Haimacho had become garrulous as he undressed and got himself ready for the Sabbath. She had never heard him talk so much before. He talked about fish, about the live trout, about how they opened their mouths and moved their gills, about how the *mahala* had been all agog to see live fish in his basket; he told her how he had earned two *zwanzigs*, one from the Macedonian and the other from Kucho the money-changer, and how Sason would be selling live fish straight through until Yom Kippur. He talked and washed, changed, stepped out onto the veranda, went into the kitchen, dipped his finger in the basin full of water and walked back into the room thinking about how cold the water-melon would be. Standing on the step as he left for temple, he reminded her:

'Don't forget to keep changing the water! Don't forget!'

Luna shut the door and sat down on the divan. She pressed her thighs together, pulled in her legs and curled up into a ball.

That afternoon, as soon as she had finished her chores she had gone to the *mahala*. She had gone quickly, her mind addled by passion. 'Today, it will happen today!', she kept saying to herself as she walked up the hill. She had turned into a burning desire for it finally to happen; it had been waiting to happen for so long. Today she would not pull away, she would not. She knew that the Dervish-effendi's family had left for the countryside on Wednesday and she was sure that Alia would be waiting for her, even though they had never spoken about it, and in her mind she had imagined what it would be like and could hardly wait to get there. But when she found herself in the courtyard and when Alia came out and stood before her, she was so surprised, so frightened, that she forgot everything and did not know whether she had walked into the room on her own or been carried in by Alia. She wanted to pull away and scream, but somehow she could not move and later when she felt the mattress underneath her, she began to shake and she simply shut her eyes.

Even now, were it not for the pain she felt all over her body, she would not believe all the things that had happened to her, to pock-marked Luna.

She was not sorry, not sorry at all! Let it have happened, let it! She was talking to herself now, the blood rushing to her head. She thought she heard, yes, the courtyard door opening and, Alia coming up the steps! Curled up, peering through half-closed eyes, she expected him to burst into the room and say breathlessly:

'Lunia, I've come to take you. I've come! I can't wait any more ...
Come ... It's time for you to live like a woman ... It's time ...'

Alia had kept saying that to her all afternoon, lying beside her
on the mattress in that room, holding her in his strong arms.

Even now it was as if those arms were there, as if she could feel
Alia's burning arms and hands, the fire in his body and the smell
of his sweat.

She remembered how she had secretly looked at him once or
twice when he was on top of her and seen that his eyes were bulging
and red. Seeing a man so close to for the first time, she could hardly
believe it was she and not some other woman lying there beside
her crumpled clothes, wearing only her top and one stocking (on
her right leg). She felt tired somehow, and heavy. Had it not been
for his hand stroking her back and thighs so passionately, she would
have dropped off into a pleasant dream, her breathing deep and
even, her body sprawled out on the mattress. But Alia kept wriggling
next to her, he kept talking to her, pressing her against him. And
she lay there with eyes closed, saying nothing, thinking nothing,
except that she ought to remove the other stocking as well, the
one on her right leg with the red band holding it up, and then
everything would be all right.

That afternoon she was not afraid of anything and she found
that strange. When Alia went into the bathroom to wash, she
remembered it was nearly the Sabbath and she had to go home.
Alia barely let her get dressed. When he walked her to the door he
put his hand on the latch and took Luna by the hand:

'But, come back, you hear me? All right, you can have Saturday,
but on Sunday I'll be waiting for you right after lunch and don't
worry about being seen. None of the Dervish-effendi's family
will be poking their noses around here for at least a month. I hope
they have a good time at their country house in Mrkojevici, and
we'll have a good time here!', said Alia, leading her back into the
middle of the room; and while Luna stood there like a condemned
woman, begging him to let her go, he slipped his hands under her
blouse and, fired with passion, took off her clothes again, and then
his own.

When he finally let her go out into courtyard, he threatened that
if she did not come back he would come and get her, he would
convert her and make her a Muslim and then marry her. 'I will, I

39

swear I will! But first I'll wait in your street for that miserable husband of yours and beat him to a pulp. He won't move a finger, no; he won't have time to know what hit him. The swine, he'd keep you and let you die without you ever knowing what it's like to be a woman, without you ever knowing the meaning of life and pleasure! That son of a bitch!'

His threat did not seem at all menacing now, or likely. 'But why should he kill him, why?', Luna wondered. Haimacho looked even older and more pathetic to her now, as if he suffered from some terrible, incurable disease. 'Let him be, let him live … God made him that way … God!' She felt sorry for him but at the same time she felt free of the sin she had committed so consciously today, the sin she had been preparing for so many weeks.

She was surprised that she had been so afraid, that she had not done it long ago. But she had been so terrified of that particular sin. It made no difference that she had tried to forget herself, to fool herself, to close her eyes and let him have his way with her. She had flinched away each time, all the same. She agonised, as every day she kept missing better and better opportunities, playing dumb, as if she did not know that Alia was looking at her with desire in his eyes, that his hands were invisibly reaching out for her, just waiting for the right opportunity. It made no difference that she was burning with passion herself, that she was trembling with this one desire, and that at night (and the nights that summer were humid) she could not fall asleep until almost daybreak. Each time she regretted that there had not been a better, more suitable opportunity and decided that the next time she would give herself to him no matter what! But when the next day came and she was near him, when she felt her pulse quicken, she would blanch and try to save herself anyway she knew how, swearing that she would never go back to the *mahala* again.

Whenever Luna was in the *mahala* Alia was always there, calling her silently, waiting. 'Ah, if only she would say yes, there would be no stopping me!', Alia would say, sorry that Luna was missing one opportunity after another. 'And she wants to, she wants to, she's on fire, I can see it, she's on fire. If she didn't have that cloudy eye, she'd be like a *houri*.'

Once he secretly pinched her. Luna blushed and broke out in a sweat. When she got home and examined the bruise on her skin, she was beside herself. Now she knew that she would sin, she knew it, and it would be with that man, the Turk, she a Jewess, and Haimacho's wife! And she knew that she would die if anyone ever found out, that she would be beaten and flogged by all those old people who were out in the street at daybreak, going to the holy temple with her Haimacho. All of them, so peaceable and serious now, would raise their hands against her and beat her without mercy. As if in a dream, she saw how the old women would enter her courtyard, shouting like lunatics, and then pull her out of the kitchen and push her down the steps, dragging her along all sorts of narrow little streets, while her shawl slipped from her head and her cap was knocked off, and the women would pull and push her towards the iron door in the stone wall around the big temple. Hundreds of hands would reach out from inside, pulling her into the yard, and while some of the women would be reading aloud from big, fat books, others would be tearing at her clothes, flogging her bare back with rods and ropes. They would beat her and scream at her, and she would drop to her knees, her hands shoved into her lap, her head bowed, her eyes shut, moaning, groaning, bearing it. And all bruised, bloodied and dishevelled as she was, they would try to pick her up and throw her out of the courtyard through the other door that opened onto a tiny little street. Meanwhile, women would be banging at the iron door, yelling through the keyhole, telling them to beat her to death, to break every bone in her body, to finish her off like a beaten dog, the blind bitch! She would put up a fight to stop them from throwing her out there alive and pray for the earth to open and swallow her up.

She also saw other torment awaiting her because of the sin she was preparing to commit, and, tossing and turning on her blankets at night, she would whisper a short prayer, the only Hebrew prayer she knew: 'Adonai, Adonai! Lord of the world, Almighty God!' She would pray to God, in her plain Spanish, to protect her from evil and ruin, and at the end she would add a silent prayer for God to forgive her sin should she transgress. 'Just once … just once … and never again.'

And now, in the wake of that sin, she was surprised she had been so afraid, she could not understand it … All women do it … She was a woman but she could not do it with her husband … so she had sinned with another ... another ... she had had to do it ... it just happened ... it happened.

It happened, it just did ... Luna repeated to herself, somehow feeling all the better for it, and she raised her head as if awakening from a dream.

Darkness had gathered and the *muezzin's* voice rang out. A*ksham*. Luna quickly pulled herself together and shut the window curtain. She stood in front of the candelabrum, her trembling hand barely managing to light all the wicks. She was unable to say the prayers or fold her hands on her chest. She stood there as the *muezzin's* prayer echoed clearly through the air. Luna listened and something made her silently repeat his every word. When the *muezzin* stopped, a silence spread around Luna like a huge, vast space, empty and distant. There was only the flames sizzling. That same instant, Luna was gripped with fear, an uncomfortable, overpowering fear. She went rigid. She did not dare move even her eye, she had the feeling that someone was peering in through the window and was about to shout: 'So, you bitch! You call that a prayer do you? That?! That?! ...' Slowly everything began to swim in front of her eyes. Beads of cold sweat broke out on her forehead and she collapsed onto the floor by the divan. She realised that somewhere something hard had hit the wood, and the sound of it reverberated throughout the room. She vaguely remembered the watermelon in the basin, round and chilled. 'Perhaps someone knocked the basin over?' That was her last thought before passing out.

When she regained consciousness and lifted her head, the first thing she did was to look and see whether her dress was unbuttoned, then she wiped the sweat off her brow with her sleeve and stood up.

A little later, Haimacho came in.

'*Shabbat shalom!*', he said in a loud, cheerful voice, walking from the steps onto the veranda and following Luna into the kitchen to check whether the water-melon was nice and cold.

VIII

Haimacho's joy lasted barely two Fridays. By the third it had vanished. He was plagued by his old misgivings again. He even stopped looking at the trout, to see how they breathed, how they moved their fins and tails; he threw a wet cloth over them, afraid to see their live, petrified eyes and the bright rings around their pupils. He was afraid. He was afraid of everything.

The days passed slowly and he could hardly wait for the New Year and Yom Kippur. Never had he prayed more devoutly than that Yom Kippur. He bowed, beat his chest, fell to his knees, recited the prayers. Along with the other worshippers in the crowded temple who were suffocating from the close, heavy air of the many candles and lamps, Haimacho, wrapped in his *tallit* and hungry from having fasted, spoke God's name with fervour, listened to Rabbi Perera's voice thunder from the black twisted pulpit and quaked from the visions that besieged him at the end of the prayer. That day he saw the sky open up and Jehovah appear, enveloped in huge flames and smoke. He read and he read but not once did he voice, not even to himself, his one great wish for that year. He had buried it somewhere deep down inside himself and believed that the Lord would thus be merciful, that He would learn of this wish and would do everything necessary to protect him from the misfortune looming over him.

And indeed, he calmed down a bit after Yom Kippur. Luna was quiet and withdrawn and Haimacho hoped that everything was all right, that there was nothing wrong in his life. It had all been his imagination, his imagination, Haimacho would say to console himself. Sometimes he felt he had wronged Luna because of the bad thoughts he had had about her and then he would take a *zwanzig* or two out of the chest drawer and buy her chintz or a trinket for the house.

Autumn was rainy. Haimacho threw a sack over himself as protection against the rain and, hunched over like that, tramped through the mud, delivering the fish. The whole city was shrouded in fog, wet and melancholy. Roofs began to leak and the sound of water was everywhere. It was as if, after the frenzy of summer, people had now taken ill in these foggy mornings and nights, and were barely able to get through the day. Only the children had no feeling of sadness. Their trouser legs rolled up, they tramped barefoot in the mud, splashing through the puddles, splattering muddy water on passers-by.

That autumn they often sent Luna cheese and milk from the *mahala* above. She bought potatoes and beans at a cheap price

43

there and Alia would bring everything down to her, twirling his short, drooping mustache. He began to chop wood in Luna's neighbourhood and later even at Luna's own house, where he would drink coffee, sit and talk with Haimacho about how the world had changed, how none of the old *hajis* were left, or the good people who used to give the poor one penny out of every seven in their pocket and let them earn an extra something from working in the field, the house, the shop, summer and winter. Haimacho nodded his head, each time repeating how hard it was to make ends meet in winter, and how whatever one managed to put aside and save on food over the summer would, by mid-winter, go on firewood and shoes.

When Alia left, Haimacho would pace the room, stoke the fire in the stove, potter around the kitchen, look in the chopped wood for gnarled logs which could burn through the long winter night. He would undress and go to bed early. Luna would be in the kitchen sewing.

Just before Hanukkah it snowed and the city looked as if it had been levelled to the ground. Footsteps were muffled and a bluish smoke hung over the city like haze and froze in the cold. As dusk gathered, the jackdaws flocked together and flew to the other end of the *mahala*. People stood on the street corners, frozen, wrapped up in their shawls, sipping *salep*. The Albanians poured out the drink, as smoke rose from the yellow liquid in the cauldrons, melting the surrounding snow. Like every year at this time, the smell of baked black *halvah* wafted through the Jewish *mahala*, announcing the start of the seven days of Hanukkah.

Haimacho was increasingly edgy from the first day, and then came the seventh, last day of Hanukkah.

It was not yet dark and one could still see the dirty footprints in the snow. Haimacho, poor wretch, stepped in the footprints, one by one, counting them. Entering the courtyard he coughed (to make his presence known) and on his way up the steps he took a small prayerbook from his pocket and began to leaf through it. He had been doing this for the past six evenings. He would move awkwardly around the *menorah*, looking this way and that, examining it, touching the wicks and then, after coughing again, he would start to read the prayer. He did the same thing this evening. He lit all seven flames himself, all seven plus the one above. He did not let

Luna light any of them. She stood behind him. Her pocked face was pale and spotted. Her head was bowed and as soon as Haimacho had lit all eight flames on the Hanukkah *menorah*, Luna went into the kitchen, closing the door slowly behind her. Haimacho did not move, but when the door closed he lifted his head and only his eyes followed her. Then he closed his prayerbook, put it on the shelf by the window and picked up the book of psalms. He sat down on the divan and turned up the lamp.

IX

The shadows cast by the triangular *menorah*, with its seven flames on the bottom and one on top to the left, crept into all the corners of the room, and the long, spindly flames sizzled, crackled and burned a bright yellowish-red, ending in thin, quivering wisps of sooty smoke. The wicks grew glowing red heads.

Peering through half-open eyes, Haimacho thought how sad the beautiful flames of the Hanukkah *menorah* looked this year. They were burning a yellowish-red, whereas last year the room had been ablaze with their light, and his psalms had shaken even the ceiling.

'They haven't got the same light, no they haven't …', he said to himself, and felt an invisible finger poking at him, repeating the words: 'No, they haven't, they haven't …'

He sat down, rocking back and forth, and watched.

The third flame on the right was beginning to die out to the sizzling of the oil. When even the glowing wick died out and the smoke detached itself, Haimacho turned out the lamp and quickly began singing one psalm after another: 'Hallelujah … Hallelujah …'

At the fourth psalm he suddenly stopped reading and listened. He looked at the *menorah*. Another two flames had gone out.

'The oil is no good, it's no good … it's been mixed with water … it's no good …'

He stood up and, with book in hand, walked to the door, opened it and called out hoarsely:

'Luna … Luna … what kind of oil is this? …' Seeing Luna at the kitchen door, his eyes immediately wrapped themselves around her hips. Luna said something but Haimacho suddenly felt so faint that it left him deaf, and he heard nothing.

He went back to the divan and sat down again. He barely managed to finish reading the psalms.

He ate dinner, his eyes on his hands, while Luna spread out the mattress and went into the kitchen.

Haimacho undressed, turned out the lamp and went to bed. The last flame of the *menorah* went out. It died abruptly. The oil sizzled two or three times, the flame flickered, turned blue, reached up as if about to take off, and then disappeared. The smell of burning oil filled the darkness and the room fell silent. The gnarled oak lying on the embers smoked inside the stove.

There was a clatter of dishes in the kitchen and then silence there as well.

Haimacho coughed to drive away his own dark thoughts. He had been trying to drive them away for a long time. But in vain. They kept returning. They returned as if they had come from some far away place, exhausted, out of breath, sweaty, leaden ...

'Yes ... her hips are wider ... yes ...wider ... her belly is round ... it's grown ... yes ... swollen ... she's heavy. She's sinned ... she's been avoiding my eye for a long time ... she doesn't leave the house ...'

These thoughts ran through Haimacho's mind until suddenly his head was spinning. He felt as if he was plunging down into an abyss, as if he was rising up into the expanses of space. His head grew into a huge, heavy lump, his legs became longer and thicker, his fingers lengthened, went rigid, numb, and he sank down as if made out of lead, he became riveted to the mattress, to the wooden floorboards, and with them, with the darkness, with the whole house, he began to rise into some sort of cold, dark distant expanse, but something was pressing against his chest, suffocating him ...

'... She's not sinning ... she's not ... it's probably some illness, an illness, dropsy ... yes ... dropsy ... and it's made her legs heavy, her belly swollen ... that's it, dropsy ...' He would talk to himself like this in those dark heights and then he would come back down, regain consciousness and run his hands over the nothingness of his lower parts.

He listened in the silence to hear whether there was any movement in the kitchen, whether Luna would come to bed, to her blankets in the corner. He listened and he heard something, he

46

heard something like the sound of the *menorah* fizzling out. A humming sound.

'Chirrup … chirrup …'

He sat up on his mattress and listened. He tucked his side curls behind his ears and pushed back his greasy night fez.

'Chirrup … chirrup'. He thought he heard it more clearly now in the silence.

He threw back his covers and got up. A small flame appeared in the stove, casting a thin shaft of light on the floor.

Gaunt, ageing, he opened wide his eyes as if that would help him better to hear what was making that sound and where.

His thin beard, red and wispy, became rigid and began to gleam as if it were made of glass. All the lines dug deeper into his face, as if carved. A bony hand reached up and cupped his ear, and Haimacho, his knees pressed together and his shoulders hunched, walked head first towards the stove.

A greasy streak shone down his flat nose and rounded fez. Two pinpoints of light shone bright in his eyes.

'It's probably a cricket … a cricket in the logs next to the stove …'

He took another step closer to hear better. The silence was even greater and the small flame in the stove died out. He could see nothing, hear nothing.

Standing barefoot in his colourful chemise and red narrow-legged flannels, Haimacho listened. The burning oil and woollen sock on top of the stove smelled. He listened. Somewhere in the neighbourhood a cat was howling, like a small child. The flesh on the calves of his legs began to tingle and again he thought he could hear that sound.

'Chirrup … chirrup …'

Now it was by the door.

'Maybe she's had a baby!', he thought trembling.

He could hear it more clearly now. Haimacho turned around and stood by the door.

'Chirrup … chirrup …' The sound was coming from behind the door. Suddenly, he threw it open. The cold air from the veranda rushed in and crept under his shirt. It was damp, as if there had been a fresh fall of snow. The trees in the garden, silent under their white load, glistened in the dark. It was a clear, white night. The cat howled again. He could hear it clearly now. And he heard another

47

cat howl and chase after it. Haimacho saw the snow tumble off the boughs and went back to bed.

A little later, Luna came in. She opened the door softly, closed it quietly, stepped over to her corner, removed her outer skirt, took the cap off her head, let her hair down, lay down on the blankets and covered herself.

Silence reigned again.

Both were now breathing loudly and rapidly: Haimacho heavily through his nose, Luna gaspingly through her mouth.

Haimacho stretched out, lay still and listened. He heard that sound again. Over there in the corner, on the blankets.

'Chirrup ... chirrup ...'

'That's not a cricket ... no it's not ...' Haimacho said to himself, listening. He turned over on to his left arm, digging his fingers into the mattress and cover. Now it sounded as if something was knocking, rapping, tapping over there where Luna was lying.

'Yes, yes ... she's sinned ... her hips are broad, her belly round, she's pregnant .... she's heavy ... When she crossed the room a little while ago she was heavy, the floor groaned under her weight, it sagged ... yes ... she's pregnant ...'

A gust of wind swept snow onto the window pane. Haimacho was startled, he felt cold.

'Yes, everything is mixed with water, with snow, snow gets into everything, the wind drives it ... Even the oil is mixed with water and everything is sizzling ... everything is rattling ... everything ...'

Haimacho tortured himself like this until sleep finally overcame him; his hand crept under the cover wanting to reach out to that corner ... to feel Luna's tummy, to see whether she was sick, whether she had dropsy ... to feel whether this humming sound might be coming from inside her and whether her stomach was hot or cold or whether she had become broader in the hips because she had gained weight, like all barren women.

'She's not a sinner, she's not ... It's a cricket, that's what it is ... a cricket is making that noise ... a cricket in the logs next to the stove ...', Haimacho kept saying disjointedly, half-asleep, his hand now on top of the cover, asleep and exhausted.

And in her corner, Luna curled up under the blankets and waited. She waited every evening, expecting Haimacho to get up, stand tall and shout out into the darkness: 'Luna, who were you with? Who? Was it Alia?'

Waiting this night again, she kept thinking: now, now he is going to get up. She waited, but in vain. The whole room seemed to have fallen silent. And just when she thought that sleep would get the better of her, suddenly, for the first time something unusual twitched unexpectedly inside her womb. It twitched and she felt her whole body tingle. A hotness rushed over her breasts, up her throat, on to her cheeks. She broke out in a flush and tepid sweat. She ran her hands over her stomach, again felt the kick, and hysterically threw off the blankets, sat up and screamed.

'What ... what ... what is it?', Haimacho stammered, jerked awake. 'What is it? What is it?', he asked, frightened, rising helplessly from his mattress; when he shook himself awake, reality hit him. Terrible twinkling little lights seemed to pierce the darkness.

'A child ... mine ... mine ... alive, alive ...', cried Luna, sobbing as if she were announcing a miracle. 'A child ... mine ...', she gasped in delirious joy. 'Mine ...'

Haimacho reeled, clutched his knees, bent over and stood there immobile, on the verge of fainting. The little lights went out and darkness now spread around him like an abyss. The floor underneath him seemed to tilt and pull away, the ceiling seemed to lift, to open up the room, the whole house, as the walls and rafters receded and the cold rushed in from all sides. 'Where are the lamps? The books could fall off the shelves and land on me. The basin could topple over ... the water could spill ... the stove could crack ... Flames could erupt ... everything could catch fire ... and ... burn ...'

The thoughts kept coming, chasing each other through his mind, stupid, disconnected thoughts, leaping out of his head into the darkness like dark sparks, like aches of pain, dull and heavy. Then he remembered that his tooth used to give him quite a lot of trouble, that once (it must have been a long time ago) he had run through the streets, streets with shops and merchants ... past the covered market, he had run screaming like a lunatic, clasping his head, and a crowd had descended on him, men, women, children ... porters ... guards ... butchers ... a hue and cry rose up behind him like thick dust: 'haaaa ... hoooo ... haaaa ... hoooo ...', and

49

he had run and run and could hardly wait to reach some terrible deep abyss: '... haaaa ... hoooo ...'

These cries, mixed with other incredible thoughts, kept hounding him until Luna's sobs called him back to reality. He felt as if he had been standing in the middle of the room for ages; suddenly he remembered where he was and what was happening to him and to his Luna. He shuddered.

'Luna, Luna ...', he whispered tremulously. "Luna ...'

Luna had stopped sobbing convulsively and was weeping softly now, her head in her hands; every so often a deep shudder would run through her, shaking both her and the blankets.

Pattering in the dark almost on all fours, like some sick, beaten dog, Haimacho came closer and said softly, voicelessly:

"Luna ... Luna ... hush ... hush ... it's not a child..." He felt the warmth coming from her body. Luna was still weeping, but she was slowly quietening down now.

'Luna ... Luna ... hush ... hush ... it's not a child ... it's not!', he whispered like a sleep-walker. 'Hush, it's not a child ... it's a cricket ... a cricket ... a cricket in the logs ... a cricket ...'

He crouched down next to Luna and talked to her like that, more and more earnestly and freely. And even when Luna had stopped weeping, when she had fallen asleep, Haimacho still kept on talking, with almost no voice left now, barely moving his lips: 'It's not ... a child ... it's ... a cricket ... it was a cricket, a cricket ...'

The words slipped into the darkness like ghosts, increasingly quiet and infrequent. Sleep was overcoming Haimacho too now. He shook his head, opened his eyes to stay awake and ward off sleep. But he kept losing his train of thought and suddenly (as if attached to him by only the most delicate of cobwebs) it broke away, rose up into the air and evaporated. And Haimacho's head dropped onto his chest. A little later, the tense face muscles relaxed, his mouth dropped open and he began to snore. He was sound asleep.

X

In the morning he got up and went into town. He went silently, despondent, to finish what he had to do, as he did every Friday, and fatigued, at a loss, he would trudge slowly and evenly through the snow. As if, by walking like this, he was seeking a reconciliation with life.

That Friday for the first time he got the fish orders mixed up. Señora Hana got the barbel, and rich Master Mamme had chub for dinner and almost choked on the bones.

Haimacho and Luna did not live together for much longer. It made no difference that he traded in his *zwanzigs* and brought things home: a new plate, a big Turkish coffee-pot. He bought six little cups with a red design and put everything on the chest in the kitchen, saying nothing, not even looking at Luna. He slurped his coffee contentedly, as if to say: 'The coffee is good today.' And he enjoyed his food. He moved around the house, certain and uncertain, content and upset, constantly preparing to say something, to say: 'Well, it's all right about the baby ... it's all right ...' He came up to Luna, ready to whisper, to utter the words, he had been ready to say them so many times, but something always stopped him. Once Luna happened to turn away, another time she coughed just as he was about to speak. Something always put him off. And later, his strength failed him. He noticed that Luna was packing away her dresses, tying her blouses up in a handkerchief. She removed her clothes from the hangers. It was all done unobtrusively, but Haimacho kept an eye on whatever was going on in the house and he saw everything. Alia did not drop by any more, and he stopped chopping wood in the neighbourhood.

'She's going to leave ... she's going to leave ...', Haimacho kept saying to himself as he roamed the streets. He neglected his beard and side curls. He even stopped going to the barber's to trim his hair. He changed his seat in temple. He walked in with a stoop, did not bow, did not look at anyone. He sat right next to the door and on Saturdays joined the followers of Rabbi Perera. And one Saturday Rabbi Perera noticed him. The rabbi was only just back on his feet after some infirmity and was being supported under the arms by two Jews. He turned around, asked Haimacho about his health and then, breathing with difficulty, said: 'And did you listen to me that time when I told you to plant that living seed? Yes ... of course you did, of course you did. And so you should, one should preserve the law. Rabbi Hanina ben Hanaña did it this way, this way. Listen to what Rabbi Hanina said!' The rabbi rested for a minute and then continued in his learned voice: 'Listen! Do not eat seeds after *Hamisha a sara*! Do not eat them, because that is when the trees come to life, when the juices rush into the boughs and buds, and it is also when life awakens in seeds. After *Hamisha a sara* the seeds sprout and if you eat them you will be putting a living thing into your mouth and killing it.' Rabbi Perera rested and then said: 'The ancient scholars used to avoid even such sins. But what can we do? That was a long, long time ago. When wisdom ruled the earth, wisdom.'

Haimacho did not hear the end of the rabbi's story. He put his hand in his pocket to see whether he would find the odd grain of corn.

After that Saturday he was afraid even to look at the rabbi. He was afraid of running into him, he was afraid of everything. He returned home afraid that he would not find Luna there.

And one evening she was not there. He waited a long time for her. He waited and fell asleep in his clothes and shoes. The next day he did not leave the house, he just went down into the courtyard to fetch water from the well and looked carefully to make sure that Luna was not down below in the water. Breathing a small sigh of relief when he saw that she was not, he carried the bucket up the stairs, his step slow and sluggish. He spent yet another night sleeping on the divan fully dressed. That evening he did not even say his prayers. When he woke up in the morning he checked the kitchen, went up into the attic, checked the well again (more thoroughly this time) and headed for the town. He went straight to Rabbi Perera and at the top of the steps ran into old Sipura, the rabbi's wife.

'Tell the rabbi I did not plant that living seed, tell him I did not plant it, I didn't ...' he mumbled, as if the grain was in his mouth.

Old Sipura tried to detain him but to no avail. He left and went back home. And then came that strange period. People swarmed into his courtyard, burst into the room, crowding the place and creating an uproar: questions, curses, abuse, women fainting, bedlam, temples being rubbed, glasses and dishes rattling, water and vinegar being splashed onto faces, cries for help, clothes being unbuttoned, people running up and down the stairs, and Yahiel Ganhiz's deep voice cutting through all the commotion like a roll of thunder in summer. Only the children in the courtyard and Haimacho up in his room were quiet and dumbfounded.

Yahiel was the first to go to the rabbi and tell him the news that Luna had run away to the Turkish *mahala*.

'Rabbi, open all your books and cry out to our Lord that he may save us from a sin which will be our ruin! Rise and lift up your arms and cry out, Rabbi Perera, ask for mercy from heaven! Luna, the daughter of the late Machebohor, has run away with the Turk. Luna the wife of Haimacho, Luna, Luna has gone, she ran away three days ago!'

'Blow your horn! Let all women and girls quake with fear! Blow the horn as you do for Yom Kippur, Rabbi. Blow on it!'

'Luna has run away to the house of the Turk! Señor Rabbi, Señor Rabbi!'

Yahiel paced the room, waving his arms. Then he went up to the rabbi and whispered something into his ear.

'Yes ... *monjo* ... *monjo* ... and the word is that Luna is pregnant ... that she's going to have a baby, do you hear Rabbi? She's going to give birth to a Turk, a Turk! Luna, the daughter of the late Machebohor, my own relative, a woman who could not say boo to a goose! My God! Rabbi, take the horn and blow on it, blow!'

Ganhiz's deep, thundering voice shook the entire room but the rabbi sat calmly, rocking himself on the divan. He understood everything Ganhiz was saying and would himself have liked to explode because of that Jewess's incredible sin, but he waited for a more exalted form of strength with which to rise to his feet and shout with all his might: 'What! Who is this Luna? Who is she? Who is this dark woman? Who, who? Have her brought here immediately, here for us to judge her! Immediately! Immediately!'

The rabbi waited but the strength did not come! Instead he was filled with the thought that had been on his mind these past few days: 'It is not our lot! It is not our lot to live in an age when wisdom rules the world, it is not our lot ...' The rabbi rocked himself back and forth, thinking how good it would be for him to move to Jerusalem if he recovered.

Yahiel pathetically repeated his invocations a few more times and then rushed out and ran to Haimacho's house. Again his voice thundered through all the commotion.

Ten days passed. To Haimacho the uproar in his house seemed to have lasted longer. He breathed a sigh of relief when it began to quieten down. The comings and goings thinned out. Yahiel was the only one who still called on him, hurling abuse: 'Why did you get married? Why? ... Why did you get married, Haimacho, son of the cobbler Eliazar Papo, why? Did you think a wife is like a piece of wood ... a stone ... a fish? Ay, Haimacho, ay, ay, ay ...'

Haimacho would say nothing, staring with fascination at the fat, fleshy, protruding lips moving in the middle of Yahiel's thick beard, at the big mouth with its yellow, loose teeth opening and closing.

Yahiel's voice would shake the walls of the kitchen, and even the chest he was sitting on. Haimacho would just stand there, gaping.

When Yahiel rose to his feet, Haimacho would walk him to the courtyard door.

'May the Lord forgive you ... May He forgive you ...' Yahiel would mumble as he left, and Haimacho would close the latch on the door and yawn, tired and sleepy.

XI

Even the sermon in the temple, fiery, mordant, almost desperate, passed. People finally stopped talking about the imagined and unimagined peculiarities of Luna and Haimacho, and Haimacho walked through the town, stooped, sluggish and silent.

Pesach came and went. The smell of spring was in the air, a time when children congregate in squealing play.

This spring the children huddled together, whispering, as if it was now their turn to examine the reasons why Luna had run away with the Turk. And they recounted: 'A cat, a big black cat ate it ... when he was still a baby ... in the cradle ... His mother went to salt the meat ... and the cat jumped into the cradle ... and bit it off ... He barely survived ... honest! I heard old Rifkula tell my mother ... yesterday ... honest!', swore Davko.

The children all nodded their heads. They found it strange. They found it terrible. They believed it. They did not believe it. But the story passed from mouth to mouth, from street to street, and there was not a child who did not know it.

Within two or three days, the story changed: 'It wasn't a cat, of course it wasn't! I knew that! He would never have survived! The *moel* cut it off. There was an old, blind *moel* named Katan, and he cut it off ... I heard it yesterday in the shop.'

And so the stories went until one day this same Davko gathered the children around to tell them something completely new, something strange but true. Absolutely true! This was the first time that the children heard the word *monjo*. Davko said it first: 'He's neither male nor female ... he was born like that ... it makes no difference that he wears a fez, has a beard, wears trousers, it makes no difference! He's neither male nor female ... M o n j o ... He's a *monjo*. A real live *monjo*!'

'*Monjo!*'

'*Monjo!*'

'*Monjo!*', the children repeated the word which sounded strange and funny and terrible all at once. '*Monjo, Monjo!*'

The children immediately agreed to wait for Haimacho the following Friday and shout '*Monjo!*' at him.

Ten of them gathered that Friday. The motley group looked serious as it walked down the street, prepared to perform an unusual deed.

They were led by Davko, who had concocted the entire plan. At the bottom of Pehlivanusa Street, they saw Haimacho, his small basket on his stooped back, trudging slowly and evenly through the mud. He undid his scarf and threw it over his arm. As soon as they caught sight of him, the children turned into a side street, raced down and around and came up on Haimacho from behind. They kept their distance, treading carefully, breathless, blinking with terror, excitement and anticipation. Haimacho suddenly stopped in front of a door, banged the knocker and walked in. The children stayed where they were. When he came out his eyes met theirs. Some twenty eyes were watching him from that cluster of children. He instantly felt that some of them were watching him with curiosity, others in fear and astonishment, and a few looked at him with bold impudence. Something inside him exploded. He felt both fear and strength. This strength made him feel for the first time that he was growing, that he was standing straight, that he was becoming some-one else, someone who could shout, wave his arms, slam doors. The feeling terrified him and Davko's two eyes, their shrewd, unflinching stare glued to him, saw it. Again Haimacho became all confused. He slipped the basket off, took out his handkerchief and blew his nose. Davko pulled back. He had missed his chance. He turned around and mingled with the other children.

Hoisting the basket onto his back again, Haimacho then

proceeded on his way, his step even slower and more sluggish than before, even though he expected trouble.

A pebble whizzed by his head. Then another. Something hit the basket.

The children scrambled around. Somebody even ran out in front of Davko. Davko raised his hand and silently ordered everyone to stop and walk on tiptoe. Just as Haimacho was about to step into the courtyard Davko ran past him and yanked at his scarf. Haimacho merely pulled his arm back, hunched his shoulders and darted into the courtyard as if fleeing from monsters.

Haimacho stayed there for a long time and when he came out he walked quickly until a clod of mud hit him in the shoulder. He stopped and turned around. He looked at them with rolling eyes. The children realised that he was standing up to them, threatening them, and they came right up to him. Twisting his neck, Davko peered into his face, looked into his eyes and shouted: '*Buenos dias, monjo! Buenos dias, monjo!*'

That same instant, as if on command, the other children chimed in, echoing Davko's cry. Haimacho's knees were shaking. He held on tight to the rope of the basket because he was afraid it would fall off his back.

'Hey ... *monjo!* ... hey ... *monjo!* ...', the children shouted. A crowd gathered. Women leaned out of their windows. Somebody shouted at the children and Haimacho muttered a curse and bent down to pick up a rock. There was an explosion of cries and shouts and suddenly Davko appeared and pushed Haimacho. Haimacho fell forward and all the fish came tumbling out of his basket and over his head. Their nacre scales glistened in the sun, their white bellies gleamed in the mud.

'Hey ... *monjo!*' the children roared.

The same thing happened the next Friday, and the next. As soon as he appeared, the children would gather and follow him. Their cries echoed throughout the *mahala*. The children did not dare get too close to him. Haimacho's pockets were full of stones and he would hurl them, breaking windows, cracking skulls. He's gone crazy, they said, crazy. And when he came down from Banjski Brijeg, Haimacho would proceed at his slow, even pace into town. He would leave a stone in one of his pockets and walk around, waiting for someone to shout *monjo* at him so that he could suddenly hurl it with all his might. But no one shouted at him. He heard no one.

He turned customers away. He would not go to Brijeg. He delivered fish around Cemalusa, he delivered fish to Javer-effendi on the other side of the Miljacka River, but he would not go up to the *mahala*. He even emptied his pockets of the stones. He spent most of his time in the house. And when he did go out it was to the Turkish *mahala*. He would take a circuitous route that brought him out at the flat cemetery. He would walk around slowly, hungry, tired, crumpled, sluggish. And soon the local Muslim children came to recognise him.

'There's Lunia's Aimacho ...'

'Come on, Aimacho, let us take you to Lunia ... come on.' They would come up to him, take him by the hand and lead him around the *mahala* like some sort of village fool. At first Haimacho went with them, he kept hoping for something, but when he realised that they were not taking him to Lunia, he started to pull away, snarling through his teeth: 'Let me go ... let me go ...' And when he pulled free he took a different route.

Twice he found bread in his room. Both times he sat down and immediately sank his teeth into it. He ate voraciously, staring deliriously at the corner like an epileptic, until he had finished the bread down to the last crumb.

He kept hoping that Luna would come back. And whenever he came home he would cough before going up the steps. Once something upstairs in the kitchen moved. 'It's her!', he trembled. But it was not Luna. It was Bulka.

'I didn't have time to come before, this place is like a Gypsy caravan!. I'll move in with the children. You can't go on like this ... you can't.'

'There's no need ... no need ...' Haimacho replied quickly, panic-stricken, staring at Bulka like a cornered animal. 'No need!', he was defending his house. 'Someone is coming ... I've got someone coming ...'

'You're a fool ... a fool ...'

Initially Haimacho turned Bulka down (a relative on his mother's side who wanted to move in rather than pay rent 'over there' for nothing) because he hoped Luna would come back, but later it was because he wanted to be alone in the house.

He would spend days on end in the courtyard. And when spring

57

was in full flush, he walked barefoot on the cobblestones, collected all the leaves and clutter in a pile, brought out the blankets, lay down on them and basked in the sun.

XII

On the Friday before *Shevuoth*, he came home breathless and happy. He was carrying a bowl and inside it was a great big live trout.

'Live fish, live fish!', he had heard Sason say again that day. 'Live fish, live fish!' The words echoed inside him like a voice from the distant past. He felt something warm touch his heart. And as he listened to Sason a kind of light seemed to glow inside him, it grew and blossomed like a flower, big, yellow and bright. As bright as the sun. And this inner light radiated from his eyes as well.

His eyes shone as if they had been washed, healed and cleansed. And Haimacho, happy as a child now, carried his bowl, smiling and gazing contentedly at the fish in the water. It splashed around, swimming in the clear water, alone, terrified, turning first one way and then the other. Its dark silvery back glistened in the sun, bursting into a hundred pearly colours. Haimacho crouched next to the well, looked at the fish and counted its red speckles. Then he tossed it into the bucket, slowly unwound the rope and lowered it into the water. He stood there leaning over the well for a long time until he saw the trout surface in the water down below, creating ripples.

Every day he would spend hours looking down into the well. He would get up early, toss it breadcrumbs, look for worms in the garden and drop them into the well. It gave him immense pleasure. And the fish would appear down below, taking the food that dropped on to the water's surface.

Haimacho started to come back to life. Now if some child shouted *monjo* at him he would just smile as if he was pleased. He would stroll in the garden, catch hold of a bough, drink in the fragrance of the blossoms, and stretch out in the sun. He removed the roofing over the well and the railing so that the trout could enjoy the sun too and when the fish jumped playfully to catch its food, he would grow taller and mutter to himself. He felt as if he had woken up from a long sleep. Everything made him happy and he groaned with contentment as he basked in the sun. 'Soon it will be time for the *ashlamas'*, he thought hopefully, walking through town. 'Red, sweet juicy *ashlamas'*. He longed for them. His mouth watered. That was his one wish. A*shlamas, ashlamas*! But he did not live to see them.

XIII

He had obtained a piece of liver for his trout. And he was hurrying home to dice it up and feed it to his fish. He was hurrying because dusk was gathering and he wanted to see how the fish would leap up for this particular morsel of food. He was looking forward to it. He would cut up the entire piece and throw it down to the fish, bit by bit. He walked up to the well and leaned over. He held out the meat, holding it with the tips of his fingers.

'Look what I've brought you, look, look ...'

He leaned over a bit more and noticed something white on the water. He looked and went faint. He stood up to catch some air, to clear the blood from his eyes. He tore off a piece of meat with his nails and dropped it straight down into the middle of the water. It hit the water, creating little ripples. Nothing moved. The piece of meat sank, and the water became smooth again. It gleamed like glass. It was dark and it reflected the yellowish sky. It exuded a coldness and the smell of moss. And the odour of fish. Haimacho scanned the entire surface and again he saw that whiteness by the stone of the well wall.

'Dead!', Haimacho thought grimly, and the liver dropped out of his hand on to the ground. He unwound the rope and lowered the bucket into the well, pulling it one way and the other, barely managing to hoist it back up. The dead trout was lying belly up on top of the water. He took it into his hands and looked at it. He saw its eyes. They were bulging and glazed. The gold rings and black pupils were invisible. He turned the fish over in his hand and looked again at its eyes. He remembered Luna's left eye. He remained crouching by the well like that for a long time. He was startled by a cat eating the liver beside him. He turned his head. It was like an apparition. The cat looked at him, hissing and switching its tail. Haimacho smiled and tossed it the fish. And then he saw the cat's

59

two gleaming eyes focus on the dead fish. The cat leaped on the fish, picked it up in its mouth, and then slowly, hissing more and more loudly, went off into the garden with it. Haimacho watched the cat go and had the impression that it was growing, that it had turned into a calf. He had the impression that it even turned around to look at him with its eyes as big as the moon. The dead fish shone white in its mouth. He followed it, chasing it.

He quickly returned to the well. Lost in thought, unable to move, he stood there for a long time. The moon behind his back rose over the roof. And in that moonlight, his thoughts and his questions became clearer. Why had it died? Who had done it? Why? Why did they take this away from him too? Who was it? Who was doing this to him ... taking everything away? Who?

He looked down into the well to see whether there was anything there, whether he could learn something. He leaned over. The water was still rocking slightly, and down below he could see the sky, it was white now and bright. He leaned over further to look. There was someone down there! There was. He could hear them ... see them ... But what was it he saw? He saw the water receding, flowing away, and deep down inside a shadow, a hand. Its fingers were moving. He leaned over to get a better look. And he saw that it was his own hand, because it was he who had reached out his hand, and the moon was up in the sky behind his back. But there was something else, something else ... Something that was hiding ahead of him ... there, he could hear it ... yes ... Now he would see what it was, who it was! Suddenly he felt himself moving, losing his grip on the stone. It occurred to him that he could fall down into the depths and so he put out his arms to protect himself. It was too late. Hitting his head against the stone, he splashed into the water.

He fell like a bag of cement.

And in the morning he was discovered by the cat which had spent the entire night meowing around the well. They hoisted him up with the windlass and Haimacho the son of the cobbler Eliazar Papo was buried that same day at the top of the Jewish cemetery. Rabbi Perera was feeling very frail but no one could stop him from attending the funeral.

Until recently, the Jewish cemetery had been a desolate, barren place, with nothing to enclose it. It had been that way since the sixteenth century. Not a single tree grew there. Only tombstones. The big elongated tombstones dotted the central part of the cemetery, and at one end stood the curved ones. Their white roughly hewn stone looked like fragments from an unfinished sphinx, the front of which had been sliced off to leave room for the inscription.

Today there are also other tombstones in this cemetery. There is one in the shape of a pyramid, a ball resting on its flat top. Trees have been planted and a huge surrounding wall of dressed stone was completed two years ago. And so, after four long centuries, the cemetery was finally enclosed. The enclosed part of the cemetery is enormous but not all the graves are inside it. Some down near the bottom and some up at the top remain outside the wall. Haimacho's grave is bound to be one of them.

Translated by Christina Pribićević-Zorić

Gabriel Gaon

People in the town spoke a great deal about Hanucha's death, about that whole horrific event. They talked more by gesture of their hands and their eyes wide open in horror than with words.

They told me about it the same winter it happened. I shook all over when I heard.

The terrible picture of Hanucha's death came frequently to haunt my dreams for a long time after the event. Vivid and cruel, it coiled in me. With time it gradually began to pale and to appear less often, until I finally forgot both poor Hanucha and her child.

A long time has passed since then.

Two months ago, the event again appeared in my memory, just as horrific as it had ever been.

For a long time I struggled to discover why it had returned to my consciousness so suddenly and unexpectedly. I reflected on everything that could have had the slightest connection with it. So it was that I recalled quite vividly all the people who had related the event to me so long ago.

Among them was a Jew who sat uneasily, with a frown on his face. He said nothing, but jerked his hand from time to time as though he was going to say or announce something.

I made out the figure of that Jew increasingly clearly in my memory. At first I saw him just as he had been when he was jerking his hand, and at that time he was troubled, bad-humoured and scowling.

Later, appearing to me more and more frequently and spending whole hours with me, as I thought about Hanucha, his face became increasingly bright and a kind of gentleness spread over it.

He kept coming to me. No sooner had I sat down at the table and begun to think about Hanucha, than there he was. He always sat facing me and as calmly as I did. I lowered my eyes and gazed at the shiny edge of the glass. He too. The gleaming light from the polished glass contracted the pupils of my eyes. His too. I sat silently. He too.

He was always silent, but nevertheless I knew his voice. I knew it well, as though I heard it every day. His voice was clear, resonant and somewhat emotional. And I knew also that what this Jew had to say was important and that a slightly mocking tone would come into his voice from time to time.

I called him Shabetai Alhalel.

I had grown close to him, and as I sat at the table I waited patiently for Shabetai Alhalel to speak at last in his clear and somewhat emotional voice and confide in me what it was he had wanted to say when he jerked his hand. But in vain. Shabetai Alhalel remained silent.

One day at noon, as I walked along the street I heard voices, then I made out one: clear, resonant and somewhat emotional. I gave a start. I seemed to recognise the voice of my Shabetai Alhalel in the crowd of people. 'Yes, it was he! No doubt!' – I said to myself and turned to look at him. When I saw him I was surprised, but not so much because I was seeing him in reality, but because he looked different from my Shabetai Alhalel.

My Shabetai Alhalel had a calm, bright face and hands with long fingers, but this one was uneasy, his face was hard, furrowed, he was slightly stooped, and his fists were clenched. He walked with a stick and looked around him with disdain.

Was this really my Shabetai Alhalel or was the real Shabetai Alhalel that Jew who had jerked his hand when I first heard the appalling tale of Hanucha?

I followed him. This Shabetai Alhalel kept stopping. He would stare at the ground as though confused, and before he set off again, he would always tap his stick two or three times on the ground, before moving on.

Ever since that day, I kept meeting this Shabetai Alhalel in the streets. I met him often and greeted him. 'Good day!' I would say

63

and I wanted to call him by his name. But how? Perhaps his name was not Shabetai Alhalel. It could not be. That was the name of my Shabetai Alhalel. That was the name I had invented.

Shabetai Alhalel replied calmly and formally to my greeting and continued on his way.

He was always thoughtful. I said to myself: Shabetai Alhalel never speaks. But the following day I saw him in animated conversation. He spoke importantly, and sometimes a mocking tone came into his voice. I listened. Was it really he? Yes, that was his voice, that was he and none other! That was Shabetai Alhalel. It was his voice, clear, resonant and somewhat emotional.

I made enquiries about his occupation. He had none. At home he read ancient books. That was all. What did he live on? He lived with his brother. His brother said 'he is a blessing in my house'.

Shabetai Alhalel wore a black suit. His suit was worn, but cared for. Why was his fist clenched and why did he look around him with such disdain? With disdain? Everyone was surprised and answered 'he is a good man, very good. That is not disdain, take a closer look'.

I followed him and guessed that Shabetai Alhalel was talking to himself. I hid from his sight, but he noticed that I was following him. He turned round three times. The third time when he was entering a courtyard, I was embarrassed when our eyes met and I vowed, ashamed, that I would no longer steal up on him.

I began to think about Hanucha and her death again. I closed my eyes, imagining the whole event the way it had occurred, and I was so involved in it that I could hear in the silence of my room the chink of dishes and the beating of Hanucha's heart, and Hanucha shouting 'Bochka! Bochka!' I experienced the whole horror and kept waiting for Shabetai Alhalel to appear to me again, the way he had before and say 'Yes, that is just as it was'. But Shabetai Alhalel did not appear.

One evening I was sitting looking straight ahead when all at once I had the feeling that someone was sitting at my table. He had been sitting there for a long time, it seemed, looking at me.

'That will be him, Shabetai Alhalel. He has come at last!' I thought, and wanted to look straight at him, but I simply could not take my eyes from a trifling object that happened to be lying on my table.

64

Just then he moved, tapped his stick twice on the floor and coughed. I went numb. 'Who is this? This is not Shabetai Alhalel, this is that other one!' I said, startled. Our eyes met and at the same moment his voice, clear, resonant and somewhat emotional disturbed the silence in my room.

'I am that Shabetai Alhalel, I and no other,' he said, continuing immediately: 'I have come to tell you the truth about Hanucha and her last supper, because I want my eye to brighten, and my clenched fist to open, because you must hear all of this so that we might together save a joy, rare and unusual. For joys are not found like this on a garbage heap.'

I held my breath. I stared at him in astonishment, while he began solemnly and in that mocking tone that I knew so well.

'In addition to yourself, this whole tale about Hanucha the washerwoman should be heard also by the shoemaker Santo and Klarucha, otherwise known as "la comadre", and the Rabbi Moshe and that grocer Abraham, with the eagle nose and the chicken's heart. We need all to redeem together the sin which was done to her long ago, when I, Shabetai Alhalel, was reaching the end of my thirty-third year.'

Shabetai Alhalel's hand, which was lying clenched on the little table, began to open a little and I recognised its fine, long fingers. He continued.

'It happened long ago, and it happened, as you know, that winter evening. But let me first tell you the name of that woman whom you never knew by her real name, because real names are sometimes important as are the rich inheritances left us by our fathers or as inherited vices are important for our destinies.

'This Hanucha, this small woman, broad-hipped, but with a thin, lined face, in a long shawl worn over her head, and a bundle under her arm, who moved through the lanes herself like some old bundle, that woman was called what I tell you now. She was called the washerwoman Tia-Hanucha di Pardo. That was her name and none other and whoever said anything about her or mentioned her in any way always said that.

'Do not be surprised at anything, it had to be said like that, for if one had said only Tia-Hanucha, then that would be either the wife of the learned Rabbi Haim-Tsevi, the old Hanucha Altarats, or else the wife of the locksmith Salamon, Señora Hanucha de Majo,

65

or any other Hanucha of the hundreds in our town. But it could not possibly have been our washerwoman. And even when one said "Tia-Hanucha di Pardo" that was still not our washerwoman, because you should know that Tia-Hanucha di Pardo was the wife of the decorator Joseph Pardo, an always smiling Jew, still alive, while the husband of our Hanucha, Abraham, barely managed in the course of his short life to laugh heartily more than two or three times. Barely two or three times. There, that is why it was always necessary to say: the washerwoman Tia-Hanucha di Pardo, so that it was clear that it was this woman of ours who was meant. Always, when she was named thus, people knew that it was she and no other woman in our town. But tell me, when do people talk about washerwomen? People talk very rarely and very little about washerwomen and so it is no wonder that they spoke even less about our washerwoman. And when people did talk about her, it was briefly and simply. Very simply.

'This was the kind of thing people said about her:

'"Why didn't you do the washing today, it was such a lovely day!"

'"The washerwoman Tia-Hanucha di Pardo couldn't come. Her child, little Bochka, is ill."

'Or else, very simply:

'"Which Pardo was it died yesterday?"

'"The washerwoman Tia-Hanucha di Pardo's husband."

'"So, the washerwoman's ill again!"

'"Yes, the washerwoman Tia-Hanucha di Pardo."

'"Who are you preparing that meal for?"

'"For the unfortunate washerwoman Tia-Hanucha di Pardo!"

'Or else, this is the kind of thing they said about the washerwoman Tia-Hanucha di Pardo:

'"Is that woman still alive, the one with the muddy shoes?"

'"Which woman?"

'"The one who always turns into that lane, the one who's always carrying some bundle. I haven't seen her for ages."

'"Oh, her? The washerwoman Tia-Hanucha di Pardo. Yes, she's alive. She's suffering from swollen ankles. She's in bed."

'"Whose is that thin little girl, the thin and scrawny one?"

'"That's little Bochka, the washerwoman Tia-Hanucha di Pardo's daughter."

'"Who lives in that little hut? Whose muddy courtyard is that?"

'"The washerwoman Tia-Hanucha di Pardo's."

'By this hand, I swear that this kind of thing was also said of her: '"Listen to what I'm going to tell you, Tia-Ster, these clothes should be thrown on the rubbish heap or used to block mouseholes. That's right, Tia-Ster, mouseholes."

'"Not on your life! Thank God there are other old clothes-sellers, thank God you are not the only one. And if nothing else, I can give them to the washerwoman Tia-Hanucha di Pardo, she'll be able to wear them, they'll do her fine!"

'That is what Tia-Ster said and believe me, Shabetai Alhalel, that in the end the washerwoman Tia-Hanucha di Pardo was given those clothes, and she wore them until she was given others. Believe me, Tia-Ster was right and believe me that everything that was said about our washerwoman was the living truth. The washerwoman Tia-Hanucha di Pardo really did have a muddy yard. And her shoes were always muddy, and the little hut where she lived was a real mousehole, a source of swollen joints and thin, yellow cheeks. And her husband, Abraham, had died long since. And our Hanucha had buried two other children. Truly, it was all like that. It was all the living truth. No one in town ever told any lies about her. And when the news went through the town that Tia-Hanucha's Bencion was betrothed, it did not refer to our Hanucha's son, but to Tia-Hanucha di Mamolo's son. Our Hanucha did not have a living son called Bencion, but even if she had, and if he had been of marrying age, it would not have referred to our Hanucha because it was a lie, a crude lie, because Mamolo's Bencion was not betrothed. Those were just malicious rumours started by evil tongues to show that old Mamolo was trying in vain to connect himself by marriage to the greatly respected family and commercial firm Danon and Son.

'No one would ever have told such a malicious lie about our washerwoman. People only ever spoke the truth about her. Always the pure truth. But still, I have to tell you that one day a falsehood was told even about her. Yes, a falsehood. But not about such a thing, for instance, as Bochka marrying some rich merchant, or anything of that kind. Bochka, the daughter of the washerwoman Tia-Hanucha di Pardo, was still a little girl, she was not yet twelve years old. And you tell me, what falsehood could have been spoken about that pathetic, skinny child! It was nothing to do with Bochka, her

67

child, but about herself, about our washerwoman and about her child.

'One day, they were found dead. The first person to discover this horror was Mazalta, the maid of the esteemed Señora Rahela, an old, noble and wealthy Jewess. So, one day, they found our washerwoman Tia-Hanucha di Pardo dead in her little room, her and her Bochka.

'For a long time people talked about the event and about the way that maid of Rahela's, a large and hearty lass, had screamed at the top of her voice, and the way she had rushed like a mad-woman out of the dark little room into the corridor with the rotten, uneven floorboards, and then into the muddy courtyard, and then onto the path, and from the path into the lane. They said that Mazalta had been waving her arms about like a ghost and that she had stopped a passer-by, white as a shroud, with wild eyes, her mouth open, shouting a long drawn-out and frighteningly stuttering "a-a-a-a", and that she had crumpled unconscious in front of that passer-by.

'In an instant a crowd of people had gathered round her and when they brought the girl out of her swoon and once Mazalta was able to speak again, her arms hanging limply from her shoulders and her whole body bent, she spoke only one word "the wash-er-wo-man!"

'And hardly had she managed to squeeze that one word out of herself, than she straightened up again as though before some terrible apparition, stretched her arms upwards and, crying out in a more terrible voice than before that same "a-a-a-a!" she collapsed onto the shoemaker Santo who was standing dumbfounded beside her.

'One of those present realised that Mazalta must have seen something unusual in the washerwoman Tia-Hanucha di Pardo's house and sensing some strange event they rushed there, treading through the slushy snow and lumps of clay into the small courtyard, and entered Hanucha's little house.

'There was an old shawl stretched over the window in the small room, with moth holes in it in places. When the first people arrived at the door which Rahela's maid had left open, they could not see much in the half-darkness other than those holes of light in the shawl. But when they pulled the shawl off the window, they could see the little room. On the floor there was a heap of coats under which parts of a coverlet could be made out. Under the coverlet lay the washerwoman and her Bochka. The child had pressed herself against her mother and her mother had held her close with both her arms. The two of them were rigid. Mother and daughter.

'For a long time no one said anything and then someone said:

'"They froze! The child was cold. You can see that she had wanted to press into her mother's arms to keep warm," and pointed at the earthenware stove, a whole corner of which was broken off. "There," said that man, "they couldn't even light their fire, poor things!"

'Then someone else said in a trembling voice:

'"Misfortunes drag others in their wake. It's always like that. Yesterday poor Shimon Papo the cheesemaker's house burned down, almost next door, and today these two women have perished. Dear God!"

'"Strange," said Abraham the grocer to the shoemaker Santo, "strange to think that they perished in a fire yesterday over there, while here these two have died of cold. Strange!"

'"There's nothing strange about it, Abraham," replied Santo the shoemaker. "It is all as it was written, and it was all written. It is written: some will live, and some will die, some of hunger, some of thirst, some of fire and some of cold. That's how it is, my good friend. It is all as it is written," said Santo, staring at a white plate on which the fat had congealed and on which lay a shiny spoon, a greasy chicken wing and a drumstick, bitten in two places.

'Another eight pairs of eyes stared at that white plate, and that plate and the white table-cloth and the chicken soup and the shiny spoons, and the piece of bread, and the star of ground almonds with red jam in the centre, that whole dining table, richly spread out on a small crate, all of that was soon known to everyone and how and from where it came to be in the midst of that poverty, in that little room, beside the dead Bochka and her dead mother. Mazalta, Rahela's maid, told it all. The girl told everything calmly and exactly.

'The girl said:

'"Wait, I'll tell you everything."

'And while Clarucha, known as "la comadre", was tying lemon rind on her forehead, the girl said:

'"I found them like this yesterday: Bochka was crouching in the fireplace, she was leaning her head against the icy tiles of the stove, sleeping. And she, the washerwoman Tia-Hanucha di Pardo, had certainly heard someone tapping their way along the dark corridor, stumbling on the rotten boards and she had come to the door, evidently afraid. Because, when I came in she shuddered and raised her arm as though protecting herself from something. I called quickly 'Don't be afraid, it's me, Tia, Mazalta!' and she pointed, pale and trembling, towards the sleeping child, not to wake her.

'"I put down the basket and began to whisper: 'How are you, Tia? Were you frightened by the fire this morning? I'm sure you were. And where's your lamp?' I talked quietly like that. I said: 'My Señora sends her best wishes. She is sorry that she could not come as usual to see you. You know that she is godmother to Albahari's daughter and she is being named this evening. They waited six years for that child, six years, so it's a big celebration. There are thirty-two people for dinner. We've been working all day. My mistress wanted this prepared, that organised. Ah, Tia, there's not a better woman than my Señora in the whole world.'

'Here Mazalta interrupted her story and asked for water. When she had drained the glass and eaten a sugar lump, she continued, replacing the lemon rind that had slipped out from under the rag on her forehead:

'"I lit the lamp, but it smoked, flickered and went out, because the cylinder was broken. I asked Hanucha, 'How are we going to heat the soup, Tia? Goodness, how did such a big piece of the stove break off? Yes, yes, my good Señora said: "Here we are, baking almond cakes, making orange jam, and just think of poor Shimon? His wooden house has burned to the ground. And the washerwoman Tia-Hanucha di Pardo must be frightened and afraid that her house could catch fire as well!" Believe me, Tia-Hanucha, in the middle of getting ready for that feast, as soon as she heard that Shimon's house was on fire, Señora Rahela immediately thought of you. "Kill a chicken", she said, "let's make her supper to give her and her Bochka strength." That's what she said, Tia. She always thinks of you when you are in any trouble. Always!'

'"I found a little paraffin cooker in a corner by the door. 'Have you got any charcoal?' I asked her, looking around. Dear God! They had nothing, nothing. You can see for yourselves! Nothing! I had some coins in my sock, some money of my own, my very own. I took them out and gave them to her: 'Tia, my good Señora sent this for you as well. I shall go and buy paraffin and charcoal. You can't go to bed like this, you're hungry and cold. God, how icy your hands are!'

'"I went quickly out into the courtyard. The trodden snow was freezing. I hastened to buy what was needed. I came back quickly. I lit the lamp, took this little cooker outside and began to wave my shawl over it so that the fire should catch more quickly. Then I took it into the room and put the pan on it. I spread the table-cloth over the crate, placed bowls, bread and everything the good Señora Rahela had sent upon it, and when the soup came to the boil, I took the pan off the heat, poured out a full bowl and added a few pieces of chicken meat, then put the lid on the rest. Then I crumbled that little bit of charcoal, threw it on the fire and placed the little cooker on the stove. I thought: let the room warm up a little. The night is cold outside, and the room smells of mould, the walls are wet.

'"Then I left. 'I'm going, Tia,' I said, 'you wake Bochka, eat, keep up your strength. We killed the fattest chicken, that's what the Señora said. The fattest. The soup is wonderful, it smells as though it had been made for the first supper of Passover, and you must be hungry and cold. We heard that you spent the whole day sitting by your things in the lane trembling in case your house caught fire. Good night, I'll come for the things tomorrow, good night! May the dawn bring blessings on you!' Yes, that's what I said and woe is me, it brought such curses on them. Alack!"

'Rahela's maid began to weep and went on through her tears to say that Hanucha had continued to behave oddly, moving round the room, sitting down first on a packing case, then on her bundle, suddenly shaking her things out of a basket and then staring at her child who kept pressing her hands further into her lap as she slept.

'Finally Mazalta raised her head, looked at Klarucha, known as "la comadre" and said: "I don't know how they froze. Believe me, I don't know. I closed the door, I swear, and I covered the window

71

over. And I put the cooker on the stove. Believe me, I don't know what happened to them."

'That was how Rahela's maid described the whole event exactly, while Klarucha, known as "la comadre", that plump little woman, who went round the town, rubbing swollen stomachs, preparing teas for coughs and spasms, Klarucha's whole reputation confirmed every word of Mazalta's story.

'She said solemnly: "Listen to me. Mazalta is a good girl, the best of all the maids I, Klarucha, known as 'la comadre' have ever seen. And I know them all. In whose house have I not been? Tell me, whose? I tell you, I know her like my own child. Mazalta here is as trustworthy as an experienced housemaid. Did you hear when she said she took the cooker out to get the fire going. Had my hasty Sterucha gone instead of her, I tell you they would both have suffocated on unburned charcoal. And Mazalta covered the window with a shawl. There, I tell you, they whose household she is in are fortunate and fortune brings her to them as their housemaid."

'After this the news of the death of the washerwoman Tia-Hanucha di Pardo swept through the town like the wind. It went from the lanes, leapt over the fences, entered up the steps, came down them, opened windows, crossed from courtyard to courtyard, from mouth to mouth.

'There had never been any news about our washerwoman in the town, but had there been it would never have spread as fast as this news of her death.

'Everyone who heard was amazed: "The washerwoman Tia-Hanucha di Pardo frozen to death! Frozen, with her Bochka! Terrible! God forbid! Poor washerwoman Tia-Hanucha di Pardo."

'I shall tell you this as well. The day we buried them was a sad one. The trodden snow in the muddy streets stuck to our shoes. The sky was covered over with thick, grey clouds. There was fog on the hills.

'In the bottom of the grave into which we lowered them there were puddles of yellow water which had frozen on the surface. The clay stuck unpleasantly to our fingers. All the sorrowing mourners were overcome by horror, like a bad fever.

'In the evening at the meeting of our local council, Rabbi Moshe stood up and said: "You have heard what a misfortune has occurred. What an appalling thing!" The Rabbi spoke for a long time, and those listening whispered to themselves: "poor washerwoman Tia-Hanucha di Pardo!"

'On Thursday wood was distributed to the poor. A whole crowd of hungry, cold, sick and in every way miserable people waited in the hall for the door to open. And while the officials in the room were examining their lists, the poor people linked their destinies to the suffering of the washerwoman Tia-Hanucha di Pardo. When the clerk finally emerged and began to call the unfortunate people into the room, they went in humbly, raising their hands and saying: "Good people, don't let us perish in torment, like the washerwoman Tia-Hanucha di Pardo." That "don't let us suffer in torment" was spoken by these poor folk like that holy eternal pronouncement: "Hear us, Israel, our Lord is the one God!" That is just what they said and thought. But this was not a statement of the truth. No. I, Shabetai Alhalel, am telling you, for the washerwoman Tia-Hanucha di Pardo did not perish in torment.'

Shabetai Alhalel stood up and continued in a lively manner. 'There, that is what was spoken falsely in the town about our washerwoman Tia-Hanucha di Pardo! For the first and last time! And the lie that was spread remained. In vain did I say to the shoemaker Santo and the shoemaker Rafael and the grocer Abraham and Rabbi Moshe and Rahela's maid and old Klarucha, in vain did I say that the washerwoman Tia-Hanucha di Pardo did not perish in torment, but that very evening felt such warmth in her heart as never before. In vain did I tell them: "She had joy in her heart, joy!" Klarucha "la comadre", turning to me and placing her hand on my shoulder said: "Señor Shabetai, we ought to rub your eyes a little, and your head a little more, we ought, I tell you. It is no use having a head that is not worth much, I tell you, it's no use, Señor Shabetai."

'That's what Klarucha said to me, Shabetai Alhalel, I who see with my fingers better than she does with her eyes. I did not see the washerwoman Tia-Hanucha di Pardo telling Rahela's maid not to rattle the plates, not to wake the cold and weary Bochka. I did not see it, but I had felt the washerwoman's heart with my fingers and felt that heart seize up with horror when she heard Mazalta's footsteps in the hall, and later, when Hanucha lay down and pressed Bochka to her bosom, then with my eyes I saw and with my ears I heard the joy beating in her heart. Joy, I tell you, like a smiling child's.

And that is why I have the right to tell you how Hanucha met her death.'

Shabetai Alhalel sat down again. He continued his narration calmly at first, accompanying his words with gentle movements of his hands, but later he became increasingly animated, standing up, walking round the room, sometimes speaking loudly and excitedly, then sometimes in a soft, muffled tone, sometimes mysteriously, almost reverently as though he were saying a prayer. This is how he began.

I

'Every year the first snow is a miracle.

'On Sunday towards evening that first snow had begun unexpectedly to fall. When I entered the muddy courtyard it was still light enough to see. Bochka was standing in the doorway. She was stretching out her hands to catch the big flakes. I stopped and waited for her to shout like all the other children: "Shabetai Alhalel, snow, snow, look Shabetai Alhalel!" I waited in vain. Bochka said nothing, staring intently at her hands. I went up to her. I wanted to ask about her mother, but when I met her eyes I went on. Bochka's eyes were beautiful, just as everything joyful is beautiful.

'A little later I found Bochka at the window. She was pressing her forehead against the glass. The snow was falling more and more heavily. The flakes were large and soft.

'I entered the room. Hanucha was rubbing her right knee with some kind of ointment. Her left knee was wrapped in rags. Today she had been washing at Tia-Bulka's and she was tired. Bochka had not yet taken off her wet shoes. There was a bundle on a crate that had not been undone. It was already dark and cold in the room. The fire in the small earthenware tile stove had just started to burn. Through a porous tile, one could just make out a red flame. Hanucha spent a long time looking into that brilliant fiery eye and she had forgotten to cover her bandaged knees with her skirt.

'I talked to Bochka. Her eyes showed how much her soul was rejoicing.

'Bochka said: "If the snow goes on falling like this all night, it'll be up to my knees." She shivered and imagined: "Tomorrow I'll go

74

out in my socks. You can walk in snow without shoes. I'll put on those red socks, the woollen ones, which reach over my knees, the ones we got from the Izahars. Mother has darned them well. I'll walk in the snow. There won't be any mud under the snow. Dear God! Did you hear, Shabetai Alhalel? The mud will disappear, the mud which sticks to your very soul. Look through the little bit of glass I've rubbed clean. See, the puddles in the yard are already going. Do you see how the branches on the plum tree are deco-rated? Tomorrow we'll play, me and Jakitsa and Blankitsa. We'll roll in the snow. I shan't go with Mother tomorrow. I'll stay at home. With Simon's Sarah. Mother's going to the flour-seller Yaka the day after tomorrow. The children there look at me as though I had horns."

'Bochka moved away from the window, glanced at her mother and said:

'"Do not make me go with you tomorrow, let me stay and play in the snow! Tomorrow the yard will be clean. I shall be able to roll in it."

'"Oh yes, and catch a chill. That's all we need. It's enough that I can hardly walk. Come on, take off those muddy shoes."

'Bochka took off her wet socks as well and pulled on the red ones. Hanucha warmed the pan of overcooked beans, fixed an old skirt over the window, lit the lamp. She sat and watched. There was a string stretched from the door towards the stove. A muddy skirt hung from it. And some yellow shoes of Bochka's hung on the string. There were string laces in the shoes. I moved to one side while Hanucha arranged a bed in the middle of the room.

'Bochka lay down early. She was very excited. She kept getting up, going to the window, pushing the skirt aside and bending her head:

'"It's snowing, it's snowing," she said when she went back to bed and closed her eyes so as to fall asleep as soon as possible, so that morning would come.

'"Will you leave Bochka to play tomorrow?" I asked Hanucha. "The yard will be clean, white as the soul of the righteous."

'Hanucha did not reply. I shut the door behind me and left. My footsteps could not be heard in the snow.

'Hanucha stood with her back to the stove. She examined the

silk dress she had been given that day for Bochka. She wondered how to mend it and what kind of patches to sew under the armpits where the silk had begun to fray. How? How did one mend silk dresses? Hanucha felt the dress, and the silk frayed more and more, as though it were rotten.

'"What a shame! What a shame! My God! They didn't know how to care for it," Hanucha shook her head and put the dress away in a trunk. Hanucha spent some more time moving around the room. Then she felt the stove, extinguished the lamp, let her outer skirt fall to the floor and lay down beside Bochka. She covered herself with a shabby coat.

'She had not yet fallen asleep when a small, shaggy mouse appeared in a corner. It scampered up to the skirt. Hanucha had left a little piece of sugar in her pocket. The shaggy mouse had smelled it, but it could not find a way to get at it. There was nothing left for it but to gnaw through the wet woollen material. For a long time its labour could not be heard, and when its sharp pointed teeth bit into the sugar, Hanucha had already fallen asleep.

'They both breathed heavily. Both Bochka and Hanucha. As though the air was thick and heavy. The extinguishing flame began to smoke and smell through the room.

'Something was stifling me as well. I stopped down in the lane at the corner to take a breath. Here the air was fresh. It was still snowing. The flakes round the street lamp seemed to me like little moths. It was calm everywhere.

II

'Early in the morning the cylinder on the lamp shattered. I heard it crack. A thin, bright line appeared on the sooty side. Before that the flame went out.

'Bochka woke up with her hand stretched out to take the skirt from the window. She stood in amazement at the frosted glass: "I've seen lace like this at Señora Rahela's", Bochka remembered, looking at the ice flowers.

'Hanucha unlocked the door:

'"Listen, I'll leave you at Simon's Sarah. I'm just going to buy you some bread. I'll pour some oil onto the bread for you. Go on, lie down and put this bottle beside you under the covers to melt the oil. See how solid it has become. I shan't be able to pour it. Go on!"

'When Hanucha had gone out, Bochka got up to see the wonder of the courtyard in snow. She stepped into the soft whiteness.

'"Señor Shabetai," said Bochka, "Señor Shabetai, look at the decorations on the plum tree. Come on, you won't get your feet muddy. Now everything's clean. You can roll in the yard, if you like. It's wonderful. Like a story!"

'Bochka had not brushed her hair and she had wrapped a yellowish coat around her. Her red socks sunk into the snow up to her knees. She laughed so that you could see her teeth. Her rotten, blackened teeth were not ugly that day in her joyful face. She stood and looked at the whiteness of the whole courtyard, at a little black-headed bird hopping along a branch of the decorated plum tree, flapping its wings and knocking the white decoration off. "Tss, tss, tss," Bochka called to the bird. "Tss, tss, tss," chirruped the bird.

'Then all at once there came a cry. At first the cry seemed to come from behind a closed door, then from an open door. At first a small boy cried out, then a little girl, then both together. After that came the long scream of a terrified woman.

'The decoration fell from the plum tree.

'Bochka ran into the room and snuggled under the bedcovers. The bottle with the solidified oil rolled away to the stove.

'Ten minutes passed. Then Hanucha fell into the room, breathlessly:

'"Get up! There's a fire at Shimon Papo's, get up, get dressed! Bochkaaa!" Hanucha cried in agitation and began stuffing rags into the trunk. Haimole the porter came.

'"All right, lady, let me have the trunk. Whenever there's a fire, it's never in a rich house. It's as though only rags and worm-eaten wood could burn." Haimole spoke in a thick voice, as though his tongue was swollen.

'Bochka was bewildered. Everyone was rushing out into the courtyards, rushing to the fences, breaking them down. Dense smoke and a long flame ran along the ground and caught the wooden verandah at the house of Shimon Papo, the cheese-maker.

III

'Hanucha crouched in the lane, protecting her things and her bundles until midday. Bochka sat on a small crate, drumming her shoes on the boards. She held a roll in her hand. She kept rolling one bite around in her mouth. She simply could not swallow it.

'"Who gave you that?" asked Hanucha.

'Bochka shrugged her shoulders, holding out the half-eaten roll.

'"Why don't you eat it?"

'She shrugged her shoulders again.

'"Who gave it to you?"

'"I don't know," said Bochka, putting the roll into her lap.

'I, Shabetai Alhalel, watched the two women looking at each other. Hanucha was pale. Her gaze had fixed on the child's lap, on the thin, crumpled yellowish coat, where the roll lay, its soft white centre poking out of the bitten end.

'That piece of bread with its brown crust and white centre on that dirty pauper's coat seemed to the washerwoman like a terrible sign. And the child seemed more wretched than she had ever seen her. Now she saw all her own poverty heaped up on the trodden snow and remembered that the silk dress that frayed wherever you touched it was in the worm-eaten crate where Bochka was sitting.

'Hanucha lowered herself onto the bundle. An icy chill ran through her whole body from her wet feet, and goose pimples formed on the skin on her back and belly.

'She was still looking at the child's lap when suddenly instead of Bochka on the worm-eaten crate she saw a bowl of hot chicken soup on a white table-cloth. She thought she also heard a greeting, warm and gentle:

'"Good evening, Tia-Hanucha!"

'She turned round to see. She could see nothing. Just people milling about, shouting, walking or running along the lanes.

'Hanucha sighed deeply. Something seemed to break in her, she fell onto the bundle, and an icy sweat broke out on her forehead.

78

IV

'Towards evening when they took their things inside, Haimole the porter came by again. As he lowered the trunk to the ground, Haimole the porter, broad and strong, caught one end of it against the earthenware stove and broke a piece off.

'"Just look, instead of being of use to you, I've broken your stove." Haimole the porter mended the stove with clay.

'"Don't light the stove immediately, let it dry a little," he said and left.

'A little later the piece he had stuck back fell off and shattered into small fragments. Then Bochka sat down in the fireplace and began to shake.

'"Bochka, Bochka, what is it?" Hanucha should have asked the child, and got up from the crate and stroked her hair. And Hanucha wanted to get up, but her legs were like wood.

'"Let her cry, yes, let her cry," said Hanucha to herself; her right hand, which was lying in her lap, stirred slightly. "Let her cry, let her mourn this unhappy day."

'As I had done the day before, I walked through the courtyard. The snow was trodden and dirty. The plum tree had been cut down and thrown onto the broken fence. In the footmarks left by heavy shoes yellow water had collected and frozen over. Over the trodden snow were the criss-crossed tracks of the wheels used to drag hoses. Behind the fence loomed the burnt-out house.

'Everything smelled of smoke and wet burned beams and rags.

'In Hanucha's corridor I caught my foot between two boards. I pulled it free and listened: Bochka was still crying. It was a strange sound. It faded, disappeared, could not be heard, and then it began again, spasmodic, strong, stifled, as though stuck between her thin ribs or hanging onto the slippery surface of her little child's heart. It recoiled, stretched up, and then drew back and hid inside her again.

'I entered and watched. Hanucha was not listening to the child's fading sobs. She was listening to hear whether anyone was tapping along the corridor and she grabbed hold of the crate in terror.

'"They'll come, they'll come today the way they always come

when there's misfortune!" Hanucha got up twice from the crate and went towards the door.

'Twice she jumped up and twice came back and sat down.

'I sat down beside her and said:

'"Who will come? No one will come. Listen, Hanucha, there's a need in you that has not been expressed. Weep, to find ease. See how Bochka has calmed down and is playing now, pulling the threads on her yellow coat where that big button fell off."

'Hanucha sat down to undo her bundles. The open bundles gaped in front of her. Hanucha looked at them and her terrible thought returned.

'"Señora Rahela will come, she will come because of these scattered rags, because of the haste with which these bundles and boxes were saved."

'Those shiny spoons and soft white bread and plates would come. Señora Rahela would greet her from the doorway in her velvety voice: "Buenas noches, Tia-Hanucha!" The dishes would clink as Mazalta, her maid, appeared behind her mistress.

'"Mama, mama!" called the child, as though she wanted to sweep away her mother's thoughts, but Hanucha did not hear the child's cry. She was holding the broken cylinder in her hand and tearing her heart: "They will come! They always came with supper, always. The first time, what happened the first time? – Wait, Shabetai Alhalel, wait!" – Hanucha strained to remember, choking. I laid my hand on her contracted heart to ease the acute and bitter pain, for I knew when the smell of those chicken soups had first begun to waft through the room. The first time was when she buried her first child and ever since that day they had marked, one after the other, every misfortune, sorrow or pain from which she had not recovered.

'As her husband Abraham lay dying, it steamed, greasy and yellow, in a white bowl, and the steam merged with his soul when it rose like a thin shadow towards the Lord our God. It shone yellow in its fat when she had taken two days to give birth to the twins, Bochka and her dead sister. They always came whenever she had to stay in bed with swollen knees. They came when Bochka announced to the cheesemaker Shimon's children that her brother Bencion had gone to heaven. They came when little Bochka had been delirious in fever, while Hanucha, bent double over

80

her sick child had called to the Lord with her greatest prayer.

'"Hear me, Lord, my Bochka is my only child. Hear me, Lord, my Bochka is my one and only one!"

'They were always the same when they came, always with the same bowls and the same spoons; with the same bread and the same pieces of chicken; with Señora Rahela's same good and compassionate eyes and her same warm and comforting voice. For Señora Rahela always came filled with inner joy, which managed to lure forth at least a sad smile in sad eyes so that, at least for an instant, light would flare on the sad path of a life of suffering, at the end of an experience etched by nails into a human heart.

'Her heart contracted under my hand and trembled.

'"Shabetai Alhalel, yes, on my life, it is all as I say, today I knew, today I knew it all!"

'They would come today, announced in that miraculous way on little Bochka's lap in the white bread of God.

'That was what Hanucha said and she could already hear Señora Rahela's greeting, and Señora Rahela's greeting was warm, concerned and compassionate.

'"Buenas noches, Tia-Hanucha! Good evening!" That was always her greeting, and her voice was gentle, for Señora Rahela was a good woman. She would not even wrap her silk shawl round her when she set off to visit the washerwoman Tia-Hanucha di Pardo. She would put on an old shawl, she would exchange her gold headdress for one on which the coins were fake, blackened and dull. She would tuck a simple sprig of rue behind her ear instead of flowers decorated with tiny glittering stones. She would undo the string of large pearls from around her neck. She would take the expensive rings from her fingers, leaving just her wedding ring, with its square Hebrew letters, and she would come, full of sadness, goodness and concern to see and comfort the poor weeping Jewish woman, the washerwoman Tia-Hanucha di Pardo; she would come to raise her up with kind words, when she had succumbed under the weight of her suffering, and to strengthen her, hungry and exhausted, with warm, greasy chicken soup.

'"Good evening!"

'That greeting was in the beating of Hanucha's heart and I could hear it.

'Bochka called again, wearily and feebly.

81

'"Mama, mama, let me lie down." Her little, thin hands, lying in her lap, were frozen. She had bent her head and rested it against the tiled stove. She seemed as though beaten all over with a cudgel and as though her weak, thin body was covered in bruises that hurt even at the touch of her clothes.

'Hanucha did not stir this time either. She heard whenever her child called. She started a little in her thoughts, she wanted to get up, to open her eyes, to see what was wrong with her and her child, but she felt heavy and huge to herself and as though she were sinking into deep mud.

V

'Bochka had fallen asleep when footsteps really were heard in the hallway, when the clink of dishes and tapping on the door were heard. Hanucha had recognised the footsteps when they were still in the courtyard. She jumped up from the crate, completely pale. At first she did not believe it, so she listened carefully, and now she was shaking as though someone were whipping her. All her muscles moved at once and she bent double with pain, but there was no time for her to cry out, and she stepped like that towards the door. Her eyes wide, she waited, fearfully, to see who would appear. She wanted to straighten up to see better, and, standing right by the door, she raised her hand a little. Perhaps her hand went up of its own accord or perhaps Hanucha had wanted to defend herself like that from some new unexpected horror, worse than that of the morning, more cruel, which was making its appearance, tapping softly on the door. Perhaps she had wanted to hold back the realisation of her expectation, still, still, at the last moment, on the very threshold, and appalled at what was going to happen, she had raised her hand to turn it back, to drive it into oblivion, to make it disappear, into the piece of white bread on Bochka's lap out of which it had sprung, tiny, indistinct, and now, here it was, in the clinking of the dishes and the tapping of a hand on the door, merciless and terrible. Yes, that was how it had tapped when Abraham, her husband, was lying on his deathbed. And when they had taken him away on a *tabut*, singing holy songs. Just like that! And then, beside the stove, in the place Bochka was now, her only son, Bencion, had dozed as he read miraculous prayers, her son, with his little pale hands, with that pale smile, which he had taken with him to the grave. And her Bochka, still just a little scrap of life that was beginning to grow in her belly had hidden so completely, perhaps poisoned by her misery, that she, the unfortunate Hanucha, shook for hours, waiting for her child to make a sign, to announce with its minute jerks: "Here I am, mother, I'm alive, I'm alive, don't worry!"

That was how the tapping always came, at the same time, and that was how the footsteps were heard, unaccustomed to the rotten floor, on the broken board in the hall which she never stumbled on, neither she nor any of those who lived in that little room with her.

'That was how the tapping came ... like that.

'Hanucha's eyes were shining. There was just an instant left for her to doubt everything that she had run over in her mind all afternoon and to believe that Haimole would appear at the door to ask and see whether the piece of broken stove was holding. "It's Haimole, Haimole the porter, that's who!" That joyful cry was already slipping out of her. Then the door opened and there was Mazalta, Señora Rahela's maid, bearing a fresh and icy breath in her clothes.

'I went out so as not to be in the way as she spread the damask tablecloth over the worm-eaten crate, so as not to hear the thin clink of the blue-rimmed dishes and shining metal spoons.

VI

'When I returned, everything was arranged and ready. You could smell the overcooked chicken. The soup, yellow and greasy, gave off hot steam, and its surface shining brightly disclosed from time to time a brilliant reflection. In front of the lamp, between the table and the crouching Bochka, stood the washerwoman. A heavy, dark shadow fell from her, dragging itself, elongated, over the floor and from there, broken beneath the shoulders, it climbed almost halfway up the mouldy wall. Hanucha looked at the broken corner of the stove through which the sooty, black interior could be seen and she prepared, for the second time already, to swallow all that bitter spittle that had collected in her mouth, when at that moment Bochka moved. The child stretched out her leg, moved her shoulders, and took a deep, squeaky breath through her nose.

'For the first time tiny sparks leapt out of the stove.

'I, Shabetai Alhalel, said to the washerwoman Tia-Hanucha di Pardo:

'"Tia-Hanucha, good Tia-Hanucha, it seems to me that Bochka has smelled the soup and that little bit of chicken heart and wing in it."

'"There's a piece of liver in it as well," replied the washerwoman, still gazing at that sooty abyss and then she suddenly turned to me.

'"What do you mean? Should I not wake her? And why shouldn't I wake her? I shall, I'll wake her, I'll wake her, let her get up, let the child have something to eat, let her have supper, let her warm herself. The little stove can hardly manage to warm our toes. But the child will eat. Have you seen the way my hungry children eat this evening? They gnaw, chew, suck, lick their lips, swallow without pausing and their mouths and hands are all greasy. And then they start wriggling, as though they had come to life. Warm blood runs through them from somewhere, their yellow cheeks become pink and their eyes gleam. That was how my Bencion ate that evening when we had buried Abraham, his father, two hours earlier. He licked his fingers, gnawed the greasy chicken joints, sucked the yellow and red marrow from the soft chicken bones, sniffed the cakes, and when he smelled cloves in them, he closed his eyes and said, the way he had learned from his father: 'Blessed art Thou, Lord, who hast created flowers and scents!'

'"Yes, Shabetai Alhalel, you did not see my hungry children eating. And that is why I have to wake my child. I must."

'"Bochka," called Hanucha, almost without a sound.

'"Bochka," she called again in the same way.

'Bochka did not reply.

'"Why should I not wake her? Why? I know how greedily she too eats. She likes the little chicken hearts as well, and she licks the shining, greasy spoon. So why should I not wake her? Why?"

'Hanucha stood like that, gazing at the child. And from higher up, from the stove, those two holes on the stove, where the glowing coal could be seen, stared at her like two red eyes.

'The pieces of charcoal that Rahela's maid had thrown onto the

1. Isak Samokovlija (1889–1955).

2. The old Jewish Cemetery of Sarajevo. Today, the only remaining trace of Bosnia's Sephardic Jews is their big old cemetery that stands on the steep slope rising above Sarajevo's Miljacka River.

3. The Jews of Sarajevo – Kalmi Baruch's family, Samokovlija's relatives, in the early 1930s.

4. The New Sephardic Temple, built in the late 1930s, demolished in April 1941.

5. and 6 Looting the
Temple in April 1941.

7. One of the rich Jewish traders of Sarajevo. Samokovlija didn't write of them.

8. A Jewish grocer's shop in one of the side streets of Sarajevo. 'To open a shop, become a grocer and no longer struggle as a porter, that really would be something!' *Samuel, the Porter.*

9. Isak Samokovlija – his great-grandfather came to Bosnia from the Bulgarian town of Samokov (hence the surname Samokovlija, or Los Samokovlis in Ladino).

10. Isak Samokovlija's family: the parents (Moses and Rifka) and four sons (Haim, Isak, Baruh and Jakov).

11. The Ashkenazic Temple. Today a house of the Jewish community of Sarajevo.

fire flared. From time to time sheaves of tiny green sparks spurted from them. The blue and gold rims of the dishes gleamed, the white damask tablecloth glowed, while yellow rings of chicken fat glistened. White steam rose from the bowl. The soup was still warm. The little room was full of its aroma. The lamp burned festively. Shadows fell over the floor from the overturned bundles, boxes and rags.

'"Bochka, Bochka, get up!" Hanucha knelt beside the child and called her. She leaned her face, lined and cold, against Bochka's tousled hair. "Bochka, Bochka, get up, get up and eat some supper, get up my Bochka, Bochka!"

'Slowly Bochka stirred, stretched, rubbed her eyes with her frozen hands and said sleepily:

'"Mama, let me lie down, make the bed for me, please, let me lie down. I don't want any supper, I'm not hungry ... I'm not, mama, really I'm not ..."

'The sleepy child resisted, but Hanucha coaxed her.

'"Get up, my darling, get up, my treasure, have some supper, look, open your eyes, there's soup, Bochka, chicken soup, there's a little heart, Bochka, chicken heart, a tiny one, and there's leg, and chicken wing. Look, Bochka, there's a cake on the crate as well, a cake with red jam, get up and warm yourself, the soup is still steaming."

'So the washerwoman Tia-Hanucha di Pardo coaxed her child and bit by bit her heart was breaking.

'Finally Bochka straightened up and when she came to herself and saw the prepared food, she opened her mouth and eyes wide:

'"Aaaah!" she gasped, "Señora Rahela must have been ... How is it I didn't hear anything?" The child tried to stand up.

'"Wait, Bochka," Hanucha stopped her, "wait, for me to take off your shoes, they're wet, wait!"

'Hanucha sat down beside the child and as she took off Bochka's wet shoes and wrapped her chilled feet in dry rags, she heard the intestines in the child's stomach rumble twice. When she heard them a third time, Hanucha carried Bochka to the crate and knelt beside her to warm her feet with her hands and cheeks.

'The child took a spoon and lightly touched the bowl with it. A thin, silver clink echoed in Hanucha's ear. As though it changed it into a great hollow. A little later Hanucha heard in that hollow Bochka sipping her first spoonful of hot chicken soup.

'She sipped another, smacked her lips with her tongue and licked them. We watched and barely breathed: Bochka was licking the shiny spoon, picking up the chicken wing in her fingers, taking the greasy overcooked skin off the bone with her blackened teeth, staring at something and saying:

'"Do you know the last time Señora Rahela sent us cakes like this, Mama? When you were ill in the spring, you know, when you had cramps in your stomach." Hanucha said nothing, and Bochka went on talking as if to herself:

'"She hasn't sent anything since then ... And who bought a new cylinder for the lamp? Did you wash that tablecloth, Mama? God, how white it is! You know, Mama, I feel really strange today. It seems to me that today is Saturday. It's just as though today was Saturday, but it was a horrid day. It was horrid, wasn't it, Mama?" The child shook her head as though disgusted by something.

'Hanucha soaked the rags wrapped round the child's feet with her tears, pressing her feet ever more tightly to her breast and struggling to suppress a cry which had curved within her into an arch like a black gnarled branch which was just about to break in a strong gust of wind and shatter against rocks and cliffs. Hanucha braced herself afraid that a scream would burst from her, while the child nibbled the cake, clinked the shiny spoon on the plate and talked.

'"And then, Mama, now I remember, they came when they took Bencion away, and then ...", the child stared at the red jam on the cake and talked.

'I, Shabetai Alhalel, went out to take a breath of air. I went out and breathed deeply. I opened my mouth wide. Outside was a calm winter night. Here and there the sky was clear, an occasional brilliant star could be seen. When I took a step I felt that the surface of the trodden snow had begun to thaw.

VII

'I came back again.

'Hanucha had turned down the wick in the lamp, turned it down and blew at the little flame that was still flickering feverishly in it. She blew just once, sharply, then lay down beside the child.

'I held my breath and waited. It was dark. Only a few little, low flames danced in the stove, and its two eyes glowed with living charcoal. Everything had fallen silent! Hanucha, and Bochka, and the spoons, and the dishes. Not even the shaggy mouse stirred.

'Then Bochka spoke in the silence:

'"Mama, Mama!"

'"What is it, Bochka, what is it?"

'I strained my ears to hear what Bochka was going to say. I turned my head towards her, but Bochka said nothing. I could feel: she had pushed her hands deeper into her lap, pressed herself more tightly against her mother.

'"What is it, my precious?" asked Hanucha anxiously.

'"Nothing, I wanted to ask you – but what I wanted to ask I don't know myself. Ah, yes, Mama, I wanted to ask you why they cut down the plum tree. But I know why they cut it down. They cut it down because it was in the way. Those carts had to cross the yard, so they cut it down. Never mind. Never mind! You think I'm sorry about it, Mama. I'm not. Never mind that they cut it down. Never mind that they trod down the snow. Thank God our house didn't burn. But, Mama, will it snow again soon, mama, will it?"

'"Certainly it will."

'"Certainly?"

'"Yes, certainly, the winter is long, it has just begun."

'"How long does winter last?"

'"A long time!"

'"A long time?"

'"Yes!"

'Hanucha laid her arm over the child, as though by chance. The child felt warm under that arm. They were both silent. Now I could make out their bed like a heap of darkness in that little room. I could see that the washerwoman was looking too. Two tiny red reflections shone in her eyes. Those were the reflections of those red fiery holes in the stove. I did not stir. Sparks scattered from the little cooker, once, twice.

'"And do you know when Señora Rahela will send us supper again? Do you, Mama?"

'Bochka felt her mother's arm, the one lying across her, twitch a little. That shudder seemed to run through her as well from her shoulder down her back. She waited for her mother to say

87

something and as she waited, wondering why her mother did not reply, she fell asleep. Hanucha had grown rigid on the bed. She could not close her eyes, for that long somewhat crooked eye on the stove seemed to be grimacing at her and saying: Answer, washerwoman Tia-Hanucha di Pardo, answer your pale and thin Bochka, when will Señora Rahela send supper again, answer! She is waiting, waiting. Perhaps she too can guess your thoughts, listen to her heart pounding!

'Hanucha had frozen. She was as icy as the earth. A pulse was trembling right under her throat. Her consciousness began to fade again, as though some horror that had fallen on her breast was preparing to shatter her brow as well. She wanted now that the branch should break in her, and to shriek, to let out a cry no one had ever heard before, to cry for help with all the strength that now appeared in her from somewhere like a miracle, and make the broken stove and the little cooker collapse, and the plates and the forks, and the cylinder, and the window, with that shawl spread over it, shudder. And she would have screamed loudly like that, power-fully, like a giant woman, had not her Bochka been lying beside her, that child whom she was holding ever more tightly in her arms and who could have been alarmed by such a cry, clenched with terror, turned pale as a rag and never breathed a breath again.

'So as not to frighten the child, Hanucha did not dare defend herself even with her hand, but she resisted that horror with one of her shoulders. Lying like that with one shoulder raised, and holding her child in her arms, she seemed to herself reborn, as though transformed into another Hanucha, large, straight, with undamaged knees, strong thighs and broad shoulders. She began to breathe heavily. She opened her eyes still wider and looked with a terrible expression into that long eye up there on the stove, and her arm pressed her child ever more firmly to her breast.

'"They won't come any more, these suppers," she began to say to someone, "they won't, I say. I'm not giving up my child, I'm not giving up my Bochka, ever! I shall carry her in my arms, I shall take her somewhere far away, I shall hide her from your gaze. I shall feed her with my sweat and her pale cheeks will grow pink, they will glow and be redder than your very blood. I'm not giving her up, I tell you, there's been enough, I'm not giving her up. She's all I have, she's my strength and my life. I shall scream, I shall protect her,

I'm not giving her up! Hear me, Lord, Bochka is my one and only! Leave me her, Lord! I shall scream, I shall scream and I shall run with her away from here out of this grave of mine, I shall run over those broken fences, ditches and rubbish heaps, I shall run along long roads, meadows and fields, I shall cross streams and hills, I shall stumble through woods and I shall come out, with her, with my Bochka, I shall come out where you will not be able to reach or find me."

'Hanucha closed her eyes, wrapped the child tightly to her and stretching out her legs, so as to feel her strength as fully as possible, she began to talk to herself. She talked and was transported further and further into some unknown and distant regions. She felt as though she was moving, running, climbing and jumping over ditches, crevices, fences and bushes, that she was climbing up hills and down into valleys. Past her went landscapes, villages, hills; past her went oxen, horses, sheep. Rams raised their heads and looked after her. And people stopped and turned to watch her go. She felt them looking at her, hesitant and surprised.

'She would have liked to turn round and say to them: "Yes, yes, just look, it is I, the washerwoman Tia-Hanucha di Pardo, it is I! Look, my knees are not swollen any more, my back is not bent any more, and Bochka's cheeks are not yellow any more. Milk has come into my breasts, it has overflowed and spurted out, see how swollen my breasts are, how full, and how the child suckles them. Listen to her swallow, see her little cheeks filling, see the milk spilling out of her mouth and dripping down her chin, Look at her growing, filling out, my Bochka. We don't need your suppers any more! No, we don't!"

'So the washerwoman Tia-Hanucha di Pardo journeyed glowing with warmth. Even the soles of her feet which she had never been able to warm were now hot, and where the child was pressed against her she was perspiring. Something was carrying her into the distance, carrying her as though on wings, lightly, joyously, swiftly.

'All at once she saw some faces, bright, compassionate, some gentle smiling eyes were looking at her and saying: "Yes, that is she, that is Tia-Hanucha, our Tia-Hanucha." And Hanucha went towards them and could already hear them laughing with joy, she could hear her own heart beating, trembling, as though joy were radiating

89

from her cheeks and more: her whole being was swaying with the rapturous sense of this happiness. She could hardly hold herself upright, she could hardly take a step.

'She had almost arrived. "Why are those gentle eyes so terrified? Why are they anxious? No, I don't feel bad, no I don't!" she said and pressed the child to her so that she should not fall out of her arms. "No, I don't feel bad, no, this is happiness, happiness!"

'Her head bowed, she was already losing consciousness, but she could still feel good soft hands taking hold of her and propping up her head. She heard them shouting in alarm: "A glass of water for our Hanucha! A glass of water and a lump of sugar!"

'And she heard someone saying softly: "Mama, dear mama." That was Bencion. That was her Bencion. "How tall he is, how he has grown! Bencion!"

'"Darling, my darling," she wanted to say, "darling, do not be afraid, this is happiness, happiness, don't worry, the main thing is I've come," but she could not.

'"Bencion!" she tried at least to say that but she could not. She was steadily overcome by feebleness and she fell slowly onto something soft, warm and velvety.

VIII

'The washerwoman Tia-Hanucha di Pardo fell lengthily into her joyous dream and then perfect calm reigned in the little room. Their two hearts beat dully in the dark. The darkness turned into an endless space in which greenish-blue flames from the stove flickered.

'They flickered and entwined like snakes raising their heads and darting out their forked tongues.

'Sometimes a bright flame would wind out of them.

'I, Shabetai Alhalel, stood and watched.

'The flames burned strangely. Mysteriously and devoutly. They burned as though in a candlestick lit to celebrate the Lord on holy Sabbath days for giving them to us, and to our servants and our maidservants, saying:

'"That your servant and your maidservant should rest."

'The flames burned as though today were Saturday and it seemed to me that something was calling me to say the *kiddush* under that candlestick.

'I looked for a shawl to wrap around me instead of the tallis, so as to say the Sabbath prayer to our Lord.

'I turned and then I noticed: that little shaggy mouse had come out of the hole in the corner and was moving forwards. He scampered a little through the room then suddenly stopped. He raised his little pink nose in the air and began to sniff, his little black eyes rolled and he quickly turned and ran straight into his hole. He vanished in a trice.

'Then I too went outside. I, Shabetai Alhalel, but before I went out I said the following prayer to our Lord: "Bless this Sabbath peace of the washerwoman Tia-Hanucha di Pardo, your great servant and ours, Lord."

'That is what I said and I went out.'

Alhalel stood up, tapped his stick twice and suddenly vanished from my room.

IX

The following day I knocked at his gate. It was opened.

'There's no Shabetai Alhalel here,' they told me, 'Gabriel Gaon lives here.'

'Gabriel Gaon? Why yes … yes … it's him, it's him I'm looking for,' I answered confused.

When I entered the room I stopped in the doorway. Shabetai Alhalel was sitting at the table. Bent over a large old book, he was engrossed in reading and certainly had not heard me come in. His hand with its long fingers was holding tight to the left side of the book while the other lay spread on the yellowing page, which he had just read. His deeply furrowed brow had stiffened into a frown.

He was reading rapidly, but not moving his lips. Then the lines on his forehead moved and relaxed. Shabetai Alhalel raised his head and said solemnly: 'My eyes have seen all this, my ears have heard and understood it.'*

*The Book of Job, ch. XIII

91

We both looked at each other strangely.
Then I was the first to greet him:
'Shalom, Shabetai Alhalel,' I said and bowed.
He gestured for me to sit and replied:
'Peace be with you! My name is Gabriel Gaon!'

Translated by Celia Hawkesworth

The Blond Jewess

There, in the *mahala* they used to say that the finger of God would seek out sin and that all would end badly, because it had long boded no good. And that suspicion arose when her hair turned gold, as though she were noble, and he caressed the child, saying what a joy she brought her father. And he loved her, cursed as she was, no matter if the old women told him she would fall fatally ill from that curse.

'No, no one could have conjured up eyes of this colour with a spell! (her eyes were like violets). It is no curse!', he would even say as he made his way along the street and his steady voice reached high into the air. From morning till night he sold second-hand clothes and when he called 'Old clothes ...' it was as though he were a stranger coming into the *mahala*. But when he reached home, he would be smiling, bearing gifts. And he was indifferent to their reproaches.

But when his child grew up he too began to be fearful, for people would say behind his back: 'Well, if we didn't know better, we would say she was a love child!' And she was a picture. Even the wealthy rejoiced to look on her. She dressed like a figure from a fairy-tale, for she was accustomed from childhood to being pampered. She was the loveliest of all the Jewish girls, and as blond as if the sun had gilded her.

Evil beset her in early summer, poor creature.

Many loved her, but she succumbed to none but he. He was a Christian who spread his wings freely and fell on her like a butterfly, not waiting for her to regain her composure, but himself becoming

93

enraptured. And he gave her a Christian name, calling her Miryana.

'Come, Miryana, of the golden locks, come … !' the song rang out and sin drew near, and the *mahala* held its breath as it whispered in wonder. In vain did she try to break loose, flapping her wings like a bird. She was caught, disarmed, and when summer bloomed, she was bewitched. 'What shall I do? What shall I do?' She thrust her fingers deep in her soul, while he summoned her to the abyss.

I

Friday came. The last.

She opened the door and window of her room, to ease her heart a little. But to no avail. Sorrow seemed to enter at them. And the objects in the room seemed dead to her, no longer to live for her.

Something leaden and heavy fell over her, from the moment people had begun to look at her, reproachfully and sharply – one with bloodshot eyes – when they chanced to meet her with him. Since then she had grown accustomed to malicious looks and protected herself, shutting herself in her room, but from time to time she would leave the house, moving stealthily.

'I love him, Mother, I love him …'

His hand was different and more beautiful. His fingers were slender, their tips warm, and when he caressed her it was as though his hand had the power to heal.

'I love him, for his voice is like a silver bell and it rings in here, in here!'

The soles of her feet tingled. And they conversed, he and she, and it was like the scent of plucked flowers. He spoke sweetly, while Miriam drank his words as though life had been transformed into a spring.

His name was the loveliest she could imagine. While his mother Jovanka called him Milan, Miriam called him her own.

'Alack, curses on her, that my child should be beguiled by a heathen soul, a Jewess! May she be cursed!'

And Miriam heard it all, comprehending little however much she asked. And so it built up in her until one day she moaned under its weight. Her father looked at her like a drill piercing through her, a man who spoke little, while her mother cut her to the quick, crying: 'Oh, my daughter, my daughter!'

And that Friday came, a leaden Friday for her. Should she wash, for the day of the Lord, the Sabbath was at hand? Her mother prepared clean, white clothes with a sprig of rue laid in them. Should she dress and let the thin fabric rub against the white skin of her thighs and the rosy tips of her breasts, and think, not of the holy Sabbath, but of how sweet his hand was when it caressed her?

'It's sinful ... sinful,' she saw, and it came to her clearly as though a Christian hand were reaching into the aroma of the Sabbath loaves and desecrating the wine for the blessing of the seventh day, Jehovah's day.

At that something in her gave way but she could not stretch her hand to help herself. And she heard her mother chiding her and saying: 'Come my child, make haste, it is the Sabbath!'

She saw the candle and her mother lighting it.

'I am coming! I want to come too and light it! I shall light seven candles and raise my hands in prayer as you do, and if I do not whisper Amen aloud my soul will speak it to the Lord, to the God of Abraham, Isaac and Jacob. Give me a little crust of bread that I may dip it in salt and say after you the prayer holy and ancient as is the wrinkle on your cheek, oh Abraham, my father! But leave me, leave me, let my sorrow crush me, and let me suffer!'

She was entranced by the summer and by his words. When he spoke he seemed to offer her mouthfuls of sweet bread. And he called to her, transported her to unknown spaces. There birds chirruped and woods of golden leaves rustled. She melted into that abyss, deep and glowing, warm and soft. And she barely stretched out her arms to defend herself. And yet! She rubbed her eyes to see the white light of day and to refresh herself with water. And as she came to herself, she was already sorry that her hot blood was running frozen again.

Full of foreboding, she ran her hands over her dress and rubbed them against her breasts. Blood ran to their tips and her shirt greedily soaked in the red.

On whom could she call? Her good father, or the one without whom her world lost its warmth?

'What is to become of me? What is to become of me?' She buried herself as though under a deep feather bed and jumped up to kiss her mother's hand.

Those who had been to the temple came in. And there was her father! He had wrapped himself in the Sabbath as though it were a bright, pure shawl for the body and soul. His gaze went to the corners of the room, as though sweeping them with a broom, and his Sabbath eyes were beautiful and looked as though the voice of gladness and the good sunfilled sky spoke out of them. The Sabbath song from the temple still rang in him and his step was long and tranquil. The word of the Guardian and Merciful One had come down and all had been cleansed and had acquired the aspect of the Lord's day. His hand was white as a saint's and the blood ran through it so that it was warm when the children kissed it. And the little room was calm, as though it too had been dedicated when its walls were whitewashed and it knew that it was written that the seventh day was the best day of all.

The flames of the candles flickered, and the white glass and oil gleamed when her father raised his head, and his lips spoke A-d-o-n-a-i! Her mother put her palms together, the children drew close to him. It was not blood that embroidered men's souls. Their bonds were silken and a hundred-fold. So Miriam noticed that her brother's lips were red with holy words, but when she moistened her own with the blessed wine something caught and tightened in her throat. And her father spoke the Sabbath calm as though he were a man from another world and his voice was akin to that of the Lord.

And like a spirit He spread through their souls and their food. Fat glistened on their chins, while drops of oil on their plates, round and shining, entered the white mouthfuls like something living. They ate as though at a feast where joy is poured out of jugs together with the wine. And, as though the soul too suckled on fat, the head of the household spoke of the King of Kings who was the Lord of Israel, he and none other, and the people of Israel were his above all people. For the Lord said let there be darkness and there was darkness: let there be light and there was light, for he said: this is my testament.

And when the meal was done and the head of the house was left alone to sing (like a wondrous gift accompanied by cymbals and various devices); before it was extinguished, the candle flared over his slumbering lady, the good mother, who that day had washed the cobbles of the courtyard to reflect the starlight more brightly. And while she dreamed, smiling, of the good tranquillity bequeathed her, praising it in her sleep for its goodness, her daughter Miriam, stretched up to the window like a flaming torch, not to save and defend herself, but to burn up somewhere far away, drowsy, but full of strength.

I shall come, she whispered into the darkness, and one by one the stars flew up from her blue eyes to settle in the indigo sky and twinkle there brilliant and pure as though bathed in her fire. The sky too turned with her and with the earth. Then the lead poured from her soul and dropped onto the flowers, and she saw him handsome and young, as though waiting for her, and her hands were barely able to soothe her heart.

And when she went out under the quince tree to stretch her arms, to tremble all over and abandon herself, she snapped a twig, listening as though she could catch somewhere distant the meaning of a whisper and then she bent down and softly, barely audibly, began to sing (not as before when she had sung her mother's arias, but as though something profane and foreign could be heard in her voice).

'Come, Miryana, the golden-haired ...'

Her father heard as well, and it seemed like a vision. He did not at first grasp what it was, just sensed it, but something sharp caught at his heart. Yes, there was something black entwined with his happiness, close to him, he shuddered and raised his head to see his sin or for his eyes to delight him, while she glowed, like longing itself, in her Sabbath clothes, as lovely as the Sabbath itself, swinging on the swing beneath the quince tree. The white fabric of her dress fluttered, wrapping round her legs, and her hair like silken shreds of gold was scattered in the white night, rippling, like her soul, and her song ran like the loveliest prayer to some profane god.

His hand clenched into a fist and he barely remembered that this was a sin on the Sabbath day. He calmed himself and realised at once that the Lord was punishing him for some sin which must be atoned for from generation to generation: for, this is how you will respond, said the Lord, when I will punish you and you shall not dare take offence at the ill I bring you, for it has long been yours — let it be known.

And the father eased open his hand and lips, and felt fine threads around them, as though a spider had passed over his face and poisoned him with a bite. And he did not at once collect himself to chide her like a father but waited until his fingers tingled and he heard nothing but the night carrying off the melody (it seemed to him that it was stealing his daughter as well, never to return her); he leaned out of the window and stopped his cry of pain:

'Don't you know, daughter, not to profane the Sabbath like this?'

And she gave a start, fearful, as though the voice had come from up in the branches and something white had flown over her head. She ran like a child to serve him, trembling, but rebounded from his look as though she had hit herself on a stone.

'It's a sin on the Sabbath!' he said again, while she repeated only 'a sin!' — not in surprise but to confirm in her ignorance her father's teaching and, like a sinner, she touched the washed cobbles with her slippers, one by one, and closed the door behind her in fear that the long shadow which had stretched across the yard would follow her in.

Around midnight something chuckled and laughed, green, with a tail and horns, and she ran to the mirror to tap it with a pebble, and her mother moaned in her sleep and her good hand moved to protect and keep her. And when she sighed, glad that she had managed to save her, then the Sabbath calm spread over them once more, silken and sorrowful.

II

The apples glowed red, and, if you bit into them, your mouth would fill with juice.

'They're tart, that's the kind they are,' said one neighbour to another.

'This sun's so fierce that in a day or two they'll mature to sweetness.'

'No, they won't! Not even the sun can spoil their sort!'

Milan looked at them both, leaning on the fence. While down below in the lanes Miriam moved fearfully round the corners, looking round to see whether malicious eyes were following her. And her small steps hastened to emerge from the *mahala*. People watched her go, while she thought only of reaching the hill. In the lanes of Muslim houses, where there were shutters, she felt easier and when she saw at the window rouged faces with black painted eyebrows, she smiled. As though one soul could speak to another, she seemed to hear: 'Yes, me too, I too like words that touch and hands that caress.'

She moved on and when she caught sight of the fence something pierced her heart and her eyes misted over. Her step grew heavier, her hand dropped, and when he saw her he all but flew to her and melted into her gaze. His white teeth flashed and in them happiness.

He took her hand and pressed it, gazing into her eyes:

'What is it, Miryana, my sweet one?'

'It's Saturday today, Milan, you know, it's Saturday!'

'And so?'

'You know what our Saturday is, don't you?'

'I don't, and why should I know. But it's not yours, for Saturday is not for blonds.'

He glanced at her like the flick of a hook to draw her from the water.

'For blonds?'

'It's not for blonds!' he said, and she nestled against him and let him take her hand. 'Jewish girls are dark, and their hair is hard, their eyes are deep, dark and burning. But yours? Yours are beautiful and peaceful. Like flowers when they open to the sun and the whole day smiles. Your blood too is blue, you have a Christian soul, but you do not know it.'

And he told her: 'And you don't know why hearts sometimes tremble. They are touched by a hand with pink nails, when you close your eyes against the white lights. Or a voice whispers among a thousand others and you know it is yours and the sweetest. They swirl like that through the ages, from near to far, to meet and rejoice. And to meet a hundred joys and fates and draw close. And no one knows where they will spring up, like flowers in spring, or under what shrub or sun. The wind – when the flowers dry – carries off the seed and colour and scatters, one by one, each fate for itself. And mine has linked itself to your smile. And if you gave away all you have received, you'd have much for me.

'I love you and let my people curse you, they cannot defend me

99

from either ill or good. They say, you are a Jew, and so you say as well. For me you are Miryana and it seems to me that you were born long ago when your people were on the Tajo.'

'In Spain.'

'... That's where you were born golden and blue-eyed ...'

'Golden and blue-eyed.'

'Like your mother too ... the first blond Jewess.'

'Blond Jewess!'

'There on the Tajo lived a beauty, a black-haired Jewess, the wife of a rich doctor – Señor Albandari. And she had no children and was full of longing. And at a carnival, when no one had ever seen her more beautiful than at that moment ...'

'Who did the poor creature see?'

'The cavalier Don Alfonso ... A young, daring knight, he kissed her hand and his blue eyes sank into hers, into a thrall of blackness. And no one noticed the handkerchief pass into her hand. She held it tight and when she could tucked it into her bosom. At home, she shut herself in her room and spread it on her lap, trembling as she read: I have loved you for an age ... My longing fills my father's gardens. In my mother's chapel I pray to the Mother of God to grant me happiness on your breast. In love and longing!'

'That's a hateful story.'

'It's not, Miryana! That night, your smile was born, my joy was born. Listen! That's what Don Alfonso wrote to her, and the beautiful, young señora soaked the handkerchief with her tears all the rest of the night. Her days passed slowly, and behind the curtain her heart beat as the guitar beat down in the street in the moonlight. And her longing grew light and called to her. And one day the señora trembled: she was sent a basket of red roses, and under them ...'

'A silk handkerchief!'

'No, Miryana, a monk's habit. She hid it skilfully. Then the Sabbath entered Albandari's home, solemnly and quietly, bringing the peace and blessing of the Lord Jehovah.

'Roses are beautiful' sang Elazar ibn Israel Albandari as he sat down at table, and the table was adorned with roses. 'Roses are beautiful, but more beautiful are the lilies in the gardens of the emperor and the fields of Zion. All days are beautiful, but the most beautiful of all is the Sabbath.'

'Stop it, Milan ... it's a hateful story.'

'No story may itself be hateful. It is our destinies which are hateful. . And when the first candles were extinguished, when lovely night fell on the Tajo river and the gardens around it, and the moon poured its silver over the water, they took a doctor to the wounded knight Fernandez de Monte Santo. The doctor made his way with his assistants up the marble steps of the brightly lit palace, and a white-clad Dominican stood in front of Albandari's house …'

'And when the others came out …'

'… of Albandari's house.'

'Be quiet!'

'The gardens were silent, Miryana, watching the brilliant, huge ring dance of the moon. The flowers opened their centres to drink their fill of the dew and the brilliance of the stars. That night Don Alfonso held the young Señora Albandari in his arms, spoke sweet words to her, and she kissed his golden hair, while the white habit of the wonderful Dominican lay under the roses with their red fluttering petals. That night her black eyes dived into the blue lake to circle in its depths and ages. That evening those black eyes bore away the desire for a golden child.

And then: the daughter of Elazar ibn Israel Albandari was a famous beauty. She grew up without a mother (her mother died in childbirth …'

'She died to expiate her sin.'

'… to keep her happiness to herself. Elazar watched over his daughter as his only child and all his treasure.'

'He caressed her, feared for her and did he never learn of the sin she came from?'

'Never! For there was no story then, and it all had to be, in order for your smile to be born. Listen: half Spain went mad over her blue eyes and blond hair. Her father, old Elazar, gave her to the handsomest young man on the shores of the Tajo: Moreno Pereira, the son of the famous Rabbi of Cordova. That was the year 1460. And from that time on in that family, every hundred years, a blond Jewess is born. And so that smile roamed over the centuries and alighted again on your lips. Do you see, Miryana, what a story you are for me. And for you to return we have to set out on our nights, from circle to circle to enter our own.'

'From circle to circle to enter our own!'

'Our destiny!'

'Mine! Only mine, for a whirlpool shows only one centre in the circle. And all that, that is just a hateful story. I am a Jew, it makes no difference that I'm blond, Milan! A sin matured into poison. I love you, not because of your hands and voice, but because the winds are bearing me into an abyss and that's what your story says ...'

She leaned her head on his shoulder, lost in thought of what was to be. She calculated that she was the fifth and she saw all four of them like her own sisters concealing themselves with their hair. And, as though falling into a swoon, she gazed into the void and when she came to, pale and weary, she placed his hand against her cheek.

He began to comfort her, and she pressed against him as though afraid of a fever, while the evening whispered strangely through the silence. It could be heard in the grass and the branches, it rose to the heights and dispersed in the distance. The scents of ripe fruit and melons wafted in, colours ran into the warmth. Everything merged. Miriam sighed and smiled as though delirious.

He smiled as well.

'There, the story says you must go back ... Will you?'

'I will, I will, but not go back: give back. His house is by the temple. And he, the old Rabbi, is handsome, for he carries the *Torah* in his heart. His beard is silver. And his son? Like his father. I shall call him Moreno as well. His hair is curly, his face is dark as though the sun had burned it. I shall lure him with a song, another one, different from the one I sang to you. I shall call him with a song my mother nursed me on and give back ... so that my eyes fill with black, for him to drink in mine and for me to be carried away by desire ... desire ...'

And, as though in a dance, she got up and pale as she was, she placed her hand on her breast and bowed her head.

'Go on, go on, let me hear how you lie!'

Then tears shone in her eyes, and a shudder ran through her and stopped in her throat. She sobbed:

'I will, I will ... I'll give back ...' she trembled, talking as though to herself.

He stood up as well, and took her by the arm:

'Miryana, let me speak too: no one ever saw her more beautiful than at that moment!'

'No, it's not a story, Milan, it's not! I hear it here, I've been hearing it for a long time, a long time. I hear …'

She would not let him kiss her but asked him to take her up where the rocks were red in the west and whispered for him to be silent.

*   *   *

Below them the *mahala* was seething with summer. Fires appeared in the gardens, and songs intertwined linking hands and hearts. Thin shirts and brightly coloured loose breeches fluttered in the breeze, and here and there a cry rang out and the girls shivered. They swung full of longing into the darkness where they imagined feverish hands, and where pipes and harmonicas merged. Tallow lamps were lit on the slender, pointed minarets.

From the white mosque came a voice pure as silver shining in the silence. It flew up and like a white bird spreading its wings rose high over the rocks.

'*Aksham, aksham!*' it whispered feverishly in her. '*Aksham!*' and her father's eyes gleamed before her somewhere down in the town where the windows were lit. There her father was awaiting her to accompany the bride, the holy Sabbath. 'Let them all wait, let them wait … and let the Sabbath pass … let it pass …' a fine silk thread wound round her. 'Let it pass from one end to the other and return. The sin stretches from end to end!'

She did not hear the sweet words Milan was speaking to her but looked round, and when she saw the river twisting brightly far below she shivered and pressed against him and her eyes sought his: 'Do you love me, do you?' she whispered and turned to look closely at the rock cleaving the chasm.

And he seemed to understand that her pupils were growing in her blue eyes and sinking into the abyss where the road followed the water like a ribbon and he took her firmly by the arm, and his legs felt lifeless.

'Don't fall, take care …'

And she squeezed his hand with her arm and something warm ran through them. She hardly tore her eyes from the chasm and took a step back taking care not to disturb a pebble under her heel, and then looked at him and smiled as though waking from a dream.

'You don't love me.'

'I do, Miryana.'

'So why don't you carry me over there? ...' She pointed to the other side. 'Why don't you carry me the way the song is carried into the night for me to forget ...'

And the song could be heard winding its way upwards. A girl's voice trembled down below in the *mahala*, trembled like a glowing flame piercing the night.

* * *

She tore herself, late, perspiring and dazed, from his arms and, burning in the warm night, said, as she stroked his hand:

'Tomorrow, Milan, tomorrow, let me give myself, let me burn up and be carried away by longing, with you and with him, tomorrow far up there on the rocks, up there let me give myself, up there, tomorrow wait for me and caress me, caress me more, madly, caress my bosom, my hair and let the stars fall shyly into the chasm ... Tomorrow, tomorrow let me give myself, Milan dear one, tomorrow to you ... to Moreno ... to the Dominican ...'

She laughed wildly as though warming herself on the words, then gave a start and sped away through the lanes, as though borne by the winds. His lips still burned on her cheeks, and the warm air from the roofs murmured sweetly: Miryana ... Miryana ... Miryana ...

But when she stepped into her own lane her head spun and her eyes grew dim. She heard a cry in herself and saw an endless, white space. Far in the distance something glinted like the reflection of water and whispered: Miriam, Miriam, Miriam! It was calling softly and warmly from the distance, and she had never heard such a voice until then. For a moment it seemed like her mother's voice. It was calling disembodied, as though the gleam of a glance could be heard.

When she leaned against the courtyard gate and looked in through the window, she heard her mother groan. She stumbled, reaching for the wall to support her and gasped for air. Her legs would not hold her and when she gathered her strength to take a step, to go in, to show herself, a curse broke in the room like glass,

104

shattering into little pieces. Her father clenched his fist and beat it against the table:

'Bastard, you bastard! You V*lach*!'

She wanted to cry out in terror, but, as though an evil hand with sharp nails was stifling her from the darkness, no sound was heard. And she could still see a star high above the courtyard stir and fall. She leaned in that direction and lost consciousness.

Later she arose, her face pale and distorted, and went back outside and it seemed that she was passing along a corridor, tapping her way, and that the wall was rough and cold. And something sticky seemed to catch on her fingers, and a cobweb to wind round her face. And a deep vaulted and dark space stretched ahead until at last a hand appeared. Miriam moved the hair from her eyes to see, to reach for it, for the hand of the Rabbi's son. It was his, his ... And the hand appeared beside her for an instant and led her to a door. She went in, and there was something velvety and embroidered with gold flowers in front of her. When the candle was lit she made out holy letters in thread.

'You're taking me to the temple!' she reproached him to herself in her delirium. She squeezed his hand with her own and looked shyly into his eyes. 'Here, I'm tired and my hair is all over my face, but I shall make myself ready to be your bride and for all to sing of your wonderful, shining bride. And I shall kiss the Rabbi's hand and everyone's, take me there, take me there! And I shall join my palms on my lap as my mother and your mother do. I shall! Had they told me before, I should have said: I will, I will, even if I am blond ...'

She stopped for a moment to rest and to shake herself and when she crossed the lane to slip into the garden, crouching, treading softly so that her step would not be heard, a knocker sounded on a nearby door. She shivered as though scissors had glinted over her head and a lock of her hair fell on her neck. She looked crazily into the darkness. And there were her father's two eyes shining over his prayer-book, watching the locks of her hair falling onto the floor, and her mother came in through the door carrying a broom.

'Sweep up that hair, sweep it up, let the Sabbath come into the house. And prepare the candles for us to breathe their aroma as we lead in the bride, our Sabbath ...'.

* * *

Hundreds of thoughts intertwined and gleamed like sparks before going out or merging into the darkness. And from somewhere there appeared a hunchback carrying a basket, and Miriam guessed by the scent that they were red roses. 'She too, she too, the Señora came out to take the basket! How did the poor creature not guess when she pricked her finger on the handle and blood dripped onto the white habit? How?'

A barn owl flew over her head, and the night seemed to roll into a secret. She did not hear the *mahala* below her breathing in a sweet spasm, but something sad appeared to her and she drove it away with her hand: 'I must go to them, they're calling me, all four of them, they're calling me, Milan!'

And she seemed to hear them now speaking to her: 'We said, we said that you would come, young and untainted. Sit in your place and cover yourself, cover yourself with your hair. And where did they get your eyes? In what nights? Yes, let them wash out with your weeping for you to carry in your palm as we your four sisters do. Look, they are blue as violets and clear, look round and see in them that something is sprouting and pulsing under your dress, see! That is not your heart, but his, the Rabbi's, the Rabbi's in a white habit, a white one.'

She reached the path, and in front of her a shadow deepened on the yellow earth and shifted away.

'Take me too, take me, I'm afraid here, the houses are tipping over; they will fall. The glass has shattered. How shall I step barefoot over the pieces! Take me away, carry me over it, my dearest, that my father's face shall brighten, for the sin to burn up, for that frozen, hungry bird under the red dress to be calm. – What? Where is the bird? Do you see it?'

Fresh air like a wind from the mountain and frozen snow struck her face. She came out onto the rock and the sky seemed close enough for her to touch. She clambered on, panting.

'I have, I have a hungry, frozen bird!' she gave a start and shivered and seemed to intertwine with someone. 'Where is the bird? Where is it? Let us see!' She took off her dress. She stood in her undershirt. She bent over and put her hands in her lap not to be seen naked.

'Where is it? There, it's hidden in her bosom, in her bosom ...'

106

came a shout. It echoed all around, and she felt that the whole *mahala* was thronging after her shouting:

'She's lying, she's lying! How come her hair is so blond and silken? How come her arms are so white? She's stolen them, stolen! And her laughter is stolen! Ask her father, ask him! The bastard, bastard! The *Vlach*!'

An icy shudder ran over her shoulders and the skin on her stomach tightened. She remembered how Milan had taken her by the arm and drawn her back. She smiled: it's my destiny, mine! – and she let out a feeble cry, and her lips parted slightly. She saw the water silver beneath her! Dogs barked angrily. The pebbles began to shift behind her and as though there were only a moment before they caught up with her, she stretched out her hands.

'Wait for me … caress me … run your fingers over my bosom … here, here caress me … let me give myself, let me give back … cover me with your hands … your habit, I'll give it back … Mother … I'll give it back …'.

One of the pebbles rolled all the way down with her and splashed into the water below the road.

In the morning a road worker found her in a ditch beneath the cliff. He leaned back to see which rock she had fallen from and then gazed at the white thigh which, whole and unharmed, gleamed white and round in the dust. He looked around for something to cover her with and when he found nothing ran like a madman into the town.

And by then the sun had come up and high on the rock among the grey stones Miriam's red dress could be seen. The *mahala* was beginning to rouse itself from sleep. It stirred and opened itself up to be enchanted that day, like the day before, as though that were the last summer to have matured in that heat.

The apples glowed red, and if you bit into them, your mouth would fill with juice.

Translated by Celia Hawkesworth

Hanka

In spring the apple trees blossomed, turning pink. And the apples ripened all summer. A few were gnawed by worms, and their hearts were eaten away; those ones would fall of their own accord in the autumn – even when there was no wind …

… So I sat that autumn – and they were prolific – and it seemed that the very trunks were groaning under their weight. The grass was fragrant and I searched through it to see whether its seeds had ripened. Beside a dandelion an apple caught my eye. It had fallen on its red side and turned soft. I blew the ants off it and broke it in half with my fingers. Out of it, from its hollowed heart, stretched a fattened worm, with tiny wrinkles. It moved its lively body, and it looked like mother-of-pearl. Its head was hard and black, and it moved first to the right and then to the left. Then it straightened up and stopped as though watching me. I held the apple and looked at it. A little pearly, wrinkled worm.

This is her heart, Hanka's … a kind of joy whispered in me. And she appeared to me as I had first seen her. And I saw her smiling and happy.

She was lying in the garden behind the town hall. She was stretched out on boards, and people had crowded to the fence to look at her. Hanka's arm hung, yellow and cold. Green flies buzzed above her, glinting in the sun.

I don't know when the people were driven away, or when the thin, old Seida came up beside me.

'Don't let any of the men look at her, let me hold her while you open her, I beg you, good sir!'

'All right,' I said, and the dead gypsy girl smiled at me when I approached her. Her eyes were half open. They were black and still shining. But her cheeks were yellow, yellow, swarthy, with tiny dark moles scattered here and there. Her mouth was slightly open as well, and a smile was caught around it. Joyful, happy.

I went to the other side. From there I could see a red line of dried blood running down the left hand side of her chin on to her neck. From her mouth to her breast. Some of the cheap beads round her neck were bloody as well.

Seida removed her clothes.

'You see, sir, she's lovely, she's like a girl still. But she was married two or three years ago, or more, only she never bore a child. This would have been her first, poor creature. You'll see when you open her. She felt it quicken just now, after Ilen day. Ten days ago ...'

Seida threw a bit of her dress over her belly and breasts.

'So why did he stab her?'

'I don't know, sir, I don't know. They're rough types, both of them, both of them, sir. He stabbed her this morning right in the doorway ... She had started to run, and he followed her and caught up with her here and plunged his knife into her just by her left shoulder blade. He must have reached her heart, you'll see, good sir, you'll see ...'

I looked at her from the side where her smile could be seen. I looked at her and caught hold of the small nickel knife.

'But why is she smiling like this?' I wondered, and old Seida replied:

'She's not smiling, and how could she, snapped in two as young as this. How could she! True, she was defiant, hale, ruddy, and full of youth, and she was capricious, it's shameful to say it: she quarrelled with that man of hers and she refused to lie with him for a single night ever since he came back to her, the whole week. She would sit in the evening by Mushan's tent. He played his *shargiye* and she sang, and called: 'Hey, Seido, why don't you come too. See what a night it is! Let me sing to you as well.' And now this, by God's will, she's dead! Now we'll all be in trouble.'

She had relaxed, I saw, the old witch, so I said:

'Move away from her and don't cover her.'

I placed my hand on her belly and felt it.

'She's not pregnant. Why did you lie that she felt it quicken?'

'It's true, dear sir, it is, you'll see when you open her. Truly, she felt it, ten days ago.'

I turned and looked sternly at her.

'… It's true, she felt it, she felt it …' said Seida and, coming close to me, she whispered: 'She told me herself, she did. "I don't want any more to do with you! Go to that woman in Zvornik. She's thinner than me and older than me … they say she has a child of fifteen. You go to her, I don't want you. I don't, you understand, I don't want you!" That's what she told him, sir. And she told us too: "I want an older and uglier man. I want him to leave me, and I'll marry Mushan. No matter what!" We calmed her down: "Come, Hanka, don't be foolish, what do you want with Mushan when Seido's alive! Mushan's a real tramp, a tramp." – "So what" she shrieked at us, "so what, so am I and so are you …"'

The clerk arrived and with him the judge, who was interrogating the murderer in the prison house.

The post mortem began. Seida breathed heavily, rolled her eyes and tried to avoid meeting the judge's glance.

I took the heart out of a pool of clotted blood.

'See how much blood he spilt … he did reach her heart, her heart, didn't I say, sir, he reached her heart …'

I held her heart in my hand and felt the wound with my finger. I placed it on the board and examined it. The knife cut could be clearly seen, deep, right into the cavity. I washed it with icy water and felt sorry for Hanka. Poor creature! This morning this heart was alive, it was pulsating like a miracle, beating strongly and defiantly, beating and shaking these lovely breasts, and perhaps she had only yesterday turned to him, breathless and with glowing cheeks, her eyes shining, and said: 'Here, kill me, kill me, this heart is not yours but another's, mine and his … Here!' Perhaps it was she who had torn her dress and the undershirt on her breast, offering it to him. How her shining eyes must have shone then if they were as bright as this in death! But why was she smiling like this? Why had that smile remained on her lips, so happy? Why, Hanka, speak! Perhaps it is good to die passionately, to love the forbidden, but freely and openly and to offer one's breast to the knife: Here, hit me! Or perhaps it is all a lie. This one says she felt her womb stir, but there's no trace. Perhaps she fell on account of some trifle, because of some triviality. Gypsies … tramps …

'A good-looking gypsy,' I heard the judge Surak say to the clerk.
'And honest ... hard-working ...' he replied.

And I cut that heart, cut it, opened it, divided it, peered into all its corners, examined it, seeking and suddenly gave a start: what was I seeking? Nothing.

I put it down.

'Now you'll see, now, perhaps it's still alive ...' said Seida as I opened the corpse further, watching my hands.

'There's nothing, nothing,' I said, 'neither dead, nor alive, nothing ...'

'There is, there is, sir, there's Mushan's child, Mushan's ...' whispered Seida, shifting the intestines away from her lower belly.

'There's not. There, that's where it should be, but there's nothing,' I replied and looked at her.

Seida ran both her hands over the belly, then felt the little pear-shaped hard uterus, raised her head, looked at me and shouted as though in surprise: 'Are you going to open it?'

'Yes!' I said and cut it open. 'There, there's nothing!'

'She lied, she lied, the wretch!'

Seida hastened to rinse her hands in the water and, drying them on her clothes, she rushed out of the garden.

Gypsies immediately pressed up to the fence, shouting in their own language, talking and arguing.

Seida came back with a cigarette hanging from her lower lip.

'She told me herself, sir, she did, as God's my witness! Yes, gentle sir! She did, she told us and him ... she did, the bitch ... she lied ...'

* * *

And this is the truth about her, about Hanka.

The Mlava comes out at Klokote. Its water is clear, but bitter, and the pebbles on its shallow bottom in the upper reaches, before it has joined the Golden Stream, red as though rusted.

The Mlava gathers all the springs at Klokote including the ones where sick people bathe in the tepid water in summer time and that spring in which young girls wash their eyes, because they say that water gives their eyes a pearly gleam.

111

That was the kind of eyes Hanka had, and she had white teeth like all gypsies.

Towards the end of summer she went often to Klokote. She washed her eyes and came back barefoot, carrying her low shoes in her hand. She had gathered her baggy trousers in front, picked them up and tucked them into her waistband. She walked the way girls walk, upright, and her breasts swayed under her red cotton dress with its pattern of white circles. In her other hand she carried a flower or a little twig of something. She always went by a short cut, through the forest and she was always alone.

And when Seido returned from Zvornik, she did not let a single day go by without going to Klokote. But less than a week passed.

When he came, and he came suddenly, she stopped in front of him and looked at him for a long time. Then she moved away, looked him up and down, shook herself, straightened up, threw back her shoulders, glanced at him disdainfully and turned away.

'Why have you come? ... What do you want? ... Why didn't you stay on the Drina ... Yes, yes, on the Drina ... We've heard ... we've heard everything, Seido, we know about old Aikuna as well ... And you'll hear about me ... you will, Seido ...'

He had brought her a ring and a string of cheap pearls. He had brought some little shoes and a scarf with spangled tassles. Hanka could hardly bring herself to sit beside him and accept the gifts. She calmed down a little and listened to the rest of what he had to say, and, as though forgetting herself, she gazed for a long time into his eyes. She gazed and grew. But when Seido touched her with his hand she started and frowned:

'Keep your hands to yourself!'

Eventually, Seido grew angry. He grabbed her hand and held it tight.

'Break it, Hanka won't murmur!'

At noon she disappeared. (She went that day as well to Klokote and bathed her eyes for twice as long.)

Towards evening on his way back from town Seido found her beside Muikich's tent. She had put on the scarf and shoes, hung the necklace round her neck and wore her belt low on her hips. She was playing with the ring on her finger. She sat down beside the fire. The flame flickered in her eyes. Mushan had lain down beside her, playing his *shargiye*. The cherry wood clattered and the taut strings twanged feebly.

'Hanka!' shouted Seido.

'Here I am!' she replied as though surprised and stood up.

'Why are you wearing your belt like that?'

'I felt like it!'

They quarrelled the whole night.

He called her, pleaded with her, gave her a bag of coins, untied a ducat from his belt and offered it to her.

Haska, an older gypsy woman, a widow, and her two sons twisted and turned in their tent. Hearing the clinking of coins in his sleep several times, the eight-year-old Ramo got up and dazed with sleep, rubbing his eyes in the darkness with his left hand, stretched out his right hand towards the open side of the tent and mumbled: 'Give me some … give me …'

Each time, Hanka laughed out loud:

'It's like Aikuna's child from the Drina near Zvornik calling! Give him something, for God' sake, Seido, let him get the feel of it too, give him some!'

'I'll kill you with my bare hands if you mention Zvornik once more!'

'I'm not afraid of your hands, I'm not!'

Skilfully, as though she had anticipated his attack, Hanka jumped aside and while Seido stood up in surprise (he had intended only to grasp her hand, not to hit her), Hanka vanished into the darkness.

* * *

On Friday they were both in town. Hanka had blackened her eyebrows and coloured her cheeks. In a thin shirt, open at her throat, her waistcoat undone, she was sitting in front of the inn, watching the people passing along the street. She was waiting for Seido to see her like this, and call her to have coffee or a beer together.

'He'll pay for that old bitch, he'll pay,' she said to herself, scanning the street in the hope of seeing him at the crossroads. 'He'll die of longing to place his hand in my bosom … I've opened my shirt to show that my breasts have not started sagging, they're still like a girl's … He'll die …'

113

She fingered the string of pearls and tapped her foot on the ground. She ordered a beer, but when Mushan came up to take a swig from the bottle she drove him away with a look.

'Vile creature' she said to herself, as though in disgust. She drank up quickly and poured away what was left at the bottom. She thought she had caught sight among the crowd of Seido's freshly blocked fez. She stood up and raised herself on to her toes. She caught sight of Seido going into the silversmith's.

He's going to buy me earrings! flashed through her mind. She straightened the spangled scarf. She buttoned her waistcoat, because her heart was beating wildly, and, as she recalled their caresses of long ago, a warm glow ran through her. In a flash she remembered the time when he had roused her passion by the way he looked at her and the way he touched her. She remembered those evenings on the Mlava, when she had sat on the flattened grass in the field, singing songs of passion which she had invented right into his ear and she gave herself to him, panting, longing only to melt away in his arms. That whole summer she had waited for him thinking of their first nights of love. She walked by herself beside the Mlava, eating stolen pears from the folds of her clothes, one after the other, and imagining wiping each of them with her hand and offering it to him to take the first bite.

Excited and flushed, when she fell late in the evening into the tent, she would wake the whole of Zovik with her songs and laughter. The sleepy children would get up and start shouting wildly, whistling, roaming round the fire and the sooty tents, beating and throwing things at their little dogs released from their ropes. And late in the night, worn out with a secret tension, with longing and madness, she would lie down by the banked fire, stretch out on her back and gaze for a long time at the sky and the stars, making spells with words and gestures whenever a star could be seen falling across the dark sky into infinity.

Afterwards she seemed to grow ill. The life in her went numb, her cheeks darkened and her step began to flag. People whispered to her that Seido was in Zvornik, that he was lighting logs there, that he was earning money with charcoal and that he spent every single evening with some Aikuna, who had never married, but had given birth twice and one of her children was alive (he was fifteen), that he lived, drank, ate and slept with this Aikuna, a thin hag. He drank beer and brandy, and ate nothing but white meat and roasted goat. And people whispered maliciously that each evening Aikuna gave him a snack of thick dried meat 'from an uncastrated billy'.

This was hardest for Hanka to bear. Suffering in the tent, beside her cousins, the image of the bank of the Drina with tents came into her mind, and Hanka seemed to see with her own eyes Aikuna's dark face, full of wrinkles, brown and streaked with furrows and lines and in them two greedy black eyes. She saw her thin hand, full of rings and bracelets, cutting small, greasy pieces and giving them to Seido, who was draining brandy from a thick beer glass.

Hanka spent two weeks like this, and then she began to brighten: 'He'll come back ... he'll come back ...' she consoled herself, 'and he'll see what that Aikuna has done to him with her goat's meat, he'll see ...'

She was no longer mad, but cheerful and talkative. She went every day to work. She worked for a daily wage as a reaper, she weeded at the forestry supervisor's house, picked beans and paprika at the Bulgarian's, and when she returned towards evening from Klokote, she would sit for a while by Muikich's tent and listen to Mushan playing his *shargiye*.

'There'll be trouble, Mushan, when Seido appears and finds you with Hanka,' people told Mushan.

'Why, I'd like to know?' responded Mushan.

And, as though a fire was flaring in her, Hanka brightened and trembled with joy when she heard people talking to Mushan in this way. 'There will, there will! There'll be trouble, oh yes!' sang her whole inner being, her soul, her heart, her pulse ... And she bathed her eyes in the spring at Klokote, saved money for satin breeches and touched herself to make sure she had not grown thin.

And, now, Seido had returned, he had come and now he had to see just who Hanka was, lose his mind, bend double with pain and reach out his whole body for her caresses and expire, pant like a chained dog at the sight of food, but not touch it, expire ...

That was how Hanka waited for him, and now he had come.

When he came out of the silversmith's, he set off straight through the town. He was surprised when he saw her. He came up to her, threw down on to the table something wrapped in a rag and sat down.

'Would you like coffee or beer? But then you've probably had

115

your fill by the Drina. You were there the whole winter and then the whole summer. Did you intend this for me or someone else?' asked Hanka, pouring him a beer and unwrapping the little packet.

'A bracelet!' she exclaimed, 'real silver!' and she wanted to stroke his hand. She was barely able to drive the tears from her eyes by fluttering her lids. But at the same moment she wondered whether he had perhaps given Aikuna gifts as well, brought her brooches and earrings, and her throat contracted. She quickly shook her head and collected herself. She took the bracelet, opened it, put it on her arm and pushed it up to the top. She turned back the wide sleeve to her shoulder, and stretching out her arm until the downy hair could be seen right in front of his eyes, she leaned towards him:

'Do it up, do it up tight, I want it to bind my arm tightly,' Hanka spoke into his face, 'but don't pinch me!' she whispered, covering her armpit with her other hand. 'Don't look down my sleeve to my bosom, God damn your eyes!' ... she laughed, looking at him with shining eyes.

'If you only knew how I dreamed of you last night. You know where I was sleeping? In that field. Where you once looked for the mole under my breast in the moonlight.'

Hanka took the glass from in front of him and drained it.

'Come!' she stood up, 'I'll tell you on the way.'

They set off. Hanka held him by one finger and talked.

'If you only knew how fragrant the grass is! Now camomile, mint, sage and lovage are in bloom and when the valley is hushed in the evening, the water down below in the Mlava and the grass glow softly. The shallow Mlava rolls over the pebbles, and a whisper rises from it into the darkness, and the crickets hurry there with their singing, and everything merges in the scent of the ripe grass, the cut meadows and yellow apples. And everything trembles in the middle of the night as though it had descended from the sky. A bat flies over my head and I give a start, and I feel sorry that I did not catch sight of someone dear to me through its wing ... And I dreamed of you, I did, I swear by my child, I dreamed of you ...'

'What child?' said Seido abruptly and stopped.

'I'm just saying, when I have one, and I shall one day, one way or the other, I shall. Don't you believe me?' asked Hanka, gazing straight into his eyes. 'I shall, Seido, of course I shall ... but listen!

116

I dreamed of you … I dreamed: I was lying in the field, and in the morning I woke up. At the same moment the day broke. My cheeks were wet with dew. I stretched. I reached out my hand to touch yours, but you were still sleeping. That's good, you sleep on, I said, and jumped up to collect twigs, to make a fire. I ran to the tent, threw a handful of sugar into my shirt, picked up cups and a pan and the coffee grinder, and flew, flew to greet you with a cigarette when you woke up, to take a lock of my hair, and to burn it above you so that no other could enchant you.

I was out of breath with running, and I knew when I finished everything, and you woke up, you would kiss me on my ear, on my neck, in my bosom, under my breast, and you would light your cigarette from my brand on which I would spit three times, so that it would enter my soul and I would die for joy because I was yours. – That's what I dreamed. I ran, the cubes of sugar bounced in my blouse, knocked against my breasts and I was just going to climb over the fence when my breeches caught. I turned round, and there was Mushan, who had reached me and was holding me. Let go, I said, and I was afraid you would wake and see us. Let go, I struggled as I stood on the fence, and he reached for my waistband, rolling both my top and under-breeches up over my knees. You know I always wear a short undershirt, above my knees, and I cried out with shame, bathed in sweat … Then I woke up. I could see, I was lying in the field, I came to myself, I remembered that you had come from Zvornik … I rubbed my eyes. The day was just breaking.'

'Quiet, Hanka, it's all lies, you bitch! You're lying. I know where you slept. I know. You weren't with Mushan, you weren't!'

'No, I wasn't. I'm not saying that. But I wasn't with you either, I wasn't and I won't be!'

'Hush!' responded Seido, hitting her in the side with his elbow.

They reached the tent. Hanka settled herself, crushed some dry leaves in her hand and threw them on to the fire. She took some cigarettes from her shirt and began to smoke. Old Haska was preparing supper.

'Your eyes are still beautiful, Seido! And your moustache is fine. But what's made them so greasy? Hahaha! It's the dried goat's meat, hahaha!' giggled Hanka, clutching her sides. And suddenly she got up, shook herself all over as though disgusted at something and ran out.

'You'll come, my little chick, Ah-hah! You'll come this very evening, to gasp and writhe!' Seido watched her go and stretched out his legs.

* * *

Night had fallen. Dogs barked once or twice and fell silent. Seido was lying outside the tent, he had covered himself with a light blanket and waited. Hanka had not come, and nor was Mushan in Zovik. They said he had gone to Brestovsko. He was going to sell tomatoes at Enez-Effendi Muftich's the next day. He was going to spend the night at Klokote, so as to get to work while it was still cool.

Seido was thoughtful, and a thin blade of jealousy tore at his heart:

'And how do you know what might have been! She talks as though she were playing, and perhaps she wants you not to believe what you hear people muttering about her. The slut ...'

He wanted to think that she certainly had not lived with him, with Mushan, because Mushan was older and ugly, and he thought of his Aikuna, bony and thin, with her broad hips.

He stood up, poked the fire, looked around, listened and, when nothing was heard except snoring from the tents, he took a knife out of his clothes, picked up his bag of tools, removed his file and began sharpening his knife. As he sharpened it, he kept feeling the blade and the point. Then he rubbed it with earth, wiped it on a stone and held it towards the fire. The blade gleamed as though made of silver. Seido put the knife back in its sheath and lay down. Each time the dogs barked, he woke up, listened, raised his head and stared into the darkness. And each time he thought: here she comes! But Hanka did not come. He slept badly that night.

Two more strange and incomprehensible days went by. She provoked him by lying in front of Muikich's tent on both evenings.

'Seido, come here, see how nice it is here. If there were only meat and brandy, you could get drunk, and I could get married tonight.'

She sang:

'...

Does he burn in fire, or by plague expire ...'

118

'Hey, Seido, my dear,' called Hanka, while Mushan beat furiously on his *shargiye*, swaying in rapture. Seido sat carving a wooden handle without raising his head.

The fifth day after his arrival, after she had not let him touch her once (and she shook him away and ran off a different way each time), he met her in the wood, exhausted and low-spirited. He hid behind an oak tree, waiting for her to come back, because he had been told that she had been seen at Klokote bathing her eyes in the Little Spring.

And Hanka appeared, carrying her shoes in one hand, and in the other a little branch with two green acorns on it. She was singing in a high thin voice. When she came out into the open, the leaves rustled behind her, and before she could turn round, Hanka heard a voice:

'Stop!'

Hanka immediately recognised his voice and stopped, half turned and tossed back her head.

'I've stopped. What do you want?' she replied defiantly staring at the sky, but alert and watchful to notice the slightest thing happening around her.

'Where have you been?'

'Never you mind!'

Seido came up to her and stood in front of her.

'Tell me, or I'll kill you.'

'Kill me, if you dare, kill me, if you dare and if you have a reason!'

'I'll kill you!' shrieked Seido ...' I'll kill you!' and he pulled the knife from his belt. 'Look, I've sharpened it for you, I've prepared it for you!'

The blade flashed before Hanka's eyes and she moved closer to him:

'You'd be sorry, Seido, my dear! Really sorry!' she said, looking into his eyes. 'You should kiss me first, then kill me. Kiss first, and then ...'

'Where have you been, tell me!'

'I won't, I won't tell you. Why don't you tell me where you've been, ah, why don't you say? You tell me where you were all winter and now all summer too. In Zvornik, in Zvornik, cooling your feet in the Drina, while Aikuna stirred sherbet and rolled cigarettes for you. Why didn't you bring her and her child here. Perhaps it's yours, from before. I would have laid out young hay for you, made sure the children did not disturb you, and in the morning I would have served you coffee. I would, Seido, you and the grey-haired Aikuna, I would. Why not? Pshh! ...' Hanka thrust out her chest to show how young she was and set off. She turned so fast that her plaits, decorated with little speckled shells, rattled on her back.

Seido put the knife in its sheath and followed her.

They reached the log over the Mlava and Hanka went down to the water. She picked up her breeches above her knees and stepped into the water. In the middle of the river she stopped, scooped up water in her hand and drank.

'Do you want some too, to see how it puckers your mouth!. I'll wash my face with it, so that my face gets wrinkled like grey-haired Aikuna's, and then I'll come to you, so that you think I'm Aikuna ... Hahaha!'

Hanka shook with laughter, gaily, capriciously.

Seido began to curse her:

'You bitch!'

'What if I am!' Hanka shrugged her shoulders. 'You've got another, I'll find someone too if I haven't already.'

* * *

There was a crowd in Zovik. Shrieking, whistling, the sound of tambourines and *shargiyes*. The children from the town, women, men and police patrols, they were all mixed up with the gypsies here by the tents, and in the midst of the crowd stood a gypsy, with an old bear on a chain, while others led a cub round the empty space which the throng had closed off in front of them. The cub was sturdy, and it staggered as it walked clumsily after its master. It had a steel ring through its nose with a strong new chain attached.

They had come from Sarajevo, and were on their way to Travnik and were going to spend the night here.

Hanka immediately mixed with the crowd. She took a tambourine and began to beat it.

'You ought to come with us to Travnik, Hanka, we'll make some good money with these two. You should see how the little one dances. Come on, Salkan!'

And Salkan fixed a pole to the chain, stuck it into the ground and lifted up the cub which stood on its hind legs, and began to turn in circles, hardly touching the ground. Salkan hit it with a stick and sang sadly, drawling, in time to the music:

'Dani dani daaaan … Dani, dani daaaan …'

The cub twisted and turned and waved its front paws. The crowd watched, open-mouthed, the children laughed, pinched themselves, clapped their hands. Hanka beat the tambourine and carefully turned round because she could hear the old bear growling and snapping its jaws as it staggered this way and that.

'Let's go to Travnik, eh Seido, shall we?' Hanka goaded him.

As darkness fell the police told the crowd to disperse and Zovik emptied and calmed down. Hanka disappeared with the crowd. When everything had settled down for the night, Seido sneaked out and peered into all the tents, and when he reached Muikich's a darkness suddenly filled his head and his heart leaped. He took hold of his knife and wanted to shout, but he was afraid of being answered from inside the tent, there under the rags or behind the sack of unwashed wool, and that she would greet him with some ugly curse, so he only coughed. A little bare-headed gypsy child in a short shirt peered out of the tent:

'Come and see the bear cub sleeping in our house! See it snoring, come and see …'

Seido went back to old Rifa. He sat down by the fire and threw her a cigarette. Rifa first spat to one side and then took it.

'They've cast a spell on my Hanka,' said Seido angrily.

'No they haven't, my boy, they haven't. You're the one who was charmed when you were away, and Hanka's like any young woman. If she were a town girl, she'd be roaming the streets like a bitch, and no wonder, my dear! Blood is like strong drink, and when it throbs in your head, you lose your mind. And she kept herself for you, my dear, she did, right up to the moment they filled her head with Aikuna, so don't be surprised, really! You don't leave a woman. You see how you found Aikuna … And so it goes on, in a circle, until the knife hits home in the right place.'

'And so it will, just where it should! It will, Rifa, I'm telling you,' said Seido, clenching his teeth and imagining the way he would stab her right through the heart.

121

Rifa picked up her plaits, moved them from one side of her head to the other, knocking the large earrings hanging from her right ear, and dropped the plaits down her back.

'Let it be, my dear, you get up early and go away. It will be better for you and for her and for all of us.'

'Oh no, Seido won't leave her, oh no. I'll bend her another few times, and she'll dance round me like that bear cub just now. You'll see ...' Seido stood up.

'Don't do it, my child, don't!' Rifa blew out the last smoke, as the cigarette burned her fingers. 'You get up early, give her back her money and let her go to Mushan. She can't be yours, she can't.'

Seido walked as though beside himself and was startled when Hanka appeared out of his own tent. He knelt down and looked at her as though in disbelief.

'It's me, Seido. I've come, so do what you want with me. Kill me if you like.'

'Come out here,' shouted Seido, uncertain.

Hanka crawled out of the tent on all fours and slowly straightened up in front of him. He took a step backwards and stared at her.

Hanka turned into two black eyes, large and shining and she kept whispering:

'Seido ... Seido ... Seido ...'

He could see her white teeth as well.

Seido grasped her hand, and she threw herself round his neck and began to kiss his hair. He pushed her away.

'Stop! Wait!'

'Don't, Seido, let me, just tonight, at least just tonight. Let me ...' and she threw herself on his chest again, now as warm as though blood had just run through her.

Seido felt her warmth and her hot lips on his neck and he grabbed her with both arms and pressed her forcefully against his chest.

Then Hanka dragged him behind the tent and fell to the ground.

'You're drunk, Hanka, you're drunk ...'

'I'm not, see ...' and Hanka blew into his face. 'I'm not drunk, I just want you. I waited for you all summer. I wept. I rubbed my arms and legs under the covers, and thought of you. I want you, Seido, I want you, you've bitten my heart! Never mind, but I won't let you leave me any more, I won't!'

Hanka drew Seido's hands under her arms, and writhed, winding herself round him like a serpent. Seido's eyes clouded over, it seemed to him that they had filled with blood, the darkness was red all around him, and she was biting him, gnawing at his arms, pressing his face into her bosom, and then pulling away, straightening up on to her knees, shaking, brushing her wet hair away from her brow and tearing her shirt.

'Kiss me, Seido, kiss me ...'

Then she dragged him into the field, wild with passion. And Seido caressed her, touched her breasts, her hips, her shoulders, and she surrendered and resisted, teasing him. And bathed in sweat Seido reached for her and remembered how thin Aikuna had been, how he could feel all her ribs, while this one, Hanka, was round, firm, hot as though she had emerged from steaming water, and he drew her to him, pulled her shirt off her shoulder and said as though in a fever:

'How round you are ... how you have filled out, Hanka ...'

* * *

Towards dawn Seido grew tired, stretched out and fell asleep. Hanka settled herself beside him, crouched, did up her breeches, tied her shirt with a blade of long grass, buttoned her red dress and she felt cold.

Dawn came quickly. A bluish thin column of smoke rose above Zovik and the clink of buckets could be heard and an occasional shout. A white mist rolled down the Mlava, larks began to call, flying out of the stubble and singing. Voices called to one another.

Hanka looked at the large drops of shiny dew on the grass, the long thin threads of cobwebs waving in the air. Tiny droplets were glistening on them as well.

In the distance a gun fired. Hanka gave a start, caught sight of a young rabbit moving behind the fence and at the same time noticed that Seido was snoring deeply.

'Seido,' she called to wake him, 'Seido!'

Seido slept. His mouth was open and he was snoring.

'Seido,' Hanka shook him. 'Seido, in God's name, why are you snoring as though your throat was cut?'

Seido turned on to his other side. Hanka shouted sharply, offended:

'Seido, don't snore like that, you're not with Aikuna.'

Seido opened his eyes a little. Hanka made as though she was going to spit in his face.

'Phh, shame on you! Where's your strength, eh? Is that it? And have you seen what a woman is? Have you? A woman and young!'

Seido sat up.

'… Have you seen? you can't feel my ribs, no … everything is round, everything …' Hanka patted her hips and ran her hand over her belly. 'This is round too, round and full! Yes, it is, Seido, it's full. Have you seen what night is, what caresses are, well, have you? And what did you do? You wore yourself out, you wretch! You'll never come near me again, never. This, is for you to remember what you've lost! Do you hear? Now here's your knife.' Hanka bent down, moved a stone and threw him the knife. 'Have it back. I wanted to cut your throat, but why should I sully my hands? And you sharpened it for me, you brute! But if you stick it into me, wherever you hit will be soft. This is flesh, flesh, full, round and hot. Just don't stab me in the belly, there's a child in it, Mushan's, Mushan's!'

'Hush! …

'Yes, Mushan's …that's why it's so round, didn't you see …'

'Come and lie down here!'

'Ah-hah! Why should I? When you've no strength! What for? Never again! You'll never see me again, ever, and if I do come back, I'll bring you dry goat's meat to give you strength …goat's meat …'

'I'll kill you, Hanka!'

'You cur!'

Seido leapt to his feet, picked up the knife, but Hanka jumped over the fence and began to run, shouting for help.

She reached Zovik and turned round. Seido was not chasing her.

'Hanka, Hanka,' Rifa called her. 'Run away, my child, run away from here, I had a bad dream about you: I saw you climbing an apple tree to pick apples. You were young and not yet married. You climbed up to a thin branch. We were calling down below: "Hanka, come down, you'll fall!" We shouted, but not a sound from you! You hang out along a branch to take hold of an apple, a big, beautiful, red apple. "Come down!" I shout. "I'll just get this one, this one, see how beautiful it is, how red it is!" "It's worm-eaten" I shout. "No, it's not" you say and stretch your fingers, you break off leaves, you hang, and a snake appears among the leaves, stretches its head, hisses, thrusts out its thin, forked tongue, and in a moment wraps itself around your wrist and we see it slip into your bosom. You turn pale, scream and fall to the ground ... That's what I dreamed, Hanka. Run, my dear, this does not bode well!'

'I'll run, Rifa, I will, but let him give me back what he owes me first ...!' shouted Hanka.

A crowd of men, women and children had gathered, and those two gypsies with the bears.

'... And I'll tell you too, all of you!' said Hanka, turning on one foot and pointing all around, and then she went on in a quieter voice. 'Let me tell you that I gave myself to Mushan there in his tent twice, three times, fifteen times ... I did, I gave myself to him so that that dog should break, perish, that he gnawed Aikuna's bones and pinched her dried up, sagging breasts ... I gave myself to Mushan and, now I've felt him stir in my belly ... Mushan's child!'

'A cub, a little bear cub!' laughed a little gyspy.

'A child!' Hanka shouted haughtily and straightened herself. Rifa picked up a sweet.

'Take this and run!'

'Give me the whole box, give it to me, Rifa,' and Hanka swept down like an arrow and took the box from Rifa. She grabbed a handful and began to scatter sweets around.

'This is my wedding, my second wedding! Tonight I'll sleep with Mushan,' she said, feverishly, scattering the sweets. Then she threw down the box and began to run along the Mlava towards the town. The children shrieked as they picked up the sweets from the ground.

'Come with me, if you want to come to the wedding!'

Seido appeared, pale, with black rings under his eyes. Everyone looked at him, and he asked ill-temperedly:

'Why are you staring at me. I'm not a bear or one of the Ramich brothers who prance around, showing off like monkeys.'

'Ha-ha ... Ha-ha ... !' laughed both the Ramich brothers.

'You're worse than a bear. And your Hanka will bear you a monkey ... a monkey ... Seid-Bey, bright crown of the tramps!'

There was nearly a fight. Old Haska took Seido by the arm, led him to one side and began to whisper into his ear.

The gypsies went off to Busovaca with the bears, followed by the children and women, while Seido stood with the gypsy woman watching them. The younger Ramich, Salkan, turned and called:

'Hey! ... She'll bear you a monkey, and a child for Mushan ... hey, you tramp!'

* * *

Seido cut across the fields and fences towards Busovaca and fell into someone's courtyard. He felt his knife and thrust it still more deeply into his belt. He came out into the street.

He met Hanka immediately, and Hanka leapt to one side. The plump clerk Stanko passed by them carrying pieces of roast lamb.

Seido seized Hanka's arm, and she trembled.

'Let go of my arm!'

'Tell me!'

'Let go of my arm and I'll tell you everything.'

Seido released her, and she hurried on into the town, shaking all over.

'Tell me,' Seido stopped her. Hanka looked into his eyes and shuddered. Her eyes flashed, and a smile spread over her face.

'What should I tell you? I've told you everything, everything, I've nothing more to tell. Nothing. There, I loved you, I loved you, you saw that last night. That's how I loved you, that's how ...' Hanka took a step forward.

'Tell me!'

'Now I love another,' and she caught her heart, 'I love him more than I ever loved you, and I gave myself to him before as well ... and I am carrying his child ...'

'Are you really?'

'Yes, really.'

'Tell me the truth, don't lie!'

'I'm not lying, I'm not lying!'

'Aren't you? You slut!' Seido swore, reaching for his knife.

'Wait, wait,' shouted Hanka in alarm. She took hold of his shoulder, and looked into his eyes. A smile appeared on her face, light and happy. She pushed him away, and jumped aside, and as though playing, she called softly, cajoling: 'I'm not lying, I'm not lying, my great tramp, I'm not!' and began to run through the town.

She ran, breathless, feeling behind her those two eyes, furious and bloodshot and reflected in them the blade of the well-made knife.

126

She ran, panting, and waiting for the point to plunge into her back. He was close. She would have liked to turn, to stop, and say: 'Hit me, hit me in the heart!' but she did not believe there would be enough time. She ran still faster. An unknown passion overcame her and she felt as though she were flying, not touching the ground.

She turned into Chanchar's inn and there in the open doorway she felt a blow and brief pain. Something warm spilled in her. It seemed that something living was sliding down her back, she straightened up, breathed deeply, collected herself to say something, but her body slumped forwards. She fell slowly, her eyes half-open as though she was falling into a deep, long awaited sleep.

Translated by Celia Hawkesworth

Samuel, the Porter

No one, not her father, nor her stepmother nor her brother Jacob had ever given a thought to Sarucha's marriage, while Sarucha's girl-friends all had two, even three, children by now.

Sarucha would often let out a deep sigh which rose unbidden from the depths of her being. At times she felt as though everyone had forgotten her, as though no one in the entire world was concerned about her. It was hard, but despite everything, secretly, in a corner of Sarucha's heart there still lived a little shred of hope and the girl rejoiced at the thought that one day after all her father would suddenly come home and he would call, festively and cheerfully, from the courtyard gate: 'Where are you, Sarucha, where are you, my girl? Come and kiss my hand! I have betrothed you, my good Sarucha, you are betrothed!'

For years she waited to hear this news, to hear her father's call. Each afternoon she listened tensely and it did not matter that she had already been disappointed a hundred times, her heart would always flutter with joy whenever she heard her father's footsteps in the yard at an unexpected hour. Here he is – she would tremble all over – here he is, and in a moment he will call: 'Sarucha, where are you? Where are you, my girl?'

These barren thrills had rent her inner being. She struggled not to give into despair. Finally she weakened (she had entered her twenty-fourth year by then), but only for a while. A strange faith was suddenly born in her. She did not herself know how or why it

128

had come, but she had the feeling that this summer she would definitely be betrothed and, indeed, married. In a trice the dark shadows vanished from her face. Her eyes brightened. She moved about the house smiling. Sometimes she even sang.

It was at that time, when Sarucha's heart was full of that joyful expectation, it was just then that her stepmother, always in perfect health, suddenly took to her bed.

'It's nothing, she has simply caught a slight chill,' said the women. And truly, all the signs were that it really was nothing. But then, some days later, her stepmother began to rave in high fever. They summoned Tia Hanucha. The old woman left the room, shaking her head. Sarucha stared at her. Surely she could not be going to die? The thought froze Sarucha's heart.

Four days after Tia Hanucha's first visit, the patient breathed her last.

Her stepmother's death struck Sarucha like a thunderbolt. It took her a considerable time to recover. When she had begun to be herself again, her gaze fell upon the poor children. They were barefoot, their hair unbrushed, in tears and hungry. And the whole house appeared to her like the aftermath of a fire. She sighed deeply, bowed her head and set to work.

Sarucha had worked like a slave even before this. Now the whole burden of the household fell on her shoulders. She had to take care of everyone in the house. Some of her half-sisters were still quite small. While some had passed the age of ten and ran around the house and down the lane, others still crawled through the house and courtyard. She had to take care that some did not slip off the fence and others did not fall into the well. In the morning she had to wash them all, brush their hair, prepare their food, and feed the ones who could not feed themselves. They had so few clothes that she had to patch them every day in a dozen places, and at least run them through water once a week.

From morning to night Sarucha flew through the house and courtyard. She did not know what to do first: make the bread, clean the house, prepare the midday meal. In the middle of her work, shrieks and wails from the yard would jolt her from her task. 'Oh dear!' she would cry, rushing out to see what was the matter, her hands covered in dough.

Everyone else was asleep by the time she retired. But often she had no peace even then. Red-haired Jacob, her brother, would sometimes come home at midnight, or even later. She would have to open the door for him, make coffee and keep him quiet so as not to alarm the children.

At first Papucho, her father, praised the Lord that Sarucha was still at home, but when his first grief passed, he began to wonder what would become of his daughter if things continued in this fashion for several more years. She would never marry. That thought was terrible. He decided to find himself a third wife. He sought, enquired, proposed, but no one wished to give him either a child-less widow or a spinster. He was offered two or three widows with children. He very much liked the look of one of these women. But how could he take her into his house when she would have brought another whole heap of children with her. He already had too much of that bounty. He had two, Jacob and Sarucha from his first marriage. Mind you, these two had long since grown to marriage-able age, but the other six, all daughters that he had had with his second wife, were a problem because there were so many of them, and they were so young. Life was hard in any case and they slept on top of each other in the little room and still smaller kitchen. But the main thing was: what would Jacob say! It was Jacob who ran the butcher's shop, bought cattle, earned money to feed his sister, his half-sisters and Papucho himself. That was why he could not marry. How could he, who hardly earned anything any more, bring three or four more of God's creatures into this misery? Jacob, who was hasty and prone to anger, would certainly have flown into a passion, stormed out of the house and left him to starve with the widow's children and his own. In the end he shrugged his shoulders. What could he do! Life was not a wedding. She would marry when she was destined to. For now she would have to suffer, she, himself, and all of them.

He comforted Sarucha as best he could. He promised that she would be betrothed as soon as the twins Bea and Lea were grown.

'Be patient, my girl!' said Papucho, 'Why, look at Jacob! He can't so much as think of marriage either, and he's older than you. And he works so hard, dragging himself round the villages, sleeping in inns, getting into bad company, and all because of us. What can you do! It's all hard, but life must go on.'

Sarucha was reasonable. From the moment she harnessed herself to her work the thought of marriage did not cross her mind. She had forgotten herself. She ran around the house, being mother, housewife, maid and washerwoman.

The neighbours praised her.

Four years passed in this way.

The twins had grown. Sarucha sighed with relief. She began again, little by little, to think of herself. She bought scented soap and a small, round mirror.

Concealing these little things in her bodice, Sarucha remembered those distant days, when she used to arrange the fringe on her forehead and when her heart beat harder and fluttered at the merest hint of a joy just glimpsed. She hoped that something of those past days would return.

As soon as she was alone in the room, she glanced, shyly and secretly, as so many years before, at the little shiny piece of glass.

Her heart froze. She saw that her face had withered, her teeth blackened and a kind of rust begun to gnaw at them. Some of them were already quite decayed.

'Who'll take me like this!' a soundless, mournful cry broke from her. Tears came to her eyes. Sorrow filled her entire soul.

Often she would make her way to secluded corners of the house, and sit, her head in her hands, weeping.

She was increasingly quiet and thoughtful. At times Papucho grew angry with her, reproaching her.

'For goodness sake, don't look so sorrowful. If squint-eyed Luna can get married, then so shall you.'

II

Just then a chance for Sarucha to marry presented itself in the person of Samuel the porter.

Two years earlier the man had lost two children and the previous summer he had become a widower.

Papucho began at once to consider him.

'If he doesn't take her, I don't know who will!' he said to himself and began to be anxious that someone else might snap up Samuel the porter, who was the only hope for his daughter to marry. He pondered at length how to initiate a conversation on the subject with the herbalist Shimon, who was Samuel's uncle. He had to ensure that Shimon did not notice the almost desperate way he was offering his Sarucha. He would ask too large a dowry if he did. And where could he find a dowry? And who knows what Jacob would say if just a few ducats seemed a lot to him?

At last the old man decided to initiate the conversation in a roundabout way.

'Well then, Señor Shimon, is your Samuel thinking of marrying?' he asked Samuel's uncle Shimon one morning. Papucho was aware that even this question was dangerous, but he had already calculated how to brush it aside.

'He certainly is!' replied Shimon at once as though he had been expecting the question for at least two months. 'He is indeed, and soon, very soon at that!' he emphasised, coughing a little, then adding: 'but why do you ask, Señor Papucho?'

'Hm! … You want to know why I ask. Well, to be honest, I don't really know. I often see Samuel around the town … He looks neglected. His clothes are quite torn, and I feel sorry for him. The man needs a wife to take care of him and make sure his clothes are mended.'

'You are mistaken, Señor Papucho! It would be senseless for a man to heave sacks of flour on his back in his Sabbath clothes. Not sacks of flour nor baskets of plums. But leave his clothes, let us talk a little more sensibly. Which girl is it you're offering me? Let's hear you, Señor Papucho!'

'I'm offering no one, my dear Shimon! No one! I was just asking. Good day to you!'

Papucho went into the butcher's shop.

Three days later Shimon met Papucho.

'Come on now, Señor Papucho, what's the matter with you. Are you thinking of marrying your daughter Sarucha? Yes or no?'

Shimon looked Papucho straight in the eye.

'Why I am! Of course I am!' replied Papucho, good-humouredly. 'If you have anyone in mind, say a merchant or a craftsman, believe me I won't regret giving a good dowry. I mean a good one. If you like, we can go to Chucha's for coffee and talk about it.'

'I'm hurrying to the shop. It's a trading day,' Shimon answered slyly.

'Never mind. We can exchange a word or two along the way. Who would you be recommending?'

'I? Believe me, Señor Papucho, I never thought about it. I'm not in the habit of concerning myself with other folk's affairs. It's just that I met your Sarucha yesterday and saw that she had broken another tooth. It seems to me that it would be time to foist off her on someone. She has faded and aged a lot.'

'And it seems to me, Señor Shimon, that your eyesight is not good. My Sarucha has not faded or aged. And even if she had! Even if all her teeth were broken, even then I'd find a good craftsman for her. Or perhaps a merchant. Don't forget that she's a real housewife, Señor Shimon! A housewife such as can't be found for miles around. Why for heaven's sake, you know yourself that she's been running my whole household for the last ten years. You'll see what kind of an offer I'll find for her. Just be patient. Good day to you!'

'All the best to you!' and Shimon turned into his own street.

A few days later Shimon and Papucho began to talk openly and at once found themselves at loggerheads over the dowry.

Shimon was asking twenty ducats. And he would not yield.

'Twenty ducats is a great deal, a very great deal!' Papucho tried to convince him anxiously, swallowing bitter spittle.

'By no means,' Shimon insisted.

'But, please, how can you say it's not? Ducats are not that easy to come by, Señor Shimon. Just calculate how many groschen there are in twenty ducats. It's a great deal, a very great deal! Think about it!'

'You think about it. Samuel can wait. It's just a year since Rifkulina's death. He's in no hurry.'

Papucho and Shimon bargained every day. The negotiations were making slow progress, but Shimon was satisfied. He called Samuel the porter.

'Listen, Samuel!' began his uncle Shimon, rubbing his hands and blinking his small eyes. 'I have not wished to say anything until today. And I have nothing to say today either. But in five or six days time I hope that I shall. He-he!' Shimon gave a little laugh, twisting his beard in his fingers. 'Did you know that I've been talking to Papucho about you? About you and his Sarucha. And believe me, Samuel, Sarucha is a very good chance for you. She's a

133

commendable housewife. Isn't that so? And she's just the right age for you. You don't need a young wife. Isn't that so? And finally, she's a maid. And she's not ugly either. And nor are you, of course! Isn't that right, Samuel? I say, let them give you twenty ducats and you may calmly kiss Papucho's hand. Am I not right?'

'Twenty ducats?' said Samuel in surprise.

'Twenty! What do you imagine! And you'll get that, you'll get it I tell you. But say nothing to anyone. Pretend you know nothing. Until I've finished negotiating with Papucho and Jacob, you're to stay as silent as the leeches in this glass dish.'

Twenty ducats! This really shook Samuel. He thought all day and night about what he would buy with that money. As he went down to the town centre each day, Samuel the porter would pass by Sado's grocer's shop. One day he remembered that, two years previously, Sado had opened his shop with a dowry of ten ducats. Now the shelves were full of goods.

And he and Papucho's Sarucha would have twenty ducats! How would it be if they were to open a shop with that money? The idea was not far away. In a trice it flashed through his mind. Flashed through and then returned. Finally it did not leave him. To buy goods with that money, open a shop, become a grocer and no longer struggle as a porter, that really would be something!

Samuel's heart leaped.

He went more and more frequently to his uncle to ask how matters were proceeding.

Shimon replied calmly:

'Patience, Samuel, patience! Everything will be all right!'

The following week it seemed to Samuel the porter that the negotiations were taking too long. He was anxious. His uncle was asking too much, and ten ducats would be enough for him to open a shop.

'How would it be if you asked no more than ten ducats, uncle?' suggested Samuel the porter one evening.

'Not to ask more than ten ducats? What do you mean?'

'Just that, uncle.'

'Are you crazy?' Shimon frowned and went on angrily piling drugs and dried herbs into a mortar and grinding them with a pestle.

'I don't need that much money!'

'You don't need that much money! Oh, my dear boy, Salamon

Salom needs it, and he has thousands already, and you don't need it. Have you taken leave of your senses? Eh?'

'Ten ducats would be enough for me. Just ten!' Samuel insisted.

'Be off with you!' Shimon drove him out of his shop. 'I know how much you need. Don't you tell me. If you were fifteen-years-old, you'd talk more sense.'

III

That autumn, it was 1874, the porters had abundant work. There had been a very heavy crop of fruit. Every day the peasants brought hundreds of baskets of plums to the Sarajevo market place. The price was very low and people bought plums to make jam as though they were being given away. From morning to night the porters would load up the baskets and carry them up to Bjelave. At that time the children were all milling about. They went to meet the porters right down as far as Banjski Hill, waiting for them with whoops and cries, scuttling round them, accompanying them, running into courtyards and shouting at the tops of their voices to tell the housewives the plums were coming.

The porters came in, perspiring and weary. They put the baskets down on the cobbles, emptied the plums into the troughs set out for them and hurried back to the market for more.

The porter Samuel Machoro was then a man of some 35 years of age. He had quite heavy bones, but he was thin, pale and a little asthmatic. As he made his way up Banjski Hill, he became short of breath and fractious. Everything bothered him. The whole way he cursed the slope, swearing at the holes in the road and the stones he stumbled on.

He put down his baskets by the White Fountain, took off his sweaty fez, bent his tousled head and splashed water over his unshaven face. He undid his shirt and wiped the sweat from under his arms with a handkerchief. Then he sat down to rest.

Sitting there in the shade of the high cemetery wall, Samuel the porter despaired that his uncle refused to listen to him. 'Eh, my Samuel,' said Samuel the porter to himself, 'if your uncle had listened to you, the discussions would have been over long ago ... And now you would be able to say: that's it, good people, Samuel the porter will no longer make his way, bent double, up Banjski Hill. This is the last basket he'll be carrying. Let Muro the porter exert himself! He's healthy and strong as an ox, and he can do it, but Samuel cannot and will not and he no longer needs to. That's right, he no longer needs to! Sarucha will bring ten ducats with her and with the money he'll open a grocer's shop. A grocer's shop, my good people! No less!'

Samuel let out a deep sigh. Then he stood up, went over to the baskets, put his arms through the ropes of the harness, stood up and, carrying his fez in his hand, with a wet handkerchief on his head, he continued on his way to Bjelave, muttering: 'there, that's what I'd be able to say, had he only listened to me. But he knows best! Ten is not enough for him and in the end he won't have even ten. He'll have nothing. Nothing!'

He reached Bjelave with his mouth open, panting. On the way he scolded the children who scampered around him, shrieking in their excitement, and drove them away.

Towards evening he paid a visit to his uncle's shop. When his uncle signalled that there was no news yet, he frowned, threw the rope from one shoulder to the other and left.

'There'll never be any progress. That's not how you negotiate, my dear uncle! You should ask for ten, ask for ten, not twenty!' he muttered.

As he made his way through the residential quarter, his anger turned to sadness. At that time of day the lanes rang with joy. The air was full of singing. Wild cries echoed on all sides. It seemed that the earth was flowing with milk and honey and happiness and contentment were everywhere.

People were making jam in their courtyards.

A crowd of women and girls would sit all afternoon by the troughs full of plums, taking out the stones, cleaning the cauldrons, stoking up the fires, and now, as evening fell, the fires were already blazing joyfully, the thick jam was bubbling, and little red drops kept splashing out of it.

At one end of the courtyard, the men sat drinking brandy, nibbling snacks; at the other the women squatted in lively conversation. The girls stirred the hot red mass, fuelled the fire, sang, laughed. The children chased each other round the cauldron, shrieking. One minute they would hide behind their mothers' and aunts' wide skirts, the next they would fly out like mad things. They would not settle anywhere. One minute they would go up to the cauldron, take spoonfuls of the still uncooked jam, and lick it, burning their tongues, the next they would go out into the lane only to come back waving their empty spoons and shouting at the top of their voices.

In many courtyards pipes, harmonicas and other instruments could be heard. Here and there a 'maestro' would turn shish-kebab over a grill, while the children baked cobs of corn.

High over the courtyards rang a song:

> *Yo pasi por la tu guerta,*
> *Tu estavas en la puerta..*
> *Te saludi, te fiutes,*
> *Esto no me se aresenta.**

The sky was full of stars. The moon appeared over the Yellow Fortress, and a living joy ran through the night, causing it to tremble.

Samuel the porter made his way sadly home, and lay down at once on his bed.

Papucho and Shimon seemed to be enjoying their haggling. They were drawing it out, patiently, following some special plan. Each of them was giving way, but slowly and cautiously. Over the last two months Shimon had come down to fifteen ducats, while Papucho had raised his offer from five to eight.

In vain did Samuel the porter plead ever more frequently for his uncle to give in. Shimon stubbornly refused:

'Leave it to me, please, I know how to bargain.'

Then the butcher Jacob, Papucho's son, joined in:

'What? Sixteen? I'm not giving eight! That's too much! I'm not giving anything!' shouted the red-headed Jacob at his father Papucho. He was red and green in the face like an unripe tomato. 'What do you see in him? What? He's a widower, his nose is crooked. Is he a craftsman? A shoemaker? A tailor? A merchant? No, he's nothing. A porter! And broken-winded as a gypsy's horse. He can barely earn enough to feed himself. And you know that in our house Sarucha has been used to having everything, if nothing else then

---

* I passed by your garden,/There you stood by the gate./I greeted you, you ran away./Now see my sorry state.

meat for the midday and evening meal! I'm not giving her to him, even if he'd take her without a stitch to her name, let alone with sixteen ducats as well! You can forget it!'

'Listen, Jacob,' Papucho tried to soothe his son. 'Sit down and calm yourself. Yes, you're right, Samuel's nose is as crooked as though he always wiped it in one direction with his sleeve. It's true! But you tell me, is Sarucha's nose any prettier? Well, Jacob? And what about her teeth, eh? Aren't her two front teeth broken? And aren't her others as black as though she spent the whole day chewing nothing but tar, and not fat mutton, as white as snow? And let me tell you something else: she's twenty-nine years old, my boy! Other girls marry at eighteen. When I married your mother, she was not even seventeen. And something else. Look at Sarucha when you go home today. Her eyes look as though she were grieving for the dead or as though she were about to jump into a well. Do you want us to wait until all her teeth have all decayed, until she's as grey as I am? What will the poor thing do then? Be sensible!'

'I'll not give her to that man!' answered Jacob. 'I'll not and that's the end of it!'

Papucho went to Shimon to complain. He told him everything that Jacob had said.

'There, now you know it all. And believe me, it's not my fault, Shimon! What can I do? He's the one with the money, he's the one who earns. I tell you: woe betide the father who is reduced to being fed by his son. I would not wish that on my worst enemy!'

Samuel the porter shouted angrily at Shimon:

'You are to blame! You should have asked for ten at the outset, and not twenty. I told you. Ten, ten is what you should have asked!'

'What do you know about it? Had I asked for ten, they would not have offered even five.'

'They would have given ten, they would have, straight away, with no argument. I know they would! Wait, I'll go and see Jacob, you'll see, it'll all be done in a day. In just one day.'

'Haha!' laughed his uncle Shimon. 'You'll settle it! You! Do you know what Jacob said about you? He said he wouldn't give Sarucha to you even if you wanted her without a stitch to her name! He said you're not capable of earning enough to feed yourself. And he's right. Had you listened to your poor father, you would not be a porter now. But you, you always know best. You're always the know-

138

all. There, now you've heard what Jacob said. Go on, then, you go and haggle with him. Settle it all in just one day. Go on!'

Samuel's blood was up. He wanted to go to Jacob right away and tell him to his face that he was good for nothing, to tell him straight that he was a waster and a drunkard. He set off, but as he still hoped that matters could somehow be arranged, he turned into another street.

Samuel the porter waited a whole week hoping for his uncle to tell him that the negotiations had begun again. Instead he learned at Chucha's inn that Jacob had gone away to the country and would not be back for a week. He was in despair.

Jacob returned from the country a day early. He was in a very good mood when he arrived. He was driving a whole flock of young sheep and nineteen fat rams. They had been grazing all summer on Zelengora mountain. They were healthy and fat. And they were not expensive either. Jacob calculated that he would make good money on them. As soon as he arrived he sent for Shimon.

'Tell him to come, but right away!' he sent word, in his usual terse manner.

When the herbalist came, red-haired Jacob did not so much as let him sit down.

'Listen, Shimon,' he said decisively. 'You've been bargaining with my father for two months now, and nothing's come of it. Today I'm going to say two words to you, but you're not to open your mouth. I'll give ten ducats and such garments as I shall not be ashamed of. Will you take it or won't you? Yes or no? Speak!'

'Good luck to them! May they be happy!' said Shimon, holding out his hand.

IV

Samuel the porter embraced his uncle. He hardly slept the whole night. Ten ducats! He was going to have ten ducats. The next morning when he went out into the lane, the day seemed finer than it had been all the previous summer. He walked with a light step.

In the market place he attached his rope to his harness more deftly than ever before, put his back into his work and almost ran, as though he were carrying an empty basket. On his way up Banjski

Hill, the sweat ran down his back and dripped down his chin onto the stones. He was panting (his basket was full to overflowing and it was a sunny day, as though it were summer and not autumn), but none of that bothered Samuel the porter. That day he went into Bjelave like a different man, as though he were as strong as Muro. He did not stop to rest at all. He went past the White Fountain as though he had never set his load down there.

Tumultuous thoughts bore him as though on wings. Under his thick drooping moustache, his big yellow teeth grinned. Joy was swelling in him. He carried out lively conversations with himself and almost forgot that his basket was rubbing on his shoulder-blades, and his sweaty clothes were hampering him as he walked.

This day was a festive one for him, the nicest of all the days in his life. It felt like an important feast day, and as though he were wearing his Sabbath clothes, and not his greasy fez and ragged, dirty trousers.

He straightened his back under his load as best he could. His heart beat as though it were moulded from bronze. Everything around him rang: he was going to be a grocer, a grocer! And he would no longer be known as 'Samuel the porter', but rather as 'Samuel the grocer'. No more would he bend his back under bulging baskets, or bow down under sacks filled with coffee and flour. He had had enough of that these last ten years! More than enough! Now he would sit in his shop, like a man, measuring out sugar, salt and coffee for his customers, pouring paraffin and oil for them and wearing a pencil tucked under his fez just behind his ear, like the grocer Sado, the grocer Mento and the grocer Yuso.

He walked with ever firmer tread, clenching both his hands as though he were carrying the ten ducats in them. Cheerful thoughts kept coming to him from all around, slipping over one another, like spawning fish. Each one of them glistened in its delight.

He would open a shop! A grocer's shop! He'd acquire this and then that! On empty boxes by the door, he'd place two or three large baskets. One of onions, one of potatoes and the third of dried pears. Just as Sado had, when he opened his grocer's shop two years before.

Customers would come from morning till night. They'd buy things and pay for them. In the evening, when it was time to close the shop, he'd take the coins from the cash box, count them, put

140

them into a bag, hang the bag round his neck, lock up the shop and set off slowly home. Sarucha would be waiting for him with the evening meal. He would go slowly, unhurriedly, into the house, take off his shoes, sit down on the sofa, take out his cigarette box, roll a cigarette and tell his wife all about what he had sold, how much he had earned and who owed him what. After supper he would undress, but not the way he did now, quickly, piling his clothes in a heap, tired as a dog, just so as to rest his legs as quickly as possible, but slowly, gradually, he'd take off one piece of clothing after another, and then stretch himself out on the mattress, cover himself with the quilt, a long, wide quilt, and say to his wife: 'Come on, turn off the lamp and come and lie down yourself, you can wash those dishes tomorrow.'

So Samuel the porter mused happily, handing plums to children along the way as though they were his own.

When he was on his way back with his empty basket on his back, he stopped by the White Fountain, washed, sat down, rolled a cigarette, smoked and sank into ever more in toxicating dreams: a Grocer! He'd be a grocer and his hard life would start on a new wide and straight road. No longer would he drag himself from one side of the town to the other, no longer would he climb up from the market to the top of the Bjelave *mahala*. And in the winter he would no longer have to squat by the warehouses of the merchants Mair, Elishah and Salamon, waiting for the carts and pack-horses to arrive, then take off the bales and boxes, sacks and wineskins and bend double under their weight as he carried them into the warehouse or took them out to be loaded on to the hired horses. And in the hardest days of winter, when drifts blocked the roads, and there was no way across Ranjen and Vucja Luka, he would not stumble from house to house, his teeth chattering, looking for any kind of work just to earn a crust of bread. There would be none of that torment: he would sit by the brazier in his shop, stretch his hands towards the heat, watching the sparks leap out of the coals and warming himself the way the grocer Sado, the grocer Mento and the the grocer Yuso did each winter.

And he would earn ten times more than he did at present, and he would not have to struggle all year round, as he did now just carrying one basket of plums from the market to the top of Bjelave.

Let Muro the porter struggle with this work now. Muro was fit and strong as an ox. He'd be able to bend under weight for many years, without coming to any harm. Whereas he, he was already quite asthmatic, and his right knee hurt. Sometimes the pain in his bones pinched him badly in the night. He had picked up that illness in Señor Mair's icy warehouse. Ah, that Mair! That Mair! He was a bloodsucker! He'd let him wait when he returned from a delivery, bathed in sweat, for his hard-earned wages, he'd let him wait, squatting in a corner, for a whole hour or more. The stone walls and stone floor gave off icy air, and he did not wear galoshes like Señor Mair, and he did not have a brazier near his knees, and the cold got into his bones, while Mair calmly carried on reckoning, writing accounts, counting his money and smoking one cigarette after another. That waiting was very hard for him. How often had he wanted to stand up and say: 'Hey, I've waited long enough, do you want me to freeze to death for your miserable wage?'

He had wanted to say that, but how could he? What would Señor Mair have done? He would have raised his eyes from his desk and simply said: 'Get out! And don't you ever come back again. Out! Devil take you!'

That is what Señor Mair would have said, and that same day Señor Salomon and Señor Liachokan would hear about it, and then what would become of him? He might as well hang himself on his porter's rope. That's what!

But now, now Señor Mair wouldn't be able to offend him like that, he wouldn't have to crouch and put up with the masters' manners any longer. Now they'd speak differently to him. They'd summon him to strike a bargain over the price of oil, paraffin, coffee, sugar, salt. Yes, they'd summon him and offer him coffee, as they did the grocer Sado, he had seen with his own eyes! Coffee and tobacco! That would be life, real life!

And Sarucha wasn't sickly as his late Rifkula had been. If God granted him children, and He would, they would not die like Rifkula's, and when they grew up, they'd help him. And who knows? They said of Señor Elishah that he used to have a little shop in the Bascarscija, selling trinkets and second-hand fezes. And now he had a large warehouse, built of hewn stone, with a large green-painted door, with windows with iron grilles on them, and it was filled with goods: bales of cotton, heaps of felt, velvet and silk, countless stacks of fezes, scarves and every other kind of expensive goods.

It was past midday when he met up with Muro the porter. They were both squatting beside empty boxes in the little lane near Señor Mair's warehouse. They were eating their lunch of pitta bread and meat balls which Chichi cooked in hot fat in a frying pan shouting all day long: 'Chevapchichi! Hot chevapchici!'

'Good luck to you, Samuel, good luck,' Muro congratulated Samuel on his engagement and biting off an enormous piece of bread went on: 'And is it true that you're going to get ten whole ducats?'

'Yes!' Samuel confirmed.

'Ten, really?'

'Ten!'

'Good for you. And what will you do with that money?'

Samuel the porter did not answer immediately. He pushed his greasy fez a little to the side, scratched his tousled head, bit off a piece of bread with his teeth, and after he had chewed the mouthful, said:

'To be honest, I don't know myself what I'll do with it. But I think I'll leave it in a trunk. Just in case. A man can get sick. Isn't that right?'

Muro said nothing. They finished their lunch in silence. And ate a handful of plums each. Muro wiped his mouth, moustache and beard with his hand. Then he nodded his head, and, slowly, rolling a cigarette, took up the conversation again.

'So, you'll leave the money in a trunk, you say?'

'And what else should I do?'

'If I had ten ducats, you'd see what I could do with so much money. Ah,' sighed Muro, 'but to tell you the truth, I got more than ten ducats with my Bea and I did nothing, nothing at all with it. I put it into a trunk. And now it's gone. I was a fool. Ah but now, if I had that money now! Now I'd know what to do with it.'

Samuel the porter looked at Muro.

'Come on, let's hear, what would you do if you were me?'

'What would I do? I know what I'd do. But you have to have brains, to know what to do with so much money.'

Samuel the porter laughed.

'Don't worry. I'm not going to leave it in a trunk. Not me! I've got brains as well! I know what I'll do with it. You'll see!'

'Ah, my Samuel, I thought I had brains in my head too. But I didn't.'

'You'll see! I have it all worked out already,' said Samuel proudly, and he stood up and returned to work.

V

At that time Samuel the porter began to enquire, in the course of conversation, how much sacks of salt might cost, and how much were jars of paraffin, skins of oil and loaves of sugar.

Biño the merchant coaxed the secret out of Samuel.

'You want to open a grocer's shop? That's good. Good,' Biño patted him on the shoulder and began to counsel him. 'But you must be careful, Samuel, when you're selecting the place. You can't open a shop just anywhere. Here in the centre, it's good, but there are no empty shops here. So look up in the *mahalas*. There are still some good places. Up on Banjski Hill, on Meitas, on Bjelave. Look there, keep your eyes open. Try to find something like Sado did. Something like that. Only not just anywhere. If you find something let me know and I'll tell you if it's any good. If you find something good, I'll give you a loan, Ten ducats for another ten in ready cash. And good luck to you!'

Something like Sado the grocer's! Like Sado the grocer's! echoed in Samuel's brain.

Samuel the porter heaved his baskets onto his back and roamed through the *mahalas*, searching. He looked to the right, he looked to the left, but there wasn't an empty shop anywhere to be found. In Tuzlina Lane he found a little hole. Yudache had once had something like a little grocer's shop there, but it had not done well. It had devoured his capital, he had fallen into debt and now he was in trouble. He did a different kind of job each day. One day he'd sell pies in the street, the next day soap, the next lemons, but still he'd need to go seeking alms on Fridays.

I shan't let the same thing happen to me! I'll keep my eyes wide open! thought Samuel the porter.

On the seventh day after his engagement, Samuel was downhearted. He was concerned that he simply could not find a suitable place for his grocer's shop and afraid that he never would.

At about noon he was passing by his uncle's herbalist's shop. Shimon was standing in the open doorway and called to him.

144

'What is it?' asked Shimon in surprise, seeing him so downcast. Had he had words with the red-haired Jacob? They had been invited that evening to a gathering at Papucho's. Had anything happened? He knew that Jacob was a hasty fellow. Had he said anything? He was capable of anything. That Jacob, who spent all his time hanging round the villages, arguing with the peasants, bargaining over the price of stock, who slept in inns with hired men, coachmen and butchers, and who was forever quarrelling with shepherds, that red-haired Jacob was becoming more and more churlish with every passing year. Even as a child he had been insolent. And now, as Papucho himself said of him, he was irascible and as snappy as a puppy.

Like all butchers, Jacob the butcher wore a leather belt with three sharp knives in it. He smelled of raw meat and fat. Everyone in his household was afraid of him, but they respected him as the head of the family, since he was the one who worked and earned to support them all. Papucho would be in the shop only when Jacob had gone to the country. And then he stayed only until he had sold the remaining meat, fat and offal. Then he would lock up the shop and go to a cafe to play dominoes and cards all day long.

Had Jacob not been there, Papucho's family would have gone hungry. He was a very able merchant. He had the best meat and the best fat. That was why he had the best customers. He was very brusque, even rude, to everyone, but it was enough for a customer to ask when he was going to get married, for his mood to change.

'When am I getting married?' he would repeat in his husky voice and then he'd start: 'I have seven sisters to marry off before I can think of myself. Seven! There, that's when I'll marry! Imagine, I have to feed them all and still leave enough for a dowry for each of them …' he talked for a long time as he carved the best pieces of meat off greasy sheep carcasses and threw them down on the scales. His customers went away satisfied, but they reproached him silently for his petulance and pitied the poor girl whose lot it would be to marry him.

Red-haired Jacob had another fault as well. Several years earlier he had become blood-brother to a certain Turkush from Anatolia, a bearded and infamous drinker. Jacob would often get drunk in his company and then he behaved very badly. When he was drunk he would quarrel with everyone he met. Including the Turkish contables. When dancers came to town, he would go to watch them dance each evening. Frequently he ended up in gaol. (When Hadji Loyo had started an uprising four years later, red-haired Jacob set off with a knife in his teeth to protect Bosnia from the 'filthy Hun').

'You have not quarrelled with Jacob?' Shimon asked anxiously, remembering Jacob's grumbling which he had told Samuel about in his anger.

'Why should I quarrel? I have not set eyes on him,' said the porter calmly, although the question irked him.

'So what is it, then?'

'Nothing. I have a bit of a stomach ache.'

'A stomach ache? Today? Today when we're going to Papucho's where there'll be food and drink? Go straight to Chucho's and have a glass of bitter brandy. You must not have a stomach ache today! Go on. Call for us this evening and don't forget to bring a lantern.'

Samuel the porter wandered through the streets for a long time, wondering why his uncle had asked whether he had quarrelled with Jacob. He could not work it out. He went into Isaac's barber's shop. The grocer Sado was there.

Sado was sitting on a chair. He was wrapped in a brightly coloured sheet. Isaac the barber was cutting his hair. He was cutting off the locks of hair that fell over his forehead and face, and Samuel the porter would never have recognised Sado, had he not been in conversation with the barber Isaac.

At first Samuel could not grasp what they were talking about. Then he gathered that Sado was leaving his grocer's shop to open a large shop down in the centre. He was leaving his shop? Had he heard right?

He simply could not believe his ears.. Then Sado said clearly:

'I've earned quite a lot up there. But that's nothing. There's no work outside the town centre. It's all small beer up in the *mahalas*. Small-time customers, small-time earnings. A hundred days, ninety *groschen*. A grocer's shop is a grocer's shop, commerce is something else. Something else! Isn't that right? It is in commerce that a man must test himself.'

Samuel the porter could not control himself. He joined in the conversation.

'You're moving out of the grocer's shop?'

'If that is what you call moving out. I'm opening a commercial business. Do you know what that means, Samuel?'

When he left the barber's, Samuel the porter was beside himself. He kept looking at the clock-tower and waiting for it to get dark. As soon as he was at Papucho's he would initiate a conversation about his intention to open a grocer's shop. They would all be surprised when they heard this and they would all agree it was a very sensible idea. And when he told them that Sado the grocer was leaving his shop and moving into the centre, Jacob would get up and say: 'Samuel, go and put a deposit on that shop first thing in the morning. First thing! Here's the money! How much do you need? Tell me!'

With these thoughts, he went into another shop and bought a candle. Then he had a good wash, put on his best clothes, took his lantern and set off to his uncle's.

VI

Papucho's courtyard smelled of roast meat. Simha met the visitors at the door, with a tambourine, to sing them a song of welcome. There were two lamps in the living room. They had found a long table somewhere and decorated it with flowers. The celebration began as soon as they arrived. Brandy was poured, dishes of food served. The mood steadily improved. At the end of the table sat red-haired Jacob. He drank his brandy slowly as the others did. But he soon began holding out his empty glass increasingly often.

It was not wise to pour too much brandy for a man such as red-haired Jacob. That was why the women had already agreed to hold back and pretend that they did not see when he wanted his glass filled. And that is how it was. As soon as Jacob held out his glass, one of them would make a joke and everyone would burst out laughing. Jacob would laugh as well. He was in a good humour. But it could not last long. Jacob was annoyed that he was not being paid enough attention. He began to frown and then to grind his teeth.

Unfortunately this grinding could not be heard. There was too much noise in the room. People sang, talked at the top of their voices, told stories, and the dishes clattered. And the benches and chairs scraped. Old Papucho had warmed up so much that he winked at Estera, who was swaying back and forth, wildly shaking her tambourine. She raised her shrill voice as best she could, while Haimacho, her husband, a tinsmith from the Tinsmiths' Street, a well-known reveller, adjusted his voice to his wife's, waved his arms and closed his eyes, in rapture.

Sarucha sat in her place. She stared straight ahead of her, growing increasingly pale. She was terrified that Jacob might make some kind of trouble.

Samuel the porter, the betrothed, sat formally in his Sabbath clothes, listening to the talk and the singing, one minute taking a piece of chicken, the next a piece of roast lamb, he ate, smacking his lips, and waiting for a suitable moment to launch the discussion of his grocer's shop, and working out how much to ask when Jacob offered him money for the deposit. He could not decide. Lost in these thoughts, he kept forgetting to eat. Then the women would cluck:

'Why aren't you eating, Samuel? – Give Samuel some more brandy! Bring Samuel the dish of chicken! Have a cucumber, Samuel! You're not eating anything! Nothing at all!'

Samuel would give a start and begin eating again.

Samuel the porter had just taken a greasy chicken neck and was pulling off a piece of soft skin full of fat, when red-haired Jacob suddenly leapt from his seat:

'What is it?' he began to shout. 'Am I alive or aren't I? It's only him you take notice of. "Eat, Samuel. Drink, Samuel. Would you like some of this, Samuel? Would you like some of that, Samuel?" And what about me? Am I here or am I not? Bring that brandy here? I want to drink and get well and truly drunk too! Bring the brandy here!'

The way he shouted was alarming. (No one else other than Ahmet the Anatolian knew how to shout like that.) He was quite blue in the face and trembling. Simha came quickly with the bottle of brandy but red-haired Jacob had already banged his fist on the table. The blow was so hard that the glasses leapt in the air like frightened chickens. The dishes clinked. A fork flew towards Erdonia. If the woman had not happened to bend down, it would have hit her in the forehead.

A chicken wing in a thick sauce was jolted out of the shallow dish in front of Samuel, splashing his face and rolling down his new suit.

Old Erdonia, terrified by the shouting and the fork, lost consciousness, bending further and further forward until she tumbled onto the floor.

Papucho fixed his eyes on Jacob. His beard, which curled towards his chest, was shaking. It was clear that a storm was brewing in him as well. Papucho had never yet been angry with his son. But this time he could not control himself. While people were raising Erdonia from the floor, and Samuel was wiping his face and suit with the end of a towel, Papucho got to his feet and, pointing towards the door, began to shout:

'Out, you wretch! Get out!'

The long curling locks that hung at his temples swayed like a bunch of disturbed leeches.

Everyone froze. They were seized by the fear that Jacob would take a knife from his belt and set about cutting their throats one by one. But red-haired Jacob said calmly and obediently:

'I'm going, father! I'm going!'

He had set off. He had opened the door, taken a step outside, but then he suddenly turned round and began quietly, collectedly:

'You're driving me out like a dog. Never mind. That's all I am. And I'm going. I'm going so as not to disturb you, and just you carry on eating and drinking and enjoying yourselves. I'll go and find Ahmet the Anatolian and get drunk. And you'll get drunk as well. But don't you forget that none of you would be sitting there if I had not opened my purse. None of you! If I had not promised ten ducats for my sister Sarucha, you would not be gnawing chicken bones and filling your stomachs with fried eggs seasoned with pepper, brought from India by Señor Mair.'

Haimacho began to soothe him.

'Silence, when I'm speaking!' shrieked red-haired Jacob. He took a step forward, put his hand on the handle of his large knife and went on in a more decisive voice:

'I just want to say this: I, red-haired Jacob, could easily remove from your stomachs all the roast meat you've been guzzling and the brandy you've been swilling. I could say to Samuel the porter: "If you wish, take Sarucha just as she is, in the clothes she stands up in, without a cord to her pants, and instead of ducats you'll get nothing." That's what I could say. Then Samuel the porter and his

149

uncle Shimon would get up and leave, because it's not Sarucha they're taking but my ten ducats. It's true, Samuel the porter, don't wriggle in your seat and jerk your legs like a ram with its throat cut. It's all as I say. Of course! You've spent two months arguing over those ducats. This evening, you haven't so much as glanced at Sarucha. Your heads are full of ducats. Ducats! And the women are dancing round you: "Take some of this, take some of that. Fill Samuel's glass! Give him some meat!" Psshh! Shame on you!'

Papucho moved and wanted to shout at his son, but red-haired Jacob reached towards his belt and screamed:

'Don't get in my way, father! I shan't hurt anyone. I gave my word. I want to redeem it. Here, here's the money. Five in silver coins, and five napoleons.' He took out his purse and clinked the money. 'Here you are, may you be satisfied, Señor Samuel. And you, Sarucha, scamper after him like a little bitch. But remember, if he could he'd take the money and leave you with our crazy Papucho ...'

He threw the purse on to the table.

Everyone drew back, as though he had thrown down a bomb that was about to explode and blow them all to pieces.

'Take the money, Señor Samuel, take it and enjoy it! There it is!'

No one stirred. Only their eyes moved, now to the right, now to the left.

Samuel's throat went dry. What should he do? What should he say? Should he take the money? If he did, tomorrow all the talk in the town would be about how Jacob had tossed him the money the way one tosses a dog a juicy piece of meat. And Jacob was right. He, Samuel, had been dreaming about those ducats. About his grocer's shop! Without the ducats Sarucha would not have crossed his mind. It was all true! And now the money was lying in front of him, he could take it, he had only to stretch out his hand. But how could he do that? How could he? Everyone was watching to see what he would do. Everyone was wondering: would he take it? Would he?

'Samuel,' his uncle Shimon interrupted the silence, saying decisively: 'Take the money, and let's carry on celebrating the betrothal.'

Samuel was about to stand up and take the purse of ducats, but he was suddenly seized by a fearful vision: if he took the money, one of the lamps on the wall would go out, and it would be the one that gave most light. The room would be plunged into half-darkness, everyone would fall silent and no one would stir from his place. Simha would drop her tambourine on the floor, and Sarucha would be overcome by uncontrollable weeping, which would burst from her, threatening to rend her heart.

He stood up quickly and, trembling all over, he said:

'Simha, give him back his purse!'

'Samuel!' warned his uncle Shimon briefly and sharply in his shrill voice.

Samuel's head was beating. His eyes had clouded over. He repeated:

'Simha, give him back the money! I don't need his money!'

'Don't talk nonsense!' shrieked Shimon. 'Take the money when I tell you!'

'No, I shan't,' all at once Samuel's tongue was freed. He shouted: 'I shan't take it, I don't need that kind of money. I'm not taking Sarucha because of the money. I'll live without it. I'll take Sarucha just as she is, in the clothes she's wearing. I'll live without his ducats.'

'He'll live! Hahaha! He'll live without my money!' red-haired Jacob roared with laughter.

'Yes, I will, I will!' Samuel turned towards him. 'I'll live!' He leant over the table, took the purse and threw it at Jacob's chest.

The purse hit Jacob hard in the chest and fell onto his knife-belt.

'There you are! I'll live without it, yes I will, you red cockerel! Red drunkard!'

'Hahaha!' laughed red-haired Jacob.

Someone made a signal. Simha beat her tambourine, shaking and jingling it, and Haimacho began to sing. Estera shoved Jacob outside.

Samuel the porter fell back onto the bench wearily. He was pale and trembling. When the song was finished Papucho stood up, he took a long chain with a silver watch from his neck. With his own hands he placed it round Samuel the porter's neck and tucked the watch into his belt. He did not say a word. Then he took his glass and raised it in a toast:

'Friends, you are witnesses. God gives and God takes away! That was my own son, but this is the one God has sent me. Samuel! *Lehaim!*'

151

Samuel took his glass, clinked it against Papucho's and said:

'Let the wedding be next week. Whatever is ready, is ready. I don't need more. Samuel the porter will work and live!'

'*Lehaim!*'

'*Lehaim!*'

Old Papucho and Samuel the porter drained their glasses, then embraced and kissed one another.

Sarucha leant her head against Shimon's wife Miriam's shoulder. She was shaking. She wept, and one could see that it was from deep joy. And Erdonia pulled off the bandage they had wrapped round her head. She waved it like a banner, crying: 'Besimantov! Besimantov! Good luck! Good luck!'

The festivities lasted until after midnight. When they set out for home, Shimon grabbed Samuel by the sleeve, dragging him along and reproaching him:

'What have you done, you ass? Ai! Ai! Ai!'

Samuel the porter waved the lantern and replied calmly:

'I have done nothing!'

'What do you mean!' the little man, Shimon, was wracked with misery. 'Ten whole ducats! Five silver, five gold, and you threw them into the water. Ten ducats, you ass! Do you think a man gets married ten times in his life? Do you, *asno*? Do you, you ass?' Shimon shook Samuel, as he held him by the arm. 'And who did you give the money back to? To Jacob Kavezon, a drunkard! Did you see the way he shouted? Well?'

'Let me go!' Samuel the porter pulled his arm away from his uncle Shimon.

'Hold on, hold on, I'll let you go, but first let me ask you, let me hear, do you know what that red-haired devil is going to do with that money? What he'll do this very night? Do you know? He'll drink it, with that Ahmet the Anatolian, he'll drink it and give it to the dancers.'

'Who?' Samuel the porter turned towards him.

'The dancers!'

'The dancers?' Samuel stood stock still.

'Yes, the dancers!'

Samuel the porter had lifted the lantern high and was staring fixedly at Shimon. Shimon's little eyes glistened like sparks.

'What are you looking at me for? He'll give it to the dancers.

That's what he'll do,' the little herbalist hissed angrily. Samuel shrugged his shoulders sadly, lowered his hand with the lantern and continued on his way.

VII

The following day, later than usual, Samuel the porter went down into town. He was wearing his old clothes, with a basket over his shoulder and a greasy old fez. He walked dejectedly. His heavy tread rang dully in the lane. He had not slept. His head ached.

'What happened last night?' Muro asked when they met.

Samuel the porter said nothing. He began unwinding his rope calmly.

'I heard that you gave those ten ducats of dowry back?'

'That's right! I gave them back!' said Samuel the porter decisively, looking Muro in the eye.

'Eh, well done! Very well done! Couldn't you think of anything more intelligent to do with them?'

'No!'

'No! Well, what did I tell you, you have to have brains, to know what to do with money. Brains!'

That day, as he climbed up to Banjski Hill, Samuel the porter panted heavily, wiping the sweat from his brow, cursing the steep slope, the rutted cobbles, the holes, and from time to time, bent double beneath his full basket, he mumbled to himself: 'He'll have given it to the dancers. For sure!' And he did not so much regret losing the money, as the fact that Jacob had given it to the dancers! Dancers!

Samuel the porter had only seen dancers once in his life. He had seen them through a broken board in the fence of a café on Bentbasha. But he had heard about those girls and women and their seductive movements.

That day he saw in his mind's eye fat Sadigdye from Solun: she was standing in the middle of a room. In front of her was a little rug and on it silver coins were set in a circle, with a heap of gold ones in the centre. She was standing there, without a blouse on. Yellow armbands gleamed on her full bare arms, bracelets clinked on her wrists and shining stones flashed from her fingers. Her loose

153

pantaloons were tied under her navel, a silk waistcoat was drawn tightly over her bust. Her white skin gleamed, her large eyes stared, unblinking, at the money, and then she began to move. A greedy smile played around her painted lips and powdered cheeks, her eyelids with their long lashes closed, her thin eyebrows rose and fell, she threw her head back and, sticking out her stomach, revolved it slowly, and it rose and fell as her hips moved now forwards now backwards. Her hands snatched at the empty air. Large yellow beads of amber, threaded round her neck bounced about, bumping against the silk on her breasts. Dark yellow curls of hair could be glimpsed under her arms. Large drops of sweat rolled down her white skin.

Samuel watched all of that and he could still hear red-haired Jacob, who had settled down on the sofa, laughing to himself. Beside him sat Ahmet the Anatolian, staring at the woman, he was drooling, his gaze fixed on Sadigdye's navel, and grunting like a pig.

Samuel put down his basket by the White Fountain, took his arms out from under the ropes, shook himself all over from some terrible revulsion and spat.

'Phh!'

Then he took off his fez and bent his head under the tap. The cold stream of water refreshed him more than it ever had. He felt as though his head were cooling down and his pulse returning to normal.

'Ah! Ah!' he crowed with satisfaction, rubbing his head with his calloused hands more and more vigorously, the head which the barber Isaac had cut so short the previous day. 'Ah! Ah!'

The wedding took place the following week.

Translated by Celia Hawkesworth

Davoka's Tale of the Living Truth

Everything I shall relate here about Behara, the Jewess of Gornje Bjelave, I heard from an acquaintance of mine, someone whom everyone almost always called Davoka rather than by his given name David – David Bararon.

I shall not call him any differently myself. In fact I feel that if I were to call him David or David Bararon, it would not be the same man but someone else, someone quite different. The nickname suited him so well that it was as if Davoka, not David, was his real, given name.

When I say Davoka, I can see him instantly, I see him the way he is, the way he really is in everyday life. But if I were to say David, it would be a different man standing before me. That too would be Davoka, of course, but Davoka in a formal pose, with a set expression in his eyes, looking as if he had been squeezed into a new suit in which he felt distinctly uncomfortable and not himself. Nothing about him would be the real Davoka.

Davoka had his mannerisms. They were in his walk, in his gestures, in the way he held his head, and in his voice. He cut a unique figure, one all his own. Just a glimpse of that figure, of the corner of his head, say, or a bit of his shoulder, sufficed to recognise him, and even from afar he could be recognised by his walk or by his footstep if he was walking behind us.

Davoka was on the small side, with a short neck and broad shoulders. His movements were quiet, measured and completely controlled. Ever since I knew him he had always been taciturn and reticent, and with the passing years he became more and more withdrawn. He was a loner. Many people regarded him as peculiar, some even thought he was slightly 'cracked'. He was always wrapped up in his own thoughts, as if immersed in or transported by them, yet as far as I could judge, he also always had presence of mind, and a very astute, perceptive eye.

I did not see him often.

I knew Davoka from long ago. We had met many years before the war. From the very beginning, ours had been a rather superficial friendship and it remained so all those years. We would exchange a few pleasantries whenever we ran into each other in a smaller crowd of people, which was usually in a café or the foyer of the theatre.

As far as I recollect, we never stopped to talk in the street. We would greet each other, politely and respectfully, and then each proceed on his own way.

That is how it was until the ill-fated year of 1941.

From the outbreak of war until the final victory over Hitler, we did not see each other even once. Sometime towards the end of the second year of the occupation, I heard that Davoka had not been taken away to the notorious Jasenovac camp, as had been assumed, and as one unfortunately always had to assume when pondering the fate of a Jew.

They told me that he had managed to find refuge somewhere from Ustasha and Nazi persecution of the Jews.

Later I learned more details. They told me that Davoka had decided to stay and share the fate that awaited and ultimately befell other Jews. And there is no doubt that he would not have been spared that fate had it not been for a relative who appeared at the last moment and almost forcibly took Davoka away with him. They made it safely to Mostar, and moved on from there. They told me that Davoka and his relative had even managed to get out of the country.

When we met after the war, again we exchanged only a few words. We stepped into a small street and, standing off to the side, enquired about one person and another. Both of us were curious to know how everyone had fared during those terrible years. As we talked, we were both surprised to be alive at all, to have escaped the perils of fascist executioners, Hitlerites and Ustashas throughout the occupation and war, which had lasted not a few days, not a few months, but four long, hard years.

156

Davoka had lost weight and aged. In his worn, crumpled suit, with several days' worth of stubble on his face, he looked unkempt, shabby. His eyes seemed to have sunk back into their sockets, and they exuded a great sadness and despondency. I sensed that unspeakable events had left deep, cruel marks on his soul.

I felt sorry for him.

'We're free again now ... A new life is beginning ...', I said, trying to cheer him up a little.

Davoka nodded.

'Yes, we are free', he said. 'I feel it. I do indeed. I rejoice at the sun, I rejoice at everything. A new age is dawning, a new era. But ... there is something right here that troubles me, that weighs heavy on me. It is eating away at me like an open wound.'

He promised to tell me one day about his trials and tribulations as a refugee abroad, about the thoughts that tormented him even in his dreams, and about many other things. He emphasised these 'many other things', his eyes boring deep into mine, and then he added softly, in the kind of voice of patients who are starting to recover from a long, serious illness:

'... Yes, yes, we have suffered greatly, you, I, all of us. How many of us are left? Barely ten out of a hundred. And how much those ten have been through! And what about the other ninety?', he said, shaking his head. 'They were taken away to Jasenovac, to the death camps in Dachau and Birkenau ... Taken away and gone, all with heads bowed ... Yes, heads bowed ... A terrible fate ... It breaks my heart even to think about it. It breaks my heart ... but', he waved his hand, 'it will all be forgotten ... We will forget the dead ... Even we who survived will forget our sufferings ... Time, time heals, time levels everything ... That's what they say and as long as they say it, I suppose it must be true. These wise sayings and expressions reflect age-old experience', he said, taking his leave.

As he spoke these last words, I noticed an almost imperceptible smile, sad and faintly mocking, brush his lips.

We shook hands. He squeezed mine with much more warmth than ever before.

'I will, I'll drop by one day, soon perhaps. There is so much I would like to talk to you about', he said and then departed. I watched him go. He went with hands clasped behind his back, head bowed.

Months passed. I kept expecting him to drop by, but as far as I knew, Davoka made no effort to see me, either at home or anywhere else.

And so Davoka and I reverted to the relationship we had had before the war. We would run into each other, say hello, and move on.

A whole year passed.

Yesterday when we met at the exhibition of our painters, I found it strange that he did not come over to me, even though we had nodded our greetings as cordially and respectfully as ever when we noticed each other.

It seemed all the more strange because he was constantly hovering around me. I was already beginning to think that I must have offended him somehow. Perhaps I had failed to notice him in the street somewhere, and he had taken it wrongly. I was about to walk over to him when I noticed that he was coming my way. He approached me. He did so several times, never for any lengthy conversation, but simply to ask how I liked this painting or that (they were always portraits or compositions), only to drift away again.

I watched him, needless to say, as inconspicuously as possible. I do not think he noticed. I saw him remove his spectacles and wipe the lenses at length, first one and then the other, with a worn scrap of soft yellow leather, pinked at the edges. Then he held the spectacles up to the window, checking carefully to see that each lens was properly clean and spotless, and when at last he was satisfied, he turned around, put them back on and slowly returned to the paintings, giving them his undivided attention.

He studied each one carefully and with great interest.

As I was leaving, I noticed that, although there were still plenty of people at the exhibition and Davoka was on the other side of the room, he too was getting ready to leave. In the street, I sensed that he had come out of the building and was walking behind me, though I did not turn around to look. I was expecting him to fall into step with me, but Davoka kept his distance, which was considerable. When I turned into one of the busier streets and began labouriously pushing my way through the crowd, I lost sight of him, if that is the right phrase, because I could feel rather than actually see Davoka still behind me. Finally, thinking that he was probably no longer there, that he had turned off into another street, I almost forgot about him. I headed for home.

When I arrived and walked up to the open gate of the old house in which I lived, Davoka suddenly appeared out of nowhere.

'I am sure, Doctor, that you still vividly remember that painting in the flat of your good friend Eliazar Daniti', said Davoka without preamble.

'Let's go inside', I said quietly.

And we went in.

When we reached my room, Davoka slowly took out his spectacles, wiped them clean, and began, with singular curiosity to examine the furniture, the books and the pictures. He looked at one side of the room and the other, and then, accepting the offered chair and returning his spectacles to his pocket, continued in the same tone he had used at the front gate.

'I think you will find what I have to say interesting', he said. 'The reason why I think so is that I know you were very fond of that picture. Once I even saw you myself, standing in front of it, gazing deeply into those eyes, at that face, that set expression around the mouth, that spirited turn of the strong shoulders.'

Davoka spoke slowly, pronouncing each sentence separately, with pauses, emphasising particular words.

I wanted to say something, to make an observation, but Davoka quickly raised his hand and stopped me with a gentle but firm gesture; pulling his chair over to me, his speech flowed more rapidly now, pouring out in a torrent of words.

'I know what you want to say. You want to say it was just a portrait. Yes, you're right. It really was just a portrait. Still, I know you saw the whole woman in that portrait. Yes, that's right. The whole woman. And she was an unusual woman, Doctor. Close your eyes for a minute, it will help you to remember. Close them and you will see her as if she were standing here in front of you right now. You haven't forgotten her, I know you haven't. She is unforgettable.

'Do you remember what Eliazar Daniti used to say? "It's a magnificent work! Magnificent! It was the artist's lucky day when he painted that picture". That's what Eliazar Daniti used to say, and his voice was always excited. He was happy that everyone liked the picture so much, that everyone was so taken by it.

'I am sure, Doctor, that you too knew many details in connection with the painting. And you haven't forgotten them in all this time, yet it has been a most unusual time. Ninety per cent, ninety per cent of our number died, only ten per cent, ten out of a hundred, are left!', Davoka said, with a wave of his arm. 'To return to the point. It was a painting of a poor Jewish woman. She was no longer young. *The Jewess of Bjelave*, that's what we used to call her. You probably remember that too. She was listed under a similar name in the catalogue at the Autumn Exhibition, where we saw her, both you and I, for the first time. That was in 1936 or '37. The date is not quite fixed in my mind. No matter. I remember it well because I saw you myself standing in front of that picture in Eliazar Daniti's flat. The painting was hanging on the wall in a dark wide frame. I can see it now, as if it were right here in front of me. And the frame, as you probably knew yourself, had been designed by the artist himself. You, Doctor, were standing – I was observing you carefully – you were standing in front of the painting, looking at it. You were completely engrossed in it, utterly captivated by it. I found nothing strange about that. Because in honesty, in honesty, Doctor, there was so much in that painting to captivate, to delight, to rivet the viewer to the spot.'

Here Davoka broke off. He leaned his elbows on his knees and buried his head in his hands. He was saying something, he was upset and shaking. He seemed to be talking to himself now, quite divorced from what he had been saying to me. Although I could make out some of the words, I could not understand what they meant.

'Why, why didn't you speak out before? Behara! Behara!', he said. He wrung out each word in convulsive anguish and grief. This upset me. Something was going on inside this man, a personal drama of his own perhaps.

Behara? Who was that? What had this painting got to do with Behara? Irrepressible curiosity took hold of me. Though I was sitting quietly, my impatience for Davoka to calm down, to collect himself and resume his story, was palpable.

When he raised his head, he released a few sobbing sighs, nodded, took out his handkerchief and wiped his brow and face. Surprisingly, Davoka immediately picked up his story in the same clear, exalted voice he had used before.

'"Something quite extraordinary radiates from that woman's

160

face ... " Remember those words? They are the words of your friend Eliazar Daniti. I heard those words of genuine admiration myself. I heard them from his own lips. Eliazar Daniti was my friend too. Just as he told you and so many others, so he often told me how the painter kept begging him to give him back the portrait, he was even willing to pay three times the price he had sold it for, or give him some other painting in return; Daniti could choose from any of the paintings in the artist's studio.

'Eliazar Daniti told me, as he must have told you, how the artist would often drop by to look at his canvas, and how, gazing at the painting, he would always say that only now did he realise how much he had put into the woman's portrait. "I know", our Eliazar Daniti would say in his soft, almost solemn voice as he stared into the distance, "I know that this painting, this *Jewess of Bjelave*, certainly has much more meaning for the painter, as its author, than it can have for me. But I cannot", and here Eliazar's eyes would stray back to the painting and he would pause, "I cannot even imagine parting with her. If I were to part with her I would feel a desolate void in my house. Look at her; doesn't it fill you with a kind of faith in life to behold her? Good portraits reveal the person, and when they have something good to reveal they are as gripping as a good book."

'Our poor friend Eliazar was right. I think you probably agree with him and with me. It's true, you felt vibrant strength in that woman standing there in front of you, looking back at you from her heavy picture frame, you felt a life that had not been lived in vain. Yet she was just an ordinary person, an ordinary woman: a working woman, a laundress. She was a woman whose life had been an uphill struggle but who had made her own way. She had gone forward. Looking at her you realised that one does not live in vain. She gave you an incentive to live, she sparked in you a kind of joy, a kind of bright, powerful view of the future. And let me also say this – although I don't know whether I felt it at the time or whether it came to me later: the more I looked at her the more I felt that this woman was the beginning of new generations.'

Davoka came to a halt in his story and gave me a penetrating look. 'Yes, new ones, new generations!', he said and then lowered his eyes again. He stared in front of him as if watching a cigarette burn in the *kilim*. Gazing fixedly at that spot, he resumed his story. One could feel that everything he was saying came from the heart.

'I love painting, I love paintings if they are real works of art. Like you I often stood in front of *The Jewess of Bjelave* and looked at her. It was a lovely work of art. To me, works of art are great, powerful revelations.'

Davoka kept looking at that same spot in front of him. Then he raised his head and transferred his gaze to me.

'Do you know what happened to that painting?', he asked after a brief pause. I did not have the time to answer, because Davoka did not wait for a reply:

'It was in 1941. The second month of the occupation. We had already been outlawed by then. One day, shortly before noon, two SS-men burst into Eliazar's flat. The flat, as you know, was on the second floor of that big, four-storey building. The SS-men had a tenant from the first floor with them. They came and pressed the door bell long and hard. You could clearly hear its shrill ring in the corridor. It rang like a menacing threat. But to no avail. No one answered. There was deathly silence inside the flat. The door was locked. They began banging on it with their fists. Again, nothing. Then, without giving it much thought they quickly and expertly broke down the door and walked in.

'There was no one in the flat. The rooms were in perfect order, as if the tenants had just stepped out for a walk. Only the painting was missing from the wall. Its heavy, dark frame was lying on a little round table. The frame was empty. One of the two SS-men picked it up and began examining it.

'"It must have held an old, valuable painting", he said loudly and then, like a disappointed thief whose hopes of laying his hands on a rare treasure have been dashed, he sat down despondently in one of those dark blue leather armchairs. He did not gnash his teeth. He just sat there quietly, as if concocting a plan. Meanwhile, the other SS-man in the next room was opening the three-door wardrobe with its bevelled mirror, and pulling the drawers out of the wide walnut dresser. He worked slowly and noiselessly. Silence reigned in the flat even now. Suddenly, steps rang out in the corridor, immediately followed by the appearance of a woman at the open door. The SS-man glowered at her. The first-floor tenant quickly explained that this was Maria, the concierge.

'The woman was carrying a long, large, neatly wrapped package. When she pulled it out from under her apron and the SS-man saw

162

it, he leaped up from the armchair. His blue eyes suddenly turned unusually bright. "Maybe that's the painting", he thought, shooting a quick glance at the empty frame on the little table.

'Written in big block letters on the cardboard wrapping were the words: To Mr. Roman Petrović the Painter, The Attic, Old Post Office Building, Sarajevo.

"Give me that!", said the SS-man.

'The concierge asked if she could say something first and immediately proceeded to speak. She said that the owner of this flat, Eliazar Daniti, had disappeared a few days earlier. He had probably taken his wife and little girl to Dalmatia, where some of the Jews sought refuge in the hope that under the Italians they might at least be able to save their lives.

"He won't save his! That's a promise!", said the SS-man, interrupting the woman.

"The woman was startled, flustered.

"Go on!", ordered the SS-man.

'"The day before he disappeared with his wife and child was a Sunday", said Maria quietly, her voice trembling. This man Eliazar had come to her with the package asking her to take care of it as if it were her own, and to deliver it personally to the painter whose name was on the wrapping. He explained where the attic was. "Please, deliver this into his hands, into the hands of the painter only, nobody else!" He had stressed that several times.

'The very next day she looked up the said gentleman, but he was not there. His studio was locked. She went back several times. She had been there yesterday, too. She had rung the bell, knocked, banged on the door, all to no avail. She had enquired about him, but it was no use, no one could tell her anything.

She had decided to try again in a few days' time, but when she heard them opening the Jew's flat just now, she thought she would come and tell them about the package. She did not want any trouble if they should search her flat and discover the package in her possession.

She knew nothing about the package. She had not opened it, she could swear to it.

The concierge now held out the package. Quickly but carefully, the SS-man tore off the wrapping. It revealed a rolled-up canvas.

'"Rembrandt it isn't, but it's certainly a valuable old painting," said the SS-man, grinning broadly at his *Kamerad* as he unrolled the canvas.

'"A painting!", Maria cried out in surprise, stepping closer.

'The SS-man stared at the picture, muttering as if to himself: "It's not an old painting ... it's modern, but ..."

'"Is it worth anything?", asked the other SS-man in German, showing scant interest in the answer as he moved off to the other room.

'"*Das glaube ich!*", replied the first SS-man, emphasising each word, still staring at the canvas. He looked at it for a long time and then suddenly turned to the first-floor tenant and asked:

'"Do you know who this is maybe? Whose portrait this is?"

'"No", said the man, shrugging his shoulders. "It looks like a Jewess", he added as an afterthought.

'"A Jewess?", the SS-man repeated in surprise, a frown quickly darkening his face. He cast a sharp look at the man from the first floor.

'"Yes, a Jewess", affirmed the rattled tenant as if it was somehow his fault.

'The SS-man looked at the picture again. He shook his head and after a few seconds said to the man from the first floor:

'"Yes, it is a Jewess, I can see that myself now. Come here and hold the picture upright there, by the top corners, hold it out so it's fully stretched!"

'The tenant took hold of the two top corners. Holding the bottom edge of the painting with one hand, the SS-man shouted:"hold it tight and steady!" and with the other hand he unsheathed his bayonet, his bright eyes fixed on the painting. And this Jewess, this laundress, this mother, this Jewess *of Bjelave*, calmly stared back at him with her dark eyes. (Do you remember that look of hers, Doctor?) She looked at him without blinking. She did not blink even when the SS-man lifted the gleaming blade and began to rip her cheeks open. She did not blink even when he gouged out her eyes with the tip of the blade. *The Jewess of Bjelave* did not even scream. That's no surprise! Since when can a painting scream! But poor Maria the concierge, now pale with fright, screamed in her stead. It was a voiceless scream, but full of horror. The woman felt as if the blade had flashed in front of her own face, as if it was about

164

to rip into her own cheeks, into the living pupils of her own eyes. She threw up her hands to try to protect herself. Her eyes were full of terror.

'Poor woman, poor concierge! Horrified by the scene, she slowly backed out of the room, step by step. When she reached the corridor, she turned around to run, to get to her own flat as fast as she could and lock herself in. She wanted to fly away, to escape, but the poor woman barely managed, with only the greatest effort, as often happens to us in our dreams, to drag one foot after the other. Even when she reached the stairs, she was unable to run. Her legs were like dead weights. She could barely lift or move them. Poor woman, she hauled herself down the stairs, with the ever-present feeling that the SS-man was drawing his knife and now, now, was going to stab her in the back, rip open her ribcage, scrape the blade against the hard bone or ... (oh, how horrible!), that now, now, the SS-man was going to grab her by the hair, swing her around and gouge her eyes out with the tip of his blade ... Ah Doctor, who knows all the things such a terrified woman must have felt at a moment like that.'

Davoka nodded his head.

'Now listen to what happened next. As the concierge withdrew, the SS-man calmly returned the bayonet to its sheath, crumpled the canvas of the disfigured *Jewess of Bjelave*, tore it up and shoved the pieces into the stove. Then he kneeled down, slowly took out his lighter, flicked it on and placed the flame against a piece of the torn canvas. It burned very slowly at first, but bit by bit it caught fire and the flame grew. The stove drew the dark red flame and its thick, dirty grey twirl of smoke up towards the chimney. The blazing fire began to glow brighter and brighter through the open door of the tiled stove. One could hear the oil sizzle and smell the grease burn.

'Still kneeling, the SS-man gazed at the fire. He flared his nostrils and sniffed. Suddenly a desperate scream rang out on the staircase, immediately followed by the thud of something tumbling down the stairs on to the concrete landing.

'"Maria! Maria!", a voice rang out, then another, then a chorus of anxious voices, as commotion broke out. Cries of "Water! Water!" could be heard.

'Meanwhile, the other SS-man was busy carrying the sheets and

165

other linen from the wardrobe and dresser to the plush sofa. He worked quietly, examining each piece separately, admiring its dazzling clean whiteness ...'

Davoka stood up, walked over to the window and peered out. The window overlooked the garden.

There was the promise of a mild spring evening outside. The west was still in the full glow of the sun. And burning light flooded my room.

'What a beautiful end to the day!', Davoka said, still standing at the window, as he turned to look at me. 'I shouldn't have picked such a beautiful day to tell this terrible story. But ... it's done now, I've told it ... That, Doctor, was how the painting of The Jewess of Bjelave, the painting of that laundress, disappeared.' Davoka moved to the middle of the room. 'I had known her since she was a child. I knew her well, both her and her father. The name of this Jewess from Upper Bjelave was Behara.'

'Behara?', I repeated, surprised to hear again the name that Davoka had mentioned so emotionally at the beginning of his tale.

'Yes, Behara', Davoka replied. 'She had three children, two married daughters and an unmarried son. She was widowed when Naum was three. She lived in Bjelave, at the top of Upper Bjelave. The widow Behara died in Jasenovac.'

Suddenly Davoka fell silent. He seemed to be trying to make up his mind about something, but then, as if cutting himself short, he went on:

'I'll tell you what happened some other time, yes, some other time. About Eliazar you know. You certainly know more than I do. I heard that during the third year of the occupation the Germans captured him in a small Dalmatian town, him, his wife and their little girl. They were reportedly taken away to Germany, to some camp, in Dachau or Mathausen, no one knows for sure. And there they died, like millions of others.'

Davoka gave another dismissive wave of his hand, as was his wont. He looked at me unblinkingly. His face assumed a grim, dark expression. He held out his hand in a wordless good-bye, and moved to leave. His hand was already on the doorknob when suddenly he stopped. He turned around, took a small notebook out of his inside coat pocket, and donned his spectacles. He flicked through the notebook and then read something silently to himself, making brusque, sharp movements with his head. He looked up from the notebook.

'There is one more thing I should tell you about Behara today. As I said, Behara died in Jasenovac. She was shot dead. They killed her', said Davoka, reading from his notebook now, emphasising every word. 'They killed her when she rebelled, when she ran out from those packed rows of prisoners, stood in front of them and cried out: "Long live the struggle! Go and join the partisans like my Naum! May luck be with you, with you and with all fighters, and with my Naum!"

'The prisoners stood there, craning their scrawny necks, gaping at this woman in amazement. Then she swung around to the *Ustashas* and swore at them: "You bastards! Do you hear me? My son has joined the partisans; he's gone to fight! And he has my blessing! He and all fighters! And remember, one day those partisan fighters will judge you for everything you have done. You'll see, you bastards!"'Her voice was strong as she raised her arm, clenched her fist and shook it threateningly.

'The *Ustashas* reached for their weapons, but she was faster, tore open her jacket and shirt and cried out: "Shoot! New generations will rise from the blood you are spilling. You'll see, you bastards!"

'Behara's cry rang out so loudly, so powerfully, that it shook the air and the prisoners' eyes lit up. Shots were fired. One after another. Three pistol shots. One bullet hit her in the chest, the other two missed her. Yes, they missed her! That's how powerful that woman's voice was. Behara fell to the ground, her arm flung out, her fist clenched. She lay there without twitching once. Like a toppled statue which would be put back up again and returned to its place.'

Davoka suddenly fell silent. He looked at me, and then, putting his face close to mine, said:

'This, Doctor, is the truth, the living truth! I wrote it down, look, it's all here, word for word. I heard it from Menachem who escaped from Jasenovac after Behara rebelled and went off to fight.'

Davoka stared at me.

'What is it? You're looking at me as if you don't believe any of this.' He stood there, his eyes boring deeper and deeper into mine. 'But I tell you, I, David Bararon, known as Davoka, I tell you that this is the living truth about Behara, the living truth! And I beg you, guard this truth for me just as I shall guard Behara's promise. Guard it ...'

Davoka's words seemed to cry out to me. It was as if they echoed the power of the rebellious Behara herself. I looked at Davoka. His eyes were glistening with tears, his face was flushed now, burning with emotion. He put his notebook and spectacles back in his pocket, repeated the words: 'Guard the truth', and walked out of the room.

An overwhelming silence befell the room when he left. I sat down wordless. The scent of ripe apples wafted through the open window. The telephone wires that stretched between the roof-tops hummed as they usually did on such serene, warm evenings. But this time I did not hear them. I kept listening to the words Davoka had wrung out of himself with such convulsive anguish at the beginning of his tale: 'Why, why didn't you speak out before? Behara! Behara!'. His words kept ringing in my ears like the refrain of a sad song, of a stirring ballad.

I think I understand their real meaning now.

Translated by Christina Pribićević-Zorić

ZDENKO LEŠIĆ

Isak Samokovlija, Life and Work

Isak Samokovlija was a descendant of the Sephardic Jews who, expelled from Spain at the end of the fifteenth century, found refuge in the Ottoman Empire. His great-grandfather moved to Bosnia as a salesman from the small Bulgarian town of Samokov. Hence the surname, Los Samokovlis, in Ladino, or Samokovlija, in Bosnian. (A branch of the same family refused the 'Balkan' name, and adopted an old Sephardic name, Baruh, instead.)

Isak was born on 3 December 1889 in Gorazde, a little Bosnian town on the banks of the Drina river, where his grandfather Isak ben Moshe, after whom he was named, had a grocery shop, After primary school, he moved to Sarajevo in order to continue his education, staying with his mother's family and attending high school there. (His schoolmate Ivo Andrić later became the first Yugoslav to receive the Nobel Prize for Literature.) In 1910, after finishing high school, he went to Vienna to study medicine, with a scholarship from La Benevolentia, a Jewish cultural and educational foundation. He graduated in 1917. After the Great War he returned to Bosnia to work as a doctor, first in Gorazde, then in Fojnica, and finally, from 1925, in Sarajevo. Whilst working as a doctor in the Kosevo hospital he co-edited the journal of the Jewish community in Sarajevo, *Jewish Life*, where his first short story appeared in 1927. His first collection of short stories, *From Spring to Spring*, was published two years later (Sarajevo, 1929), when he was already forty. Later, in an interview given in 1954 to a Belgrade journalist Siniša Paunović, he explained his relatively late start as a writer:

I did not have much time, because I was very busy as a doctor. I worked in the hospital and also as a GP in my own surgery in the afternoons, so I wrote mainly after nightfall. After completing my medical duties I would devote myself to literary work; and that was my greatest joy. I enjoyed writing immensely, and I also liked the things I wrote. But I kept them in my drawer for too long, without bothering to have them printed. I had my people, I had my themes, and I wanted to present them, to say something about them in the form of the short story.*

When his first book of short stories appeared, both the critics and his readers realised instantly that an extraordinary writer had emerged; one who indeed had his own people and his own themes, one who indeed had something to say about them, and one who indeed knew how to write in the form of the short story. And this was confirmed by his second volume, *Short stories* (Belgrade, 1936), which finally launched him as one of the best story writers in modern Serbo-Croat.

When the Second World War started, the Germans occupied Bosnia, which then became a part of the Independent State of Croatia, and Samokovlija was immediately sacked from the hospital. But he was soon mobilised as a doctor to fight the typhus epidemic which was threatening to decimate the whole population of Bosnia. Wearing the yellow strip with the star of David, he was often humiliated and bullied by Croatian fascists, but he carried on curing the sick of typhus fever, first in Northern Bosnia, and then in a detention camp for refugees near Sarajevo. In the early spring of 1945 he finally succeeded in fleeing from the *Ustashas*, and then waited for the liberation in hiding. After the war he lived in Sarajevo, working as a professional writer, translator and editor. He published three more volumes of short stories: *Samuel, the Porter* (Sarajevo, 1946), *On Trial for Life* (Zagreb, 1948), and *Selected Short Stories* (Belgrade, 1949). He began to write a novel about the life of the Jews of Sarajevo, but left it unfinished in fragments. He died in 1955, and was buried in the old Jewish cemetery on a slope above Sarajevo. His *Collected Works* in three volumes were published in Sarajevo in 1967 by the Svjetlost publishing house.

*Siniša Paunović, *Pisci izbliza*, Belgrade, 1958, pp. 88–125.

Like all genuine narrators, Samokovlija spoke about his own world. This world, which came directly from real life, permeated his stories, and defined their character through its own authenticity. As Ivo Andrić has written: 'This Bosnian writer of Jewish origin depicted the life and mentality of Bosnian Sephardic Jews.' Characteristically, when introducing Samokovlija to Slovene readers in a preface to a Slovene edition of his short stories (Ljubljana, 1955), Andrić spoke less about Samokovlija's stories ('so vibrant and fine in their simplicity'), than about 'the environment which spawned him' which 'preserved its distinctive self in his work', as if underlining the obvious fact that the world of Samokovlija's stories was made of real-life material, of 'the life and mentality of Bosnian Sephardic Jews', and that it could not be properly understood without knowing that life and that mentality. (That is why the editor of this book considered Andrić's text on the Bosnian Sephardic Jew to be the most appropriate introduction for an English edition of Samokovlija's stories.)

But of the large Jewish community to which he belonged – before the Second World War every eighth inhabitant of Sarajevo was of Jewish origin – Samokovlija was attracted only to the poor. In the interview with Paunović, he admitted:

While I was a young boy, I used to climb these steep streets of Bjelave (in the northern part of Sarajevo) and watch a whole tribe of manual labourers, porters, laundresses. With my eyes wide open I absorbed those people, impressed by their poverty and misery. And later as a doctor I kept meeting the same people year after year. I was amazed by their life, with all its peculiarities and religious fanaticism, consisting mainly of misfortunes.

In most of Samokovlija's stories, as if on the stage of a naturalistic theatre, it is indeed the life of the Jewish poor that is vividly displayed: The epileptic orphan Miko and his stepmother, the unfortunate widow Sarucha (*The Kaddish*), the poor laundress Hanucha and her little daughter Bochka, who suffers from tuberculosis (*Gabriel Gaon*), the wretched impotent fishmonger Haimacho whose wife left him for a Muslim man, disgracing the entire Jewish community (*From Spring to Spring*), the poor but proud

171

porter Samuel (*Samuel, the Porter*), and so on. But in Samokovlija's stories their lives are presented in such a warm light that some critics have appraised Samokovlija's writing as an almost impossible combination of a naturalistic obsession with human misery and romantic compassion for the miserable.

However, the world of the poor that peoples Samokovlija's stories is only the material, the material of real life, which this immensely talented story-teller is remodelling all the time. And although his characters are very similar, the narrative structure which brings them to life changes from story to story. Thus, for example, *The Blond Jewess* has an intense poeticality and two-fold composition. The story *From Spring to Spring* evolves as a mosaic and develops into a whole little novel. *Gabriel Gaon* is a unique experiment in narration with a double narrator and a double point of view, while *Hanka* reminds us of gypsy romances and *Samuel, the Porter* is constructed like a well-made play with a strong plot. Having found *his* world and *his* people, Samokovlija sought novelty only in terms of narrative structure. That is why the life of his characters appears in his stories in such peculiar perspective: their world is made of real life material, but variously modelled, with each new story following a different structural principle.

However, this does not mean that Samokovlija did not have preferences as a short story writer. In spite of an obvious diversity of narrative devices, most of his stories (and all of those published before the Second World War) follow the same narrative matrix. In these stories Samokovlija's 'heroes' are caught in a crucial moment of their life: when Fate calls on them to play their final act. From the relative safety, stability and conformity of everyday life each one of them has to step into the centre of a stage and face his or her destiny. Samokovlija also preferred to begin his stories by announcing the final dramatic climax. At the beginning of *The Blond Jewess*, for example, he announces: 'There, in the *mahala* they used to say that the finger of God would seek out sin and that all would end badly, because it had long boded no good.' *Gabriel Gaon* also begins with an ominous hint: 'People in the town spoke a great deal about Hanucha's death, about that whole horrific event. They talked more by gesture of their hands and their eyes wide open in horror than with words.' *From Spring to Spring* begins in this way: 'One could imagine his life from the manner of his death, and

172

people simply shrugged their shoulders in that manly way that was their wont when dealing with someone else's pain, but the children were stunned by the unexpected news that his corpse had been winched up from the depths of a well.' *Hanka*, again, begins with a whole scene (the autopsy of a beautiful gypsy girl's body), which casts a dark shadow on the love story which is to follow.

In fact, all of Samokovlija's 'heroes' live in the shadow of death: Hanka, Haimacho, Hanucha, Miko (the epileptic from *The Kaddish*), Miriam (from *The Blond Jewess*). And they all enter the story in the same way: having been living in conformity and with the certainty of everyday life, they are suddenly compelled to face an abyss of which they had not been aware, and which betrays the supposed safety and stability of their – and our – lives.

Samokovlija never rushes to the dramatic climax which he predicts at the beginning of his stories and, even when he does come to it, he prefers to depict it more as a state of mind than as an actual event. Whilst Miriam is plunging into an abyss (*The Blond Jewess*), Haimacho into a well (*From Spring to Spring*), and Hanka into a lethal sleep having been stabbed by her lover's knife (*Hanka*), we are brought to witness the happenings in their minds rather than the physical act of their fall; as if the most exciting moment of the drama of life lies there, in the very last flicker of consciousness.

The falls (Miriam's from a cliff, Haimacho's into a well, Hanka's into 'a long-awaited lethal sleep') are the fatal events predicted at the beginning of his stories. Samokovlija calmly depicts the life his 'hero' has been living up to that moment. He shows him, or her, moving around, laughing, eating, talking, crying, as if he or she were one of us. So Samokovlija's narration is never dramatically hasty. On the contrary, it flows slowly, with characteristic retardations and many apparently insubstantial details. This is because *ambiance* for him is not just a frame for life, but rather a form of existence. For him, man's destiny is ultimately determined by the possibilities of life which are contained in the form of existence in which he is compelled to live.

Samokovlija is one of those story-tellers who are unable to tell their stories *in abstracto*. His people cannot appear on a bare stage void of all the concrete and specific things which fill everyone's daily life. ('For the first time' – he wrote in one of his stories – 'I realise how much a man is part and parcel of the things which surround him.') For him *ambiance* becomes a constituent part of the narrative because it contains the real possibilities of man's life which intrinsically determine his (or her) destiny. Therefore, in his stories, depicting the details of a specific environment is as important as developing a plot. In fact, it is precisely these little particles of everyday life which make up the fine and invisible but fixed and unbreakable web of life in which all of Samokovlija's 'heroes' are caught.

It is also because he paid so much attention to depicting the peculiar details of the everyday life of the Jewish community in Sarajevo that he became 'a Jewish writer'. One need only read *The Kaddish* to see how much he reveals 'the life and mentality of Bosnian Sephardic Jews', as Andrić said. Sarucha's conviction that 'one has to endure evil because, like goodness, it comes from God Himself'; her concern to have someone recite the *kaddish* at her deathbed (which was why she adopted Miko in the first place); the *mezuzah* at her door; the Rabbi Yako, who used to come, every Friday evening straight from the temple to read the *kiddush* in the widow's home; the sudden concern of the whole Jewish community for Miko's destiny whilst he was in hospital ('He needed to be buried according to Jewish law, and what did those Krauts up there know about that?'); and the very climax of the story, when a religious ritual (reading the prayer at her deathbed) turns into the final act of Miko's life: all of this is distinctly Jewish. However, this is not the sole purpose of Samokovlija's writing. A*mbiance* is neither the main subject nor the pivot of his stories. Nevertheless, it is the real-life environment which makes his characters' lives possible: it is the 'fresh water' without which no 'fish' can stay alive.

But it is also because Samokovlija paid so much attention to depicting that real-life environment that his stories are so relevant today. They give evidence now of a world that is no more. For, as Andrić said, 'the dark, murderous onslaught of racism managed to disperse and destroy' the whole Jewish community that had lived in Bosnia for more than three centuries. They disappeared. The people Samokovlija brought to life in his stories, the people who, in return, determined the nature of his stories, vanished. In the Holocaust Samokovlija lost not only many relatives and friends but also the people who inhabited his stories. For him, who himself miraculously survived four terrible years of the war, it was more than a tragic experience. In the interview with him in the autumn of 1954 (almost ten years after the Second World War) Paunović unveiled Samokovlija's deepest grief:

After a long conversation about his stories, and particularly about a novel he had begun to write, we set off for a walk along the streets from his house toward Bjelave, where most of the Sephardic Jews used to live. He spoke almost as soon as we arrived there:

'Once upon a time I knew everyone here, every man, every child, every chicken, as people say. Dogs came to me, cats wound around my legs, as if they were from my own backyard. Look, many houses still exist, all the streets from my childhood, my youth, but none of the same people are here any more. Everyone is new, strange to me. Where are they? Killed, murdered, destroyed, dispersed. These who are moving around – they neither know me nor I them ...'

He was looking around vaguely, as if waiting for the people of the past to reappear, the people he had known and loved, who are now alive only in his memories and in his stories. Suddenly he strode ahead. I had scarcely caught him up, when I saw him, he was weeping ...

Such a painful experience inevitably came to flood Samokovlija's literary work, which became strongly marked with his reflections about the war, war crimes, and the Holocaust. It is characteristic of his attitude towards his pre-war literary work that he repeatedly acknowledged *Samuel, the Porter* to be the story he loved the most. For it was the first of his stories to bring the idea of resistance into a world of submissive suffering; and it was an idea that began to preoccupy him as he reflected on the tragic fate of the Jewish people.

After the war Samokovlija began to seek a narrative structure capable of conveying his emotions without challenging the very nature of narrative literature. In the early 1950s he published several stories where an internal narrator, called Davoka, appears. He is a Jew who has survived the war and now contemplates the Jewish fate. He is sufficiently individualised to be a character writing a story, and yet still able to be an omniscient narrator. With the help of Davoka, his 'double', who had taken over his emotional load, Samokovlija succeeded in expressing his own feelings of bitterness, sorrow, anger, and rage, maintaining the 'objective', impartial narrative nature of his stories. The efficiency of the 'transfer' of Samokovlija's own emotions on to the shoulders of his internal narrator might be illustrated by this passage from *Davoka's Tale of the Living Truth* (1950), where the author tells us of meeting his pre-war friend Davoka, after 'they had lived through these four terrible years':

His eyes seemed to have sunk back into their sockets, and they exuded a great sadness and despondency. I sensed that unspeakable events had left deep, cruel marks on his soul ... his eyes boring deep into mine, and then he added softly, in the kind of voice of patients who are starting to recover from a long, serious illness:

'Yes, yes, we have suffered greatly, you, I, all of us. How many of us are left? Barely ten out of a hundred. And how much those ten have been through! And what about the other ninety?', he said, shaking his head. 'They were taken away to Jasenovac, to the death camps in Dachau and Birkenau ... Taken away and gone, all with heads bowed ... Yes, heads bowed ... A terrible fate ... It breaks my heart even to think about it. It breaks my heart ...'

Davoka bows under the burden of his emotion, but he keeps it to himself, so that, although it is also the author's, it does not overload the narrative structure of the story. Through his internal narrator Samokovlija managed to express his own feelings, and also to solve a creative problem he had been trying to resolve since the end of the war: how could he continue to write about the world to which he had devoted all his attention, love and talent, when it had been entirely destroyed? And how could he carry on speaking about it without being choked with pain, horror and anger? In *Davoka's Tales* Samokovlija finally found a way to recollect his memories of people who were no more. For example, *Davoka's Tale of the Watchmaker Benzion* (1953) is full of memories of the 'old days', of the people affected by poverty and misfortune, but living their lives in piety and hope. ('I recall how strong was their passion for life: to live, to live!', says Davoka). And then – as if from a deep dream – we are brought back to reality, when all images of their former life disappeared, to make room for entirely different ones, the images from 1941 on:

They were stirring, overlapping one another, until finally one emerges, appearing in all its horror: an image of wretched people leaving their homes and setting off on a road of suffering with broken hearts, beaten by the butts of fascists' rifles, harried by their bayonets, frightened by their shouts, swearing and mockery.

Constantly changing the narrative structure of his short stories, Samokovlija remained the same in one decisive aspect: he kept listening to the restless quivering of the human soul, especially of the soul of the poor, of those who have no other role in history but the role of sufferers. Even in the whirlwind of historical events he heard the beats of the human heart rather than 'the sound and fury' of history. However, in *Davoka's Tales* he also put forward an idea of historical weight, which had first occurred to him before the war, at the time that he was writing *Samuel, the Porter* and which began to obsess him after the war. This was the idea of resistance, which preoccupied him as a historical option of the Jewish people. 'The Jews, I mean the nation, should have fought', he told Paunović. Knowing how many Jews had been taken to the death-camps ('taken and gone with bowed heads … yes, with bowed heads … dreadful fate …,' as Davoka says), Samokovlija introduced *resistance* as an idea governing the life of his people. For him it had a cathartic value, and for his stories it introduced a new principle in story-telling. *Davoka's Tale of the Living Truth*, for example, ends in a young Jewish girl's defiant act of rebellion in the hell of the Jasenovac camp:

The Ustashas reached for their weapons, but she was faster, tore open her jacket and shirt and cried out: 'Shoot! New generations will rise from the blood you are spilling. You'll see, you bastards!'
Behara's cry rang out so loudly, so powerfully, that it shook the air and the prisoners' eyes lit up.

The defiant cry of the Jewish girl resounded as a new tone in

Samokovlija's stories. In the pre-war stories 'all his characters bear their fate without grumbling about it, praising God', as the critic Jovan Krsic pointed out in 1929. Now Samokovlija resolutely questions the fatalistic trait of the Jewish mentality. In *Davoka's Tale of Jachiel's Rebellion* (1951) he sought the idea of resistance among the people he had previously written of as 'the humble people who accept both good and evil, since either comes from God'. His Jachiel now withholds acceptance of the morality of obedience and fear and dares to look life freely in the face. 'Well,' says he, 'it will be a hard life, very hard, but it will be a different one, one worth living!' However, the true significance of Jachiel's rebellion emerges later when Jachiel's granddaughter Strea, with weapons in her hands, confronts the fascists and actively affirms the idea of resistance. The story ends with a scene which underlines the whole of Samokovlija's literary work:

Davoka has gone. That evening I remained seated at the table for a long time. Whatever I started doing I failed. I could not concentrate. The wonderful girl Strea kept appearing in front of my eyes. I looked at her eyes – two shining stars. And I saw her hands, firmly holding a machine-gun. I heard the short sharp bursts of fire mowing down the enraged fascists. In the wielding of her machine-gun I heard the scream of a new, joyful life.

Perhaps these were not the most valuable lines Samokovlija's hand wrote. But they were the most exciting images to inspire him after the Holocaust. Perhaps they hindered him as a writer by diverting his imagination from the life he used to depict. But they certainly helped him to experience, at least at the very end of his journey, the joy of life for which all of his characters had yearned. In such a way the very spirit of a world that has been physically destroyed remained alive. Having lost the world he used to describe in his stories, at least Samokovlija found a meaning in life. And that was, perhaps, his greatest achievement both as a writer and as a human being.

Glossary

Adonai:	(Hebrew) God
aksham:	Muslim evening prayer
ashlama:	(Turkish) cherry
Bairam:	either of two Muslim festivals following the fast of Ramadan
djanum:	(Turkish) dear
groschen:	(German) small coin, small change
Haggadah:	Book of the Jews' deliverance from slavery in Egypt
halvah:	sweetmeat of sesame flour and honey
Haji:	title of honour; a Muslim who has made a pilgrimage to Mecca
halakha:	Jewish law
Hamisha a sara:	Jewish festival of trees and fruits waking up from their winter sleep
Hanukkah:	Jewish festival commemorating the rededication of the temple by Judas Maccabaeus
hevra kaddisha:	(Hebrew) funeral association
houri:	any of the beautiful nymphs of the Muslim paradise
huchen:	(German) large salmon-like fish found in the Danube (also known as Donaulachs)
ikindia:	Muslim afternoon prayer
jubbah:	long outer garment worn by Muslim priests
kaddish:	Jewish prayer of mourning
khoja:	Muslim teacher
kiddush:	Jewish benediction recited over wine on the eve of the Sabbath or a festival
kilim:	Turkish rug
Lehaim:	(Hebrew) Cheers! (Lit.) To life!
mahala:	(Arabic) street, part or quarter of town

menorah:	traditional Jewish candelabrum, with seven or nine branches
mezuzah:	small piece of parchment inside a case attached to the right side of the doorpost, inscribed with a Jewish prayer to protect the house from evil
moel:	(Hebrew) person who circumcises male children
monjo:	(Spanish) eunuch
muezzin:	the crier in the minaret of a mosque who calls Muslims to prayer at the proper hours
novio:	(Spanish) bridegroom
pastel:	(Spanish) meat pie
Pesach:	Jewish holiday commemorating the deliverance of the Jews from slavery in Egypt; falls in springtime; same as Passover
Purim:	Jewish holiday, the Feast of Lots, which falls towards the end of winter
rakija:	(Turkish) brandy
rushpa:	gold coin
salep:	(Turkish) sweet drink made of starchy tubers, favoured in the Balkans in winter
sechser:	(German) former small coin
sevdalinka:	Bosnian love song
shaliah:	Devout Jew who travels from Jerusalem, collecting donations for Jewish institutions in Jerusalem
shargiye:	(Arabic) stringed musical instrument
shefoch:	closing prayer of the Haggadah
Shevuoth:	Jewish festival commemorating the revelation of the Law at Mt. Sinai
Sukkoth:	Jewish festival celebrating the autumn harvest
tabut:	(Turkish) lidless coffin
tallit:	Jewish prayer shawl
Talmud:	the collection of writing constituting the Jewish civil and religious law
tia:	(Spanish) aunt
Torah:	The whole body of Jewish religious literature
Ustasha:	Croatian fascist collaborators in Second World War
vlach:	name for person of a different faith, foreigner, stranger in this case Orthodox Serb
Yom Kippur:	Jewish high holiday, The Day of Atonement
zufle:	type of woodwind instrument
zwanzig:	(German) former coin money equalling twenty Kreutzer